DALZIEL *and* PASCOE
Hunt the CHRISTMAS
KILLER
& Other Stories

Reginald Hill, who died in 2012, was a native of Cumbria and former resident of Yorkshire, the setting for his novels featuring Detective Superintendent Dalziel and Detective Chief Inspector Pascoe. Their appearances won him numerous awards including a CWA Gold Dagger, the Diamond Dagger for Lifetime Achievement and the Theakstons Old Peculier Outstanding Contribution to Crime Fiction Award. The Dalziel and Pascoe novels were also adapted into a hugely popular BBC TV series.

Also by Reginald Hill

Reginald Hill

DALZIEL *and* PASCOE *Hunt the* CHRISTMAS KILLER

& Other Stories

FOREWORD BY VAL McDERMID

HarperCollins*Publishers*

HarperCollins*Publishers*
1 London Bridge Street,
London SE1 9GF

www.harpercollins.co.uk

HarperCollins*Publishers*
Macken House, 39/40 Mayor Street Upper,
Dublin 1, D01 C9W8, Ireland

This paperback edition 2023
1

First published by HarperCollins*Publishers* Ltd 2022

A catalogue copy of this book is available from the British Library.

ISBN: 9780008430054 (PB)

This novel is entirely a work of fiction. The names, characters and incidents
portrayed in it are the work of the author's imagination. Any resemblance to
actual persons, living or dead, events or localities is entirely coincidental.

Typeset in Sabon by Palimpsest Book Production Limited, Falkirk, Stirlingshire

Printed and Bound in the UK using 100%
Renewable Electricity at CPI Group (UK) Ltd

MIX
Paper | Supporting
responsible forestry
FSC™ C007454

Contents

Foreword

It should come as no surprise to anyone that Reginald Hill won the Crime Writers' Association Short Story Dagger not once, but twice. Although he is best remembered for his four dozen novels, half of them featuring the unforgettable duo of Andy Dalziel and Peter Pascoe, he was one of the most accomplished short story writers in the genre. But because the majority of short stories appear in magazines or anthologies, their lifespan is fleeting. That this collection has been rescued from oblivion is something to be grateful for.

Here, we can sit again with Dalziel and Pascoe and their aides-de-camp Edgar Wield and Ellie Pascoe; but we can also experience some of the virtuoso range of Reg's imagination as he takes us to the Germans in the First World War, via a bargain with the devil, an impossible trail of footprints, and Elfland. And we have a front-row seat at Reg's feats of ventriloquism as he tells tales in a dazzling array of different voices. As Reg himself said, his non-series work is often 'about characters into whose lives crime comes, sometimes tragically, sometimes comically'. But always engagingly.

*

I'm often asked who I'm reading. I talk about recent discoveries, long-standing favourites whose latest books I fall on with delight, and a handful of writers whose books I re-read. Reg is one of those repeat pleasures I always pick up with the same thrill of anticipation as I get from an impending encounter with an old friend.

Re-reading is the greatest compliment I can pay a writer. My shelves are stacked with titles waiting to be read for the first time; to choose to return for a second or third time to a book whose shape and ending I already know means I believe that as well as guaranteed pleasure, there is the promise of discovering something I've missed before. In the uncertainties of lockdown, like many of us, I revisited past printed companions. Reg never disappointed.

I can still remember the delight of discovering Dalziel and Pascoe in their debut, *A Clubbable Woman*. It was one of those 1980s Grafton paperbacks with the uninspiring covers. I was in the café of the Royal Exchange Theatre in Manchester where I used to hide from my newsroom colleagues so I could read instead of drink during my lunch break.

As I read, I realized I was smiling. But not only because of the wit that permeates Reg's writing. I was smiling because I had in my hands that particular delight – a crime novel that demonstrates that it's possible to write about murder and mayhem in good prose. Well-made sentences, felicitous choices of words, and the ability to create deft shifts of mood all revealed a level of literary craft that was unusual in British crime fiction back in the mid-1980s.

For me, a fledgling crime writer struggling with her first novel, it set the bar high. And as Reg developed his skills through an impressive series of novels, he continued to provide me with a target to aim at. I always felt he was several steps ahead of me, and as well as enjoying his work, I learned from each of his novels. How to mislead the reader. How to draw on other writers' work to enrich my own. Not to be afraid to invest real emotion in the work. How to allow characters to carry the weight of their past. To have the courage to be complicated.

And to include at least one word in every novel that drove me to the dictionary . . . an eleemosynary impulse from a generous teacher.

He grew up in Yorkshire in what he described as 'a very ordinary family'. His father was a professional footballer for Hartlepool United, and his mother was a devoted reader of Golden Age detective novels, which Reg fetched for her from the library and began to read himself. A working-class lad, he made the impressive leap to St Catherine's College, Oxford, where he immersed himself in English literature. Not because he was pushed, but because he wanted to dive deep into something he loved. His books betray that love, peppered as they are with references to authors and works that illuminate what he was writing. But it's never about showing off; he was genuinely erudite and it came naturally to him to provide an allusion that enriched his own storytelling.

And those references are never heavy-handed. *Recalled to Life* opens with a perfectly crafted nod to Charles Dickens:

It was the best of crimes, it was the worst of crime; it was born of love, it was spawned by greed; it was completely unplanned, it was coldly premeditated; it was an open-and-shut case, it was a locked-room mystery; it was the act of a guile-less girl, it was the work of a scheming scoundrel; it was the end of an era, it was the start of an era; a man with the face of a laughing boy reigned in Washington, a man with the features of a lugubrious hound ruled in Westminster; an ex-marine got a job at a Dallas book repository, an ex-Minister of War lost a job in politics; a group known as the Beatles made their first million, a group known as the Great Train Robbers made their first two million; it was the time when those who had fought to save the world began to surrender it to those they had fought to save it for; Dixon of Dock Green was giving way to Z-Cars, Bond to Smiley, the Monsignors to the Maharishis, Matt Dillon to Bob Dylan, l.s.d. to LSD, as the sunset glow of the old Golden Age imploded into the psychedelic dawn of the new Age of Glitz. It was the Year of Our Lord nineteen hundred and sixty three.

Even at his most linguistically playful – in *Dialogues of the Dead*, for example – we don't stumble and lose whatever complex narrative thread he's laying out for us. We see it here in the short stories too, with nods to Border ballads, folk tales and Anthony Trollope.

And of course, we can see the influence of his deepest literary love, Jane Austen. It's there in the novels – *Pictures of Perfection*, a bucolic *trompe l'oeil* of a novel whose title comes from Austen's line: 'Pictures of perfection make me sick.' And *A Cure for All Diseases*, a modern reworking of Austen's unfinished novel *Sanditon* – but with corpses. Reg himself acknowledged this debt, saying that he occupied the Jane Austen end of the crime-writing spectrum; in other words, no graphic sex or explicitly detailed violence.

But the thread between them goes deeper than that. Jane and Reg would have thoroughly enjoyed each other's company, sharing their sharp and insightful observations on characters, subverting the conventional, and despising pretension and pomposity. Even Andy Dalziel's vulgarity would have tickled Miss Austen, I suspect. Both writers had a shrewd eye for human psychology, acute observation and vivid scene-setting. Here's a brief vignette from 'Castles', a character-led story in this collection:

People are pouring in from the crowded platform, some narked at being kept waiting, others chuffed to be catching an earlier train than expected. There's a wedding party on the platform who look like they belong to the first group. All the usual time-honoured jollities seem to have gone limp with repetition, and though the guests manage to whip themselves into a final frenzy of confetti throwing, balloon bursting, and tear shedding, they can't altogether hide their relief at being shot of the happy couple.

As I read it, I could see it, and hear the rhythms of Northern English speech.

The short story is a tricky beast, the crime short story most of all, because it demands a resolution. You can't write a successful crime short story that leaves the reader puzzling about what just happened. Somehow, in a few thousand words, the writer has to deliver set-up, development and pay-off, peopled by nuanced characters who feel authentic. It requires economy of method, a sure grasp of the key elements of the story, and ideally a twist or a reversal of fortune that leaves the reader with a nod of satisfaction.

In my experience, it's easier to write a novel than to turn in a good short story. I reckon I've written maybe five that I'm truly proud of. But Reg was one of those writers who seems equally at home with either form. When I was reading 'Brass Monkey', I was struck by the profligacy of the plot. There's so much going on, so cleverly dovetailed the construction, so rich in allusion and character possibility, so lovingly detailed, that I couldn't help feeling that another writer wouldn't have been able to resist the temptation of turning it into a novel. But Reg condenses it into a mere 17 pages and it feels neither scant nor over-burdened. It's hard to resist the thought that he had so many ideas nesting in his head that he was forever racing towards the next.

As Reg himself said, 'Good crime fiction is economical, which does not mean short, but rather that everything in a book, however apparently peripheral, incidental, or even ornamental, should contribute to the story's central dynamic. If a writer is successful in this, readers will finish the book with that contradictory sense of delight and disappointment – delight at having enjoyed such a complete and rounded experience, and disappointment that it's over!'

The characters he writes about in these short stories could easily populate the pages of a novel. They're varied, from a working-class copper to a middle-class senior teacher, from a novelist to a failed businessman, from a frustrated also-ran to a Hollywood success story. Reg's unsparing eye passes over them all. Although none escapes his scrutiny – a scrutiny that invited us to share his opinion – neither do they escape his humanity. His murderers are not monsters, they're human beings whose lives have not turned out the way they dreamed of. There are moments where I certainly felt the tingle of 'there but for the grace of God . . .' But thankfully, not the moments of murder!

When I heard the news of Reg's death in January 2012 I was on a book tour in the US. I felt the loss keenly. I was one of a handful of his fellow writers who had known he'd been diagnosed with an inoperable brain tumour, but still his death came as a blow. He'd been one of the first of my fellow crime writers to welcome me into what still feels like the best club in the world. He was always generous with his time and his conversation was a sparkle of delight. I feel lucky to have called him a friend and I still miss him, still mourn the unwritten books.

Reg was a gentle man, and a kind one. He suffered fools if not gladly, then at least politely. His wit could be pointed, but he was never malicious. He loved the fells and dales of the Lake District. He walked them regularly with his beloved wife Pat, with his dogs and with a handful of trusted old friends. He loved Mahler, and paid tribute to that love affair in the Dalziel and Pascoe novel *On Beulah Height*, where he provided his own Yorkshire translations for *Kindertotenlieder (Songs on the Death of Children)*. He could hide behind a facade of the bluff Yorkshireman, but he was blessed with a warm emotional intelligence that made the conversations we shared memorable and invigorating.

Reading these short stories brought him back to life in my imagination. Those qualities I admired and respected in the work and the man are all present here in this rich plum pudding of a collection, one that will warm the heart on a cold winter's night. I hope you come away from them feeling as I do, that the chance to revisit Reginald Hill's short stories is the best Christmas present any reader could ask for.

Val McDermid
St Monans
April 2022

Dalziel and Pascoe
Hunt the Christmas Killer

It was the first Sunday in Advent. The bell summoning the devout to morning worship at St John's church had fallen silent. The congregation, all seven of them (normally there were ten but it was a cold, wet day) sat waiting for their vicar to arrive.

After five minutes, one of the churchwardens went to the vestry door and peered out towards the gate in the wall through which the clergyman would make his way from the neighbouring vicarage. He saw a black-clad figure standing there, leaning against a sheltering yew tree as if waiting for a break in the driving rain.

Returning to his seat the churchwarden assured the others: 'He's on his way.'

Five minutes later he went to look again. The figure was still there, under the tree, and the churchwarden, irritated by the delay, advanced to remonstrate that bad weather shouldn't come between a man and his duty. As he got nearer, he saw that the vicar seemed to be embracing the yew, more like some primitive nature-worshipper than a man of the cloth.

'Are you all right?' he called. But even as he spoke, he was taking the next couple of steps which gave him his answer.

The back of the priest's skull had been crushed by a massive blow, and the only reason the body remained upright was that its hands had been nailed to the tree.

Detective Superintendent Andy Dalziel arrived on the scene with a sore head. Not normally a man given to religious observance, he made an exception in the case of St Andrew, in whom he felt a personal interest. Yesterday had been his namesake's Feast Day and the Fat Man had wassailed deep into the night. This morning it seemed a poor reward for piety that he should be dragged from his bed to view the corpse of a dead vicar, especially one who turned out to have notes for a sermon on the evils of drink in the pocket of his cassock.

A search of the churchyard quickly revealed the likely weapon, a bloodstained claw-hammer which had presumably also been used to drive the nails through the hands. The only other item of interest was a fresh cheroot butt found beneath the yew.

Dalziel was not a man to ignore the obvious and, knowing that clergymen are assaulted most frequently by those who apply to them for help and don't take kindly to being offered a sermon, the Fat Man confidently anticipated he'd be home for *Heartbeat* after picking up some twitching druggie with blood all over his shirt and prints matching those on the hammer.

Except there were no prints on the hammer. And though the mean streets of Mid-Yorkshire threw up any number of well-stained druggies, none of the stains matched the vicar's blood, nor did any of their DNA match that obtained from the cheroot butt.

By the time the second Sunday in Advent arrived, Dalziel was almost ready to apply directly to God for a sign. He got one anyway.

The vicar of St Peter's was as radical as the vicar of St John's had been traditional, an approach which didn't guarantee larger congregations but did put him top of your list if you wanted to arrange a gay wedding or, as on this Sunday afternoon, have your baby daughter christened with the names of the Leeds United first team squad.

The early arrivals were laughing at the jocular proposal of one of their number that they should fill the deep-scooped seventeenth-century font with lager instead of water, but most stopped laughing when they found it already occupied by the vicar. He had been stunned by a blow to the neck, then his head held beneath the water till he drowned.

Another cheroot butt was found, this time in the church porch. The DNA on it matched that from the one at St John's.

'Well, that helps,' said Dalziel. 'But not a lot. Any ideas, Pete?'

DCI Peter Pascoe, who had other things on his mind, principally how to deal with his pre-teen daughter Rosie's assertion that she would leave home and never speak to her parents again if they failed to present her on Christmas Day with a pair of fashion boots like Madonna's, said: 'You could advise vicars to follow their parishioners' good example and avoid churches on the Sabbath.'

'Thanks a bunch,' growled Dalziel. But he did issue a statement to the press saying that, while two didn't form a sequence, it might be wise for clergymen to proceed with caution the following Sunday.

How many clerics spent the third Sunday in Advent quivering in their canonicals isn't known, but the vicar of St Matthew's wasn't one of them. Everything was done as it was normally done. The churchwarden did offer to walk the vicar to the car park after evensong but was told in no uncertain terms that he'd do much better to hurry off to his niece's birthday party which he'd been talking about all week.

Much to his later regret, he obeyed, and the vicar set out down the ill-lit track through the ancient churchyard, whistling 'Onward Christian Soldiers' to ward off ungodly spirits. It didn't work. There was a rush of footsteps from behind, then a glancing

11

blow to the back of the head from what turned out to be a lapidary cross broken from a tombstone. The vicar, dazed but still conscious, swung around in a vain effort at resistance before tumbling on to the gravelled surface as the attacker came in for the kill. His left hand swung the cross high for the fatal blow while his right pressed down hard on the vicar's chest. Then squeezed.

'Bloody hell,' he exclaimed in shock. 'You're a woman!'

And, casting the cross aside, he fled.

A moment later the Reverend Sally Greenham heard a car speed away.

She sat upright, checked her body for serious damage, found none, gasped a prayer, then pulled out her mobile phone and rang the police.

'This makes three Sundays in a row I've been to church,' said Dalziel. 'Must be a record.'

'Let's hope you don't beat it,' said Pascoe grimly.

In fact things were looking up slightly.

Sally Greenham had glimpsed the attacker's face and was able to provide a description – male, tall, well built, slightly hooked nose, reddish hair, early twenties – sufficient to create a Photofit picture.

And the departing churchwarden, as he drove away, had noticed another car parked near to the vicar's. It was, he thought, a Ford Montego. Colour dark blue. But, best of all, he'd registered the number plate or at least part of it.

'The actual number was 666,' he said. 'I thought, hello! Revelation, Chapter 13, Verse 16.'

He paused to savour the irreligious ignorance of the constabulary.

'You mean Verse 18,' said Dalziel. 'The number of the beast.'

The churchwarden looked a bit disgruntled to be both corrected and pre-empted but at least it took his mind off his guilt at leaving the Reverend Sally unprotected.

'You sure it was Verse 18?' Pascoe enquired later.

'Listen, lad, I left school with O-levels in Religious Knowledge and Grievous Bodily Harm,' growled the Fat Man. 'If you didn't learn your texts, you got 'em knocked into you. And if that computer of thine can't track down the owner of yon car, I'll mebbe try knocking some sense into it!'

Happily for the computer, it did the trick without physical encouragement.

There was a surprising number of Montegos whose registration incorporated the figures 666. And several of them were dark blue. But only two of them were registered in Mid-Yorkshire. And both to the same man at the same address.

Mr James Christmas of Ladysmith Lodge, Greenhill.

'Now why should a man called Christmas want two cars incorporating the number of the beast?' said Pascoe. 'I like the smell of this one.'

'How many times have I told you not to jump to conclusions?' said Dalziel.

'Sorry,' said Pascoe meekly.

'Right then. Now let's go and kick a confession out of him afore he goes to bed.'

Greenhill was a once-prosperous, now rather run-down district to the west of the city centre. Ladysmith Lodge turned out to be a detached villa in grey granite.

In the driveway was parked a dark blue Montego with the number 666 in the registration. Dalziel felt the bonnet. Not very warm but warmer than the ambient air.

They rang the doorbell, which chimed the opening bars of 'Ding-Dong Merrily on High'.

The door was opened almost immediately by a tall, well-set-up man in his early twenties. He had russet hair and a hooked nose beneath which his lips curved in a welcoming smile without disturbing the narrow black cheroot suspended there. He was a dead ringer for Sally Greenham's Photofit picture.

13

'Mr James Christmas?' said Pascoe.

'That's right,' said the man, peering expectantly into the darkness behind them. 'Just the two of you then?'

'Well, yes,' said Pascoe, puzzled. He produced his warrant and introduced himself.

'Silly me!' laughed Christmas. 'I thought you were the carol singers. The church mag said they'd be out tonight, and your friend has something of a charitable look about him.'

Anyone who could think that would probably welcome Attila the Hun as an envoy of Greenpeace, thought Pascoe.

They followed the man across a bare-boarded entrance hall, their footsteps echoing as hollowly as if they'd been in an empty house, but the room he led them into was well furnished in a bright, modern style.

'Now how can I help you, gentlemen?' enquired James Christmas after he'd sat them down before a powerful woodburning stove.

'Could you tell us where you were earlier this evening, sir?' said Dalziel. 'Between, say, the hours of six and eight.'

'Well, let me see, I left Cambridge shortly after half five, so I must have been on the A1 between Huntingdon and Pontefract. I got home about ten to nine, I recall. Has there been a traffic accident or something? I didn't see anything.'

Pascoe didn't like the sound of this but the Fat Man wasn't disconcerted.

'Cambridge? You've spent the day in Cambridge?' he said, making it sound like Sodom and Gomorrah. 'Would that have been for business or pleasure, sir?'

'Neither, really. Filial duty, I suppose. My father's in a nursing home there and I drive down most Sundays to see him.'

'Sorry to hear that, about your dad I mean,' said Dalziel. 'Bad, is he?'

'Pretty bad. He had a severe stroke. Can't speak, can hardly move, but he's fully compos mentis, they assure me. So I get

14

there at lunchtime. We spend the afternoon together, I read to him, bring him up to date with the news, family and general, do what I can to cheer him up, then, after a spot of tea about five, I head for home. It's little enough, I know, but the staff assure me it's the high point of his week.'

'Very commendable, sir,' said Dalziel.

'This is nice,' said Pascoe.

He'd been wandering round the room and had stopped in front of an ornate Advent calendar hanging on the wall opposite the fireplace. Only the Sunday windows had been opened, the first two fully, the third halfway.

'Oh, that,' laughed Christmas. 'Hard to break the habits of childhood, eh? I was brought up in a very religious household. Father was a vicar, you see, down in darkest Suffolk. Naturally he got called Father Christmas, especially by the kids. It's funny, since his stroke it's been simpler to let his beard grow than try to shave him, so now he actually looks the part! I know it's sad but you've got to laugh, haven't you?'

He's enjoying this, thought Pascoe.

He's taking the piss, thought Dalziel.

He stood up and said: 'Very amusing, sir. Now I wonder if you'd mind accompanying us to the station so we can ask a few more questions?'

'Certainly, if you think it would help,' said Christmas without hesitation. 'Though, as I say, I really don't recollect noticing an accident.'

At the station, his laid-back cooperative mood continued. He gave details of his father's nursing home, provided a DNA sample without protest and even complimented them on the excellence of the canteen coffee, which made Pascoe wonder if he was building up for an insanity plea.

Or could it be that he was simply innocent, thought Pascoe as he dialled the number of the Fenny Bottom Nursing Home in Cambridge. Dalziel was clearly convinced they had the right man and Pascoe's own feeling went along with this. On the other hand that was what the Tories had thought in their last two leadership elections . . .

Five minutes later he put the phone down and was sprinting down the corridor to get between Dalziel and a false arrest suit.

The matron of the nursing home had been unambiguous. Yes, James Christmas had visited his father today as he had for the past several Sundays. She personally had seen him at regular intervals during the day and he had looked into her office to call goodbye as he left just before a quarter to six. No way, even driving like a maniac, could he have got to St Matthew's in time to jump on Sally Greenham.

The Fat Man showed surprisingly little inclination to kill the messenger. Instead, he simply disregarded the message. 'Let him go? Bollocks. He's our man. You'll see. Get him another cup of coffee, and I'll hurry those dozy b*****s at the lab along with the DNA check.'

Half an hour later the phone rang. The Fat Man listened, said 'Ta,' put the receiver down, stared blank-faced at Pascoe, then let his rubbery lips curve in a sharky smile.

'Gotcha,' he said. 'It's a match. We'll worry later how yon b****r's managed things today, but we've definitely got him on the spot at St John's and St Peter's for the two Sundays before. Come on, lad. Bring your rubber truncheon. It's time for some serious talking.'

But as they went down the stairs to the interview room, they met the desk sergeant coming up. He didn't look happy.

'Sir,' he said to Dalziel. 'There's someone just come in asking for you.'

'Oh aye? Unless he's from the Palace with my peerage, he can wait.'

'I think you should come, sir,' insisted the sergeant with such urgency that Dalziel let himself be diverted grumbling to the front office.

A man stood there reading the public service notices on the noticeboard. From behind he struck Pascoe as familiar. When the man turned, he saw why.

'Who the hell let him out?' demanded Dalziel angrily. 'Was it you?'

He glared at Pascoe accusingly.

Pascoe couldn't blame him.

Confronting them was James Christmas, cheroot in mouth, smile on face, as he held out his hand and said: 'Mr Dalziel, I presume. I'm James Christmas. I believe you've got my brother in the station.'

Sometimes the explanation is worse than the problem. Seeing the two men sitting side by side in the interview room, it was impossible to tell them apart. Same features, same voice, same gestures, same clothing and, of course, the same car, with the same number and only a minor difference in the letters.

Pascoe's heart began to sink at the implications. The Fat Man showed little inclination to do anything but glower, so Pascoe started.

'Right,' he said. 'So which of you is James?'

'I am,' said the new arrival, who was sitting in the left-hand chair.

'And so's he,' said the other.

'In fact, I'm Jim,' said the first.

'And I'm Jamie.'

'But we're both James,' they said together.

'You can't have the same name,' protested Pascoe.

'In a sense, we don't,' said Jim.

'It was our father . . .' said Jamie.

'. . . which art in Cambridge . . .' said Jim.

'. . . his father chose his son's forenames from the apostles . . .'

'. . . and our father . . .'

'. . . which art in Cambridge . . .'

'. . . wanted to continue the tradition . . .'

'. . . but when he was told he had twins . . .'

'. . . he thought it fitting that they should each have the only apostle name that occurs twice . . .'

'James,' they said together.

'But it's not strictly the same name,' said Jim. 'You see, I'm named after James the Great and he's named after James the Less.'

'No,' said Jamie. 'I think you err there, bro. I'm James the Great. You are James the Less.'

The brothers smiled at each other. Dalziel looked at Pascoe.

'Sir,' said Pascoe. 'Why don't I take . . . Jim next door and put him in the picture?'

He smiled apologetically at the new arrival for using his fore-name.

'Aye, in a minute,' said Dalziel irritably.

'I think we should do it now, sir,' said Pascoe urgently.

'Oh you do, do you? A word outside, Chief Inspector. Jennison, keep an eye on these two gents, will you?'

PC Jennison, a portly constable who'd been listening to the brothers' double act with wide-eyed disbelief, nodded as if to say, They won't muck me around!

Outside in the corridor, before Dalziel could speak, Pascoe said: 'Sir, I think we should separate them while we can still tell them apart.'

'Don't be daft. You think I'll forget that Jim's sitting on the left, Jamie on the right? Or shall I punch one of the buggers on the nose just so they've got a distinguishing mark? Don't look so worried, lad. I'm not serious. Even if you did get 'em mixed, we've got Jamie's DNA sample, remember.'

'Yes, sir, that's my point. If, as looks very much the case, they're identical twins from a single divided egg, they'll have the same DNA.'

18

'You what? You sure of that?' said Dalziel.

'Pretty sure,' said Pascoe.

They were distracted by the sound of raised voices from inside the interview room. The words less and great were prominent, then all were drowned out by PC Jennison's bellow: 'Come along, gents, behave yourselves, won't you?'

Dalziel flung the door open.

The brothers were grappling with each other. Jennison draped a burly arm round each and easily drew them apart. They glowered at each other for a moment then, smiling rather shamefacedly, resumed their seats.

Except were they the same seats they'd been sitting in before? Pascoe asked himself.

Dalziel seemed sure.

Addressing himself to the man in the left-hand chair, he said: 'Mr Christmas, Jim, why don't you go next door with DCI Pascoe and let him fill you in on what's going off here while I have a few more words with your brother about his trip to Cambridge today?'

'Cambridge? Then it's me you want to talk to,' said Jim.

'No, you're getting confused as usual,' said the other. 'You went last week, remember. It was my turn today.'

'Come on! Are you suggesting I don't know how I spent the day?' said Jim. Or was it Jamie?

'Nothing would surprise me from a man who can't remember that he is James the Less,' retorted Jamie. Or was it Jim?

Pascoe felt himself growing cold. A glance at Dalziel confirmed his suspicion that, though the Fat Man was getting irritated, he was still a long way from fully appreciating the gravity of the situation. Unless, of course, he himself was simply overreacting.

He said brightly, staring at the space midway between the two men: 'Mr Christmas, the DNA sample we took wasn't really satisfactory. Would you mind giving us another? And perhaps you too, Mr Christmas, just for comparison's sake.'

'Certainly,' said the two men in unison. 'No problem.'

But there was a problem and it got bigger. The DNA samples proved identical. Both men claimed to have been in Cambridge on two of the Sundays and at home on one. The Fenny Bottom matron was convinced she had only ever dealt with one James Christmas and wouldn't admit any possibility that there had been two of them.

The twins made no objection to being detained in custody that night, nor to taking part in separate identity parades the following day. The Reverend Sally, little the worse for her ordeal, picked out Christmas without hesitation on the first parade, then expressed some puzzlement at being asked to view another.

When she saw, as she believed, the same man on the second parade, she grew angry. And when things were explained to her she shook her head incredulously and said: 'Well, I'm sorry. In that case I definitely can't stand up in court and swear either one of them attacked me.'

The Cambridge police were asked to look into things at their end. They confirmed that, according to the records, the Reverend John Christmas had been checked into the nursing home six months earlier by James Christmas, who claimed to be his only son.

It transpired that the Reverend John had been the vicar of a remote rural parish in Suffolk for nearly forty years. Relatively late in life, he'd married a young woman and the twins were born nine months later after a long and painful labour from which the mother never recovered. She had died within the year.

After this the children were brought up by a succession of nannies, and educated at home by their father.

A year ago at Christmas he had suffered a stroke that had left him speechless and paraplegic. After several months in hospital, the twins had removed him to the Cambridge nursing home and themselves to Mid-Yorkshire.

This much the investigating officers were able to discover, but of the details of the twins' upbringing, nothing. But it didn't matter. The Christmas twins were more than happy to talk about their upbringing, so long as they were questioned together.

'It was good to be educated by Father,' said Jim (?).

'Because he knew everything,' said Jamie (?).

'What he didn't know wasn't knowledge. And he was a good teacher.'

'Oh yes. Forget your lesson once and it was the ebony ruler across your knuckles.'

'Forget it twice and it was the bamboo cane across your behind.'

'You knew where you were with Father.'

'You certainly did. Especially if it was the cellar.'

At this point they looked at each other in shared memory and nodded vigorously.

'What happened in the cellar?' asked Pascoe.

'Nothing happened in the cellar, that was the point.'

'The cellar was where you got put to reflect on your sins.'

'One night for a venial sin . . .'

'. . . three for a deadly sin . . .'

'. . . and a whole week for a sin against the Holy Ghost . . .'

They paused, this time not looking at each other but their eyes hooded as if gazing into their souls.

'But he was fair,' said Jamie (?).

'Firm but fair,' agreed Jim (?).

'If he knew that one of us had sinned . . .'

'. . . but couldn't tell which . . .'

'. . . then he'd lock us both in the cellar . . .'

'. . . and that was better, you see . . .'

'. . . you didn't mind the rats so much . . .'

'. . . and the dark wasn't so bad if you . . .'

'. . . and talking helped you forget the . . .'

'. . . and of course you were never alone . . .'

21

Silence again. 'Why'd you put up—'

'It was for our own good,' said Jim (?).

'It was all we knew,' said Jamie (?).

'And it wasn't all bad.'

'No. There was always Christmas.'

'Oh yes. There was always Christmas.'

Silence.

'What happened at Christmas?' asked Pascoe.

'We had an Advent calendar,' said Jamie (?).

'When you opened a window there was a treat,' said Jim (?).

'A jelly baby or a Malteser.'

'But you only got them if you could recite the collects for the four Sundays in Advent.'

'That's right. Each Sunday, you had to recite the appropriate collect.'

'If you got it right, then you got the treats when you opened the windows in the following week.'

'But you had to get it perfect.'

'Word perfect.'

'Comma perfect.'

'And if you didn't get it perfect?' said Dalziel.

'The cellar,' they said in perfect unison.

'What about Christmas Day?' asked Pascoe.

'Now that was special,' said Jim (?).

'If you got the collects right . . .' said Jamie (?).

'That was very special.'

'It was our birthday, you see.'

'Name of Christmas, born on Christmas Day.'

'That's right. Our special day.'

They paused and lit up cheroots in perfect unison.

'But last year it was different,' said Jim (?).

'Oh yes. It was different,' said Jamie (?).

'When we saw him at morning prayers, his voice was slurred . . .'

'. . . and then it got worse . . .'

'. . . until finally he couldn't talk at all and he couldn't move either and he just sat slumped in his chair with his mouth open . . .'

'. . . and we didn't know what to do . . .'

'. . . but our housekeeper called the ambulance . . .'

'. . . and they took him away . . .'

'. . . and later the doctor came and said he was very ill . . .'

'. . . and later still the lawyer came and said we had to make the decisions now . . .'

'. . . because we were old enough you see . . .'

'. . . in fact we'd been old enough for three years, he said . . .'

'. . . because now we were twenty-one . . .'

'. . . and one of us had to have Power of Attorney . . .'

'. . . that was me because I'm the elder . . .'

'. . . no, I think you'll find it was me because I'm James the Great . . .'

'Don't start that malarkey again!' snapped Dalziel. 'Both of you dumped your dad in the nursing home, then came up here to live. Why'd you do that?'

The twins looked at each other as if puzzled by the question.

'He liked Cambridge,' said Jamie (?).

'He went to college in Cambridge,' said Jim (?).

'We couldn't stay in the vicarage . . .'

'. . . the Church needed it for the new vicar . . .'

'. . . so we had to find somewhere to live . . .'

'. . . and Cambridge was very expensive . . .'

'. . . though Father had quite a lot of money, thank heaven . . .'

'. . . his hobby was working with precious metals, you see . . .'

'. . . he made gold collection plates and monstrances and pyx chests, that sort of thing . . .'

'. . . he was really a Roman manqué, we sometimes thought . . .'

'. . . so there was all this precious stuff lying around . . .'

'. . . as well as all our dear mother's money . . .'

'. . . which is what we used for ourselves . . .'

'. . . and his own money to pay for the nursing home . . .'

'. . . that seemed fair, and we picked on Yorkshire because we heard it was cheaper up here . . .'

'. . . and that the people were kinder up here . . .'

'. . . which from what we've seen of you, Mr Dalziel, is certainly true . . .'

'. . . so I came up here and rented our house . . .'

'. . . no, I think you'll find it was me who came up here and rented our house . . .'

'Enough!' bellowed the Fat Man. 'You're up here, your dad's down there, one of you goes every Sunday to see him. That's a hell of a trip to make.'

'It's our duty,' said Jim (?).

'And I like driving,' said Jamie (?).

'So do I.'

'And he's so pleased to see us.'

'He can't speak. And he can hardly move. But you can tell he's pleased.'

'Of course, we have to do all the talking.'

'That's right. All he can do now is listen.'

'But he likes to see us and hear us talk.'

'Especially at this time of the year.'

'We bought him an Advent calendar, you see.'

'And we recite the collects and open the windows.'

'And we feed him the treats.'

'And we tell him everything we've been doing in the past week.'

'Everything. Every detail. Especially what Jim is doing this Sunday.'

'Yes, especially what Jamie's doing this Sunday.'

'You can see in his eyes that he takes it all in.'

'You can see how proud he is of the way we've turned out.'

'All down to his efforts, we always make that plain to him.'

'He's got nothing to reproach himself with – we're exactly what he made us.'

'And when we get up to leave, we tell him what we've got planned for the following week.'

'And sometimes you can see his tears.'

'The tears of love and pride.'

'Pride and love. His little boys. Grown up and making their mark in the world.'

'Interview terminated,' said Andy Dalziel, snapping up the tape switch.

Outside, he said: 'They make my flesh creep, yon pair. Much more and I'd not have been able to keep my hands off them.'

'Old Father Christmas sounds a pretty nasty piece of work too,' said Pascoe.

'I'll not disagree. Deserves a good kicking, maybe a lot more. But killing innocent folk just so's they can watch their old dad suffer, that's really sick.'

'They clearly reckon all vicars are tarred with the same brush. Unless they happen to be female. Perhaps we can get them for sexual discrimination in the workplace.'

'Murder, that's what I'm getting them for,' said Dalziel. 'Let's go and play this tape to the CPS and see if we can get some sense out of them.'

But the lawyer they spoke to at the Crown Prosecution Service wasn't in a sensible frame of mind, not in Andy Dalziel's eyes at least.

'Look,' he said. 'The clock's ticking away. Your time's nearly up. You've either got to charge them or let them go. And what are you going to charge them with? You have a DNA sample which puts one of them at the scene of the two killings. But which one?

'And in any case, it's hardly incontrovertible evidence that they actually did the killing, is it? Your search of their house produced nothing.

'True, you have an attack victim who can identify both of them as her attacker, but as she was only attacked by one person, she is naturally reluctant to point the finger at either. Your only other possible witness is the father who can't talk, perhaps wouldn't want to talk if he could, and whose evidence would be hearsay in any case.'

'So what are you saying?' demanded Dalziel.

'I'm saying you're going to have to let them both go. Sorry.'

'Can't I hang on to them till after next Sunday at least?'

'Not if you want to keep your job, you can't,' said the lawyer. 'If they'd bothered to get a lawyer, they'd have been out of here twenty-four hours ago. I wish I could be more helpful.'

'Why break the habit of a lifetime?' said Dalziel. 'Pete, you set the buggers loose. But give us twenty minutes first so I can set up surveillance. Between now and Sunday I want them watched so close that if they drop dandruff, we can have them in for littering.'

'I'll pretend I didn't hear that,' said the lawyer.

The Christmas brothers returned home and stayed there, watched by a round-the-clock surveillance team which was, in Pascoe's eyes, a gross waste of manpower at this most criminously active time of year.

'It's what they try to do on Sunday we need to worry about,' he protested to Dalziel.

'No. We know exactly what they'll try to do on Sunday,' replied Dalziel. 'It's where they'll try to do it. Any ideas? I thought not. So belt up.'

The nearest Pascoe came to an idea was late on Saturday night. He wasn't on duty the following day and when he'd volunteered to come in, Dalziel had mocked him, saying: 'You're getting delusions of grandeur, lad. We've got them covered. Watch and wait, that's the way to sort them out. Either they'll give up or we'll catch 'em in the act!'

Nevertheless, Pascoe had gone home with every bit of paper relating to the case and he sat studying the file long after his wife and daughter had gone to bed. Why had they picked those particular vicars as their victims? Purely random? It seemed so from the evidence of surprise at discovering the incumbent at St Matthew's was a woman. So, not the vicars. What about the churches? The first was at St John's, then it was St Peter's, and last week at St Matthew's . . . was there some kind of sequence there? If so, he couldn't see it.

Then just as he was giving up, his gaze fell on the copy of the Fenny Bottom Nursing Home's registration sheet for the twins' father, the Reverend John Christmas. His name was written as the Reverend John P. M. N. Christmas.

Hadn't the brothers said he was named after some of the apostles? What a sweet extra twist to the mental and spiritual torture of their father it would be if the twins were using his own Christian names to target their murder victims.

It took a couple of phone calls and many placatory words but finally he sat back with that sense of triumph which always follows a successful deductive leap. John Peter Matthew Nathanael Christmas. And no, Nathanael wasn't a misspelling of Nathaniel.

Now they had them! All they had to do was check out Mid-Yorkshire's St Nathanael churches and hope there were few enough to lay an ambush in each.

Fifteen minutes later, his triumph had evaporated completely. Not only Yorkshire but also its neighbouring counties were entirely free of churches dedicated to Nathanael. Which prompted him to do what he should have done in the first place and check whether there was indeed a St Nathanael. There wasn't, not even spelled Nathaniel. Maybe the Rev John's parents had thought that three names were enough for God and given Mammon a look in by tagging on the name of some rich uncle in whom they had legatary hopes.

So as usual Fat Andy was right. Watch and wait. What could go wrong? He pushed the file aside and went to bed.

Next morning he was enjoying his lie-in when the phone rang. It was Dalziel.

'You not at church?' he said. 'Good. 'Cos I think one of the Christmases could be. Get yourself down here right away.'

Evading the surveillance team had been incredibly easy. At 10 a.m. both Montegos had come rolling down the drive. In anticipation of this, the surveillance team had two pursuit cars waiting. Both Montegos turned towards the centre of town. The surveillance cars followed, ready to split up when the twins did.

In a narrow one-way street in the town's picturesque medieval centre, the second Montego came to a halt. With an apologetic wave at the following cars, the twin driving it went into a news-agent's and came out a short while later flourishing a Sunday paper and a packet of cheroots. The leading Montego by now was out of sight.

The team allocated to the second Montego said a prayer of thanks and followed it to the motorway where it headed south, presumably to Cambridge. The other team, fearful beyond the hope of prayer, reported their loss to Dalziel, offering as slight mitigation some fifteen minutes later the discovery of their Montego parked within sight of Police HQ. Of the driver, there was no sign.

'Still taking the mickey,' growled Dalziel. 'Check taxi firms, but if he's on foot, that limits him.'

He ordered a check on every church in a five-mile radius. When Pascoe arrived at the station, he found the Fat Man shaking his head over the very long list.

'Jesus,' he said. 'And here's me thinking we lived in a heathen land. We've had John, Peter, Matthew. Who comes next? Any ideas, Pete? You're good at holier-than-thou. We've got just about every saint under the sun to choose from.'

'Except Nathanael,' said Pascoe.

'What makes you say that?'

'Because he's not a saint, more's the pity.'

Dalziel looked as if he was thinking about hitting him, so Pascoe explained.

When he'd done, the Fat Man regarded him with huge sorrow, shaking his head in disbelief.

'I were right after all,' he said. 'We do live in a heathen land. Let's see that list again.'

He ran his eye down the named churches, then picked up his radio mike.

'Listen in, everybody,' he boomed. 'Head for St Bartholomew's in Bigland Lane. Find the vicar and get him out of sight. I'm on my way.'

'Sir,' gasped Pascoe as he followed his leader down the stairs to the car park. 'What makes you so sure it's St Bartholomew's?'

'Because anyone with an O-level in religious knowledge knows the disciple Bartholomew who's mentioned in Matthew, Mark and Luke, for some reason gets changed to Nathanael in John. Come on. Let's go!'

Bigland Lane was about ten minutes' drive away. Dalziel seemed determined to do it in five. When they arrived, they found the church porch full of policemen.

'Where've you put the vicar then?' demanded Dalziel. 'Who's guarding him?'

Sergeant Bonnick, a relative newcomer to Mid-Yorkshire and a true muscular Christian in that he was a pillar of both his local gym and his local church, said confidently: 'It's all right, sir. He's administering Communion so we couldn't interrupt, but we've got him in plain view and he'll be finished soon.'

Dalziel looked at him as if he were mad. 'I don't care if he's administering the last rites, I want him out of there!'

He pushed through the posse of policemen and peered into the church. Bonnick was right. The vicar was nearly done. Only two people remained kneeling at the communion rail. As Dalziel watched, one of them, a woman, rose and returned to her seat. The vicar put the chalice to the last communicant's lips, murmuring the accompanying phrases: the blood of our Lord . . . drink in remembrance . . . and be thankful . . .

The man touched his lips to the metal rim, the priest straightened up, turned and bore the chalice to the altar where he placed it reverently and covered it with a linen cloth. Then he began to recite the Lord's Prayer.

The last communicant remained kneeling till it was finished then rose and came back down the chancel steps to return to his seat.

It was James Christmas.

The Fat Man opened his mouth to command his arrest but it was unnecessary.

Christmas saw him standing there, smiled broadly in recognition and came hurrying down the aisle towards him. But when he got within a couple of paces, the smile vanished from his face and with it any trace of colour. At the same time, his knees buckled under him and it was only Dalziel's strong grasp that prevented him from crashing to the floor.

The Fat Man half carried, half hauled him into the porch and sat him down on the bench. He was finding it difficult to breathe. Mixed with his gasps were words, faint and broken . . . Jamie . . . oh Jamie . . .

Pascoe said urgently to Bonnick: 'Sergeant, get an ambulance.'

Christmas suddenly stood up.

'No. It's too late,' he said in a strong voice.

'Let's get him into the air,' said Dalziel.

With his arm round the man's shoulders, he ushered him out

into the chill December morning. Pascoe followed. Behind him, he heard the vicar come to the end of the last prayer and invite the congregation to join with him in the Gloria.

Glory be to God on high, and in earth peace, goodwill towards men . . .

The second pursuit car was parked outside. One of the surveillance team got out with a phone in his hand. He came towards Dalziel, saw it probably wasn't a good time to interrupt him and settled for Pascoe instead.

'Sir,' he said. 'It's the other car. There's been an accident . . .'

Pascoe grabbed the phone.

'DCI Pascoe,' he said. 'What's happened? Are you OK?'

'Yes sir. It's not us. It's Christmas. He was driving along nice and steady then he started talking into his mobile phone and I was just thinking, 'Shall we have him for this?' when his car went all over the place, bounced off a lorry and ended up down the embankment. We got him out straight away but it was too late. He's dead, sir.'

'Oh hell,' said Pascoe.

'And another thing . . . his phone was still on. It was the matron from that nursing home in Cambridge . . . seems she'd just rung him to tell him that his father had suffered another stroke . . . and he's dead too, sir . . .'

Pascoe looked towards the other twin who was staring at him as if he'd heard every word. In the church they'd finished the Gloria and the priest was intoning the blessing . . . the peace of God which passeth all understanding . . . Dalziel, his arm still around Christmas, had caught on that something was amiss and he mouthed: 'What?' at Pascoe . . . the blessing of God Almighty, the Father, the Son and the Holy Ghost . . . Pascoe held up the phone and shook his head . . . be amongst you and remain with you always. Amen . . . James Christmas let out a great cry and did what few other men would have been able to do: hurled the Fat Man aside as if he'd been an unwanted garment, then turned and plunged back into the church.

If Pascoe had time to think anything, it was that somehow Christmas knew exactly what had happened and was now rushing back in a state of near madness to complete his purposed task of murdering the vicar of St Bartholomew's.

If that had been his intent, there was nothing they could have done to stop him.

By the time Pascoe got into the aisle, Christmas was already in the chancel and within striking distance of the vicar, who had approached the altar, picked up the communion chalice and raised it to his lips. But before he could drink, Christmas shouldered him aside, snatching the vessel from his grasp and downing its contents like a man desperate to quench a choking thirst.

Now he turned to face the approaching policemen and flung his arms out wide as if he were the priest offering them his blessing. For a moment, his face shone with the bliss of a transfigured saint. Then he doubled up with a cry of agony and crashed to the floor.

He was still conscious when Pascoe reached him.

His lips parted in a smile, or perhaps it was just the rictus of death, and he croaked: 'Looks like it's back to the cellar then,' went into a spasm, and died.

'The quack says it were cyanide,' said Dalziel. 'God knows how he got it.'

'Didn't they say their father was an amateur goldsmith? They use cyanide in their processes, I think.'

'Do they? More interesting is how he got it into the chalice without poisoning the whole congregation.'

'Easy. He had it in a capsule, something that would dissolve quickly in alcohol. He put it in his mouth as the chalice approached, and he didn't drink but let the capsule slip into the wine. He'd been at enough services to know that if there's any of the consecrated wine left over, the priest drinks it after the blessing. I think they'd have got a real kick from telling their dad they'd murdered another vicar at the altar in his own church with poisoned communion wine.'

'Sick bastards.'

'At least he saved the vicar's life by drinking it himself.'

'Aye and, more important, he saved us the cost of keeping him banged up in a nuthouse for the rest of his worthless life,' growled Dalziel. 'Still, it teaches you one thing. If you're a parent, be kind to your kids 'cos one day you may want them to be kind to you.'

'That's true,' said Pascoe. 'Which is why I'm heading home now to enjoy what remains of my day off.'

'You'll have a quick pint first, surely?'

'Sorry, I'm in a bit of a hurry.'

'Oh aye? What's your rush?'

'It's the last Sunday before Christmas and all the shops are open,' said Peter Pascoe. 'And in view of what you just said, I think it might be a wise move to take Rosie shopping.'

Market Forces

It is one thing to utter pearls of wisdom. Quite another to swallow them yourself. They tend to stick in the throat.

The pearl George Faber found himself choking on was one he had often cast before would-be entrepreneurs in his capacity as small business adviser at the Cumbrian Investment Bank.

Cornering a market is pointless unless you've cracked the distribution problem.

He had been wiser than he knew, and the getting of wisdom is a great sorrow.

For he had cornered the market in dead Mrs Fabers without giving any thought at all to the problem of distributing the remains.

Of course it wouldn't have been a normal suburban marriage if during its twenty-five-year duration he hadn't occasionally fantasized about being a vigorous widower with insurance money to burn; but his earthbound imagination had never envisaged attaining that blessed state by means other than illness or accident.

In the present circumstances, *illness* was definitely out. He looked down at the body and tried *accident* for size.

'I'd been out in the garden chopping firewood, and I got rather hot so I came into the kitchen to get a beer, and Phyllis started screaming at me not to track dirt across her nice clean tiles, and then this dreadful accident happened . . .'

He paused hoping for inspiration but none came. Even a more creative thinker than dull old George Faber might have been hard put to explain how his hatchet came to be buried *accidentally* in his wife's head.

He went to the fridge, got a can of beer and drank it while he debated what to do.

Three cans later, he opted for what dull bank executives usually opt for, which is the obvious, and decided to bury her in the cellar.

It was a Cumbrian farmhouse, tastefully modified by the addition of central heating, air conditioning, double glazing, sprung flooring, spotlighting, wall-to-wall carpeting, and vibrant Provençal colouring, all without compromising its quintessential *oldness*.

Only the cellar remained untouched.

There had been talk of pine panels and strip lights, of flood-lit pool tables and racks of fine wine, but even Phyllis Faber's springs of inspiration dried whenever she looked into those dark, mice-infested depths. In the end it came to be used as a dumping ground for items too old for use, too familiar to throw away.

A more cynical or a more fanciful man might have been amused to place his wife's corpse in this category, but it never occurred to George.

He simply covered the body with a heavy Liberty tablecloth, wishing he'd had the foresight to lay it on the floor before he axed her, thus making it easier to wrap her up and also pre-empting the gruesome task still to come of mopping up the blood from the Tuscan tiles.

On the other hand, Phyllis had been the kind of woman who noticed things like tablecloths spread across the kitchen floor. He'd wanted a carpet. He hated these cold, slippery tiles. But she'd laughed him to scorn, and later tongue-lashed him to tears when he'd had the effrontery to introduce a small rug as a stepping stone from the outside door to the dining room.

No more of that! He went out to his shed for a pick and shovel and did a little dusty dance across the tiles as he made for the cellar steps. The age of stockinged feet was past. From now on it was wellies, wellies, all the way!

Down in the cellar, lit by a single unshaded light bulb, he set to work.

It wasn't easy. First he had to shift the household rubbish to reveal that the floor was paved with rough-hewn granite slabs. At least four of these had to be levered aside to create enough space to dig a grave. This done, he wiped the sweat from his brow and went up into the kitchen to get another beer. He drank it slowly, finding himself strangely reluctant to descend the steps again. Phyllis dead and draped with a tablecloth was only a mildly discomforting presence, but down there, out of the daylight . . .

He shook his head irritably. *A man in a hurry has no time to worry.* Another pearl he produced at small business seminars. He crumpled his can in his hand, tossed it into the sink with the others, smiled at this sacrilege, and headed back down.

Now the real labour began. Fortunately, George had kept in pretty good condition, refusing to let even an arthritic knee keep him from squash in the winter and at least a dozen sets of tennis a week throughout the summer. But he quickly realized that his sporting life had developed muscles more suited to the killing smash with a hatchet than the double-handed overhead with a pick.

It occurred to him after a while (this lack of forward planning again!) that the Archimedean theory of displacement applied as much to earth as to water, and he went back upstairs to collect another couple of tablecloths to shovel soil on to.

Fortunately Phyllis had been a compulsive snapper-up of sales bargains on her trips south and the absence of a few tablecloths was unlikely to be noticed by even the most percep-tive of detectives.

The thought of detectives depressed him, however, and he unzipped another can of beer. In all his fantasies, the prospect of a wifeless life had opened up before him like a sunlit landscape seen from a high terrace where he took his ease with a cham-pagne cocktail in his hand. It had never occurred to him that beneath that terrace, dividing him from that landscape, there might be a rocky ravine of interrogation and suspicion, not to mention depression and guilt.

He shook these dark thoughts from his mind, tossed the empty can into the sink, and went back to work.

Twenty minutes later his pick drove through the packed earth and bounced back with a resounding clang. He tested to left and right with the same result. He had reached solid rock.

The hole he had so far excavated was less than three feet deep. Conventional even in these unconventional circumstances, he had been aiming at six. But now he came to think of it, the cellar steps had already taken him ten feet beneath the earth's surface, so he was way ahead of schedule.

Happy to think the worst was over, he set about shovelling the remaining loose earth on to the cloth. The bedrock thus revealed took him by surprise. It certainly wasn't granite, but more like some form of chrysoprase, highly polished so that it glowed apple green beneath the single light bulb, and smooth and as level as a ballroom floor. He could see no pockmark where his pick had impacted, and the sharp edge of his spade skidded off this surface with no hint of a scratch.

Puzzled, he touched it with his hand and drew back with an exclamation of surprise. It had that degree of coldness which almost burns like fire.

He was not by nature an inquisitive man. Professionally his strength had always been his ability to concentrate on the job in hand to the exclusion of all else. So, odd though this layer of bedrock was, his natural inclination was to collect Phyllis and get on with the task of burying her.

Instead, he found himself unwilling, indeed perhaps unable to move. He stood there quite still, his gaze riveted on that glowing green slab.

For it was a slab, he now realized. No bedrock this, but another floor level, laid God knows how long ago and covered with the earth on which eventually his own cellar floor had been set.

'Come on, Faber!' he urged himself as though he were at a conference. 'Eye on the target. Mind on the job. You've killed your wife, you're burying her body, this is no time for archaeology.'

But still he could not move away. Instead he knelt on the slab and explored it with his fingers till he found an edge. Now working with a feverish energy which made his previous efforts seem lethargic, he began to scrape away the soil along that edge, following it round till at last he had the whole slab in outline.

It was about six feet long, three feet wide. Grave size. Had someone been here before him?

He resumed his explorations into the soil beneath the edge and quickly established that the slab was no more than two inches deep. He was able to wriggle the toe of his pick beneath it, and now he threw himself against the pick handle in an attempt to lever the slab upward.

At first it resisted his efforts with a pressure that seemed disproportionate to its likely weight, but he soon found that he was exerting a leverage far beyond his normal strength.

For a period which seemed timeless, lever and weight seemed locked in perfect balance. Then the slab moved. Just a fraction. Just enough to open a crack between the edge and what lay beneath. But it was as if this tiny aperture acted as a vacuum release. There was a noise of inrushing air as though something down there, long deprived of oxygen, was gulping in huge breathfuls. And as the air rushed in, the slab twitched and creaked and groaned and finally flew open like the cover of a book in an explosion of earth, stone, and evil-smelling dust.

George shot upright. The tip of his pick shattered the light bulb. Coughing and spluttering, he staggered to the steps and crawled up into the kitchen. Even when he felt the cool tiles under his hands, he could see very little, as the dust seemed to have come up with him. Now he got the impression that its swirlings were becoming more uniform. It was twisting in an anti-clockwise direction, like a mini-cyclone, as though driven by some centrifugal force. Not just the dust but the very air seemed to be moving and there was a noise like iron-rimmed wheels sparking across a paved courtyard.

He closed his eyes and cried aloud with fear.

When he opened them again, he found he was looking at a pair of shoes.

They were slightly pointed, highly polished and ornately knotted.

He raised his head. His gaze travelled up the knife-edge crease of a pair of elegant green trousers, traversed a saffron-coloured shirt beneath a casual jacket in pale blue silk, and finally reached a face.

For a second the angle made it look like an animal's face, foxy, fanged, ferocious. He blinked, pushed himself to his knees, and saw it was the face of a young man, rather narrow and a touch swarthy, but not at all frightening. In fact his features were full of concern.

'I say, are you all right?' he said anxiously.

His voice was light, lilting, with just a trace of a foreign accent.

George said, 'Yes thanks, fine.'

He stood upright and began dusting himself down. Only there was no dust. It all seemed to have vanished.

'Who the hell are you?' George demanded with a sudden aggression provoked by the realization that if the stranger took a couple of steps backward he would be treading on Phyllis's body.

'I was just passing and I heard a noise, and I wanted to be sure everything was all right. Why don't we step outside for a moment and get a breath of air? It's a bit close in here.'

George had no objection to getting out of the kitchen. Unfortunately Phyllis lay between the stranger and the door. Which meant he must have stepped over her when he came in. It didn't seem to have bothered him. He stepped over her again without even looking down and went out on to the patio. Perhaps the tented effect produced by the hatchet had misled him into thinking it covered something else, but the outline of the legs and feet was unmistakable.

Skirting the tablecloth carefully, George followed the stranger. He found him standing with his head thrown back, drawing in deep breaths, his eyes fixed on the turbulent sky. As George joined him, he made a gesture with his left hand and forearm which brought to mind a holiday in Greece when a passing truck driver had taken exception to George's driving. But this young man's attention seemed to be focused firmly on the lurid clouds bubbling over the Lakeland fells.

Suddenly he looked round, smiled in slight embarrassment and said, 'Lovely day, isn't it?'

'If that's what you like,' said George.

'Indeed. Well, if you're sure you're OK, I ought to be pushing on. Things to do.'

'I'm fine,' said George.

'Good.'

The young man began to move away, but at the edge of the patio he hesitated and looked back.

'Is there anything I can do for you before I go?' he asked.

'I don't think so,' said George.

'Any little service. Doesn't matter what. Just name it,' insisted the young man.

40

'No, really,' said George. He didn't know what the fellow's game was, he just wanted rid of him.

'There has to be something,' persisted the stranger. 'I'd really like to help. Please.'

'There's absolutely nothing,' said George with some irritation. He turned away, meaning to go back into the kitchen and lock the door, but somehow his feet wouldn't work.

The stranger came and stood in front of him, very close. His breath smelt like the warm gust from the ventilator of a Thai restaurant. 'Mr Faber, I'm offering to help you, no strings attached. You've only got to ask. Now where's the problem in that?'

He spoke in the gentlest, most reasonable of tones, but George still felt threatened.

He said, 'There's nothing. Honestly. Nothing I need help with. Please, just go . . .'

'Nothing?' cried the stranger. 'Your wife's lying dead on the kitchen floor and you're digging her grave in the cellar, and you say there's nothing you need help with? Come on!'

George's eyes orbed in horror and shock. The case was substantially altered!

He stammered. 'Who are you . . . ? Why've you come . . . ? Where have you come from . . . ?'

His mind played blind-man's buff with answers to his questions.

An escaped lunatic? A policeman? Phyllis's lover? But how . . . ? and why . . . ? and what . . . ?

'No, I'm quite sane and I'm not a cop,' interrupted the stranger impatiently. 'Nor am I your wife's fancy man, though incidentally, she did have one, did you know that? Fellow called Freddie who owns the big furnishing store in the High Street.'

'Freddie? You mean Freddie Corcoran?' exclaimed George, dumbfounded.

Freddie Corcoran. He thought of him as a friend. They'd got most of their carpets and furnishings from Corcoran's. Freddie had given them an excellent discount . . . he'd even come round himself to measure up . . . *Measure up*! The bastard!

But retroactive jealousy was a waste of time. More important was working out how this chap breathing in his face came to know so much . . . came to be able to read his thoughts even!

'Oh my God,' said George, making perhaps for the first time in his life an imaginative leap. 'You were under the slab, weren't you?'

The young man made no attempt to deny it but smiled and said, 'That's right, Mr Faber. And I can't tell you how grateful I am that you got me out. That's why I want to help you, simply as a token of my gratitude.'

George shook his head, not in denial but for clarity. Good banking practice required that you kept a cool head and dealt solely with facts. He wasn't going to let himself be sidetracked by offers of assistance till he knew precisely what he was dealing with.

'Listen,' he said. 'Who are you? What are you?'

'You can call me Alzac,' said the young man. 'As to what I am, it's a long story and, honestly, I don't really think you want to know. Suffice it to say, I've been shut up down there for rather longer than I care to remember. I was beginning to doubt if I'd ever get out. There was an escape clause, of course, there always is. But as the years rolled by and what you call civilization ground on, it began to look more and more unlikely that it would ever apply.'

'Why?' said George, his ears alert to the whisper of small print. 'What did it say?'

'It said that the stone could only be removed by a priest or priestess who had just made a human sacrifice and still had blood on their hands.'

George looked at his hands. He hadn't noticed the blood till now.

He said, 'I'm not a priest.'

'What do you call yourself then?'

'I'm a banker.'

Alzac smiled.

'That explains it. You're in the service of my old master. I daresay he's got himself a new name now, but back in the old days he was known as Mammon.'

'Mammon? You mean the God of money?'

'Oh no. Hardly a . . . what you said,' said Alzac. 'But certainly a Power. How shall I explain it to you . . . ? Let me see. Think of it like this. A long time ago, when the human race was still finding its feet, often quite literally, the Great Powers decided on a policy of colonization. There were the usual disputes but in the end the distinctive land areas, what you call countries, were carved up and received ambassadors, each according to its own perceived potential. Your country, England, as it came to be known, fell to Mammon. Naturally there was resistance but on the whole things have worked out pretty well, wouldn't you agree?'

'Resistance?' echoed George, unable either to believe or disbelieve what he was hearing. Perhaps he'd had too much beer on top of too much stress . . .

'Oh yes. The Powers have always had to struggle. How shall I put it? They are on the side of self-determination and market forces, and very much against central control and state interference.'

'You mean, God?'

'You do like that word,' said Alzac frowning. 'But if it helps you understand, yes. In what you call your Middle Ages, Mammon foresaw the huge potential of America and headed west to prepare the ground, leaving me to finish things off here. I got careless. I freely admit it. And I paid the price. I got taken and buried and you lot . . .' he laughed scornfully '. . . you lot got art and music and literature, all that stuff you call the Renaissance. It took Mammon a couple of hundred years to

43

regain the lost ground so he didn't waste any effort trying to get me out. He's not what you'd call a forgiving fellow. But clearly he's back on top of things now, which probably explains how I've come to be released. For which I'm enormously grateful. I really owe you a favour. Have you thought of anything yet?'

'Not yet,' said George. 'I'm still thinking.'

As indeed he was, possibly harder than he'd ever thought in the whole of his life. What was happening was quite incredible, of course. But an hour or so ago if anyone had suggested that he was about to murder Phyllis, wouldn't he have found that just as incredible? The difference was, in the latter case there was evidence to convince a reasonable man. A body is a pretty large step in logic. But what test of logical consistency can you apply to something like Alzac?

He said slowly, 'Look, if you are a devil or demon . . .' (Alzac looked somewhat offended) '. . . or whatever, why are you so keen to help me? I mean, from what little I know of such things, I never thought your kind went in much for stuff like gratitude?'

Alzac flung his hands apart and shrugged in a gesture which was straight out of a casbah carpet shop.

'Listen, let's forget it,' he said. 'You don't want me to help you, that's OK. No skin off my nose, eh? See if I care.'

The hands came together dismissively and he began to walk away. When he reached the edge of the patio he paused and looked to right and left as if uncertain which way to turn. George watched and waited. Alzac tried a little step left, then a little step right, like a man whose future depended on finding the right direction.

'All right,' said George. 'I've changed my mind. I'd like you to help me.'

His strange visitor spun round, his face lit up with relieved delight as he said, 'That's great. I knew you'd see sense.'

It was the relief that finally convinced George of what he'd begun to suspect.

He pointed a finger triumphantly at the demon or whatever it was and said, 'That does it! I've got your measure, my friend. You're not wanting to help me out of the goodness of your heart, are you? What would a demon's heart be doing with goodness in it anyway? You're doing this because you've got to.'

'What do you mean?' blustered Alzac.

'You know very well what I mean. I bet it's another condition, like the priest and the blood. If someone sets you free, you can't go on your way till you've paid the debt by doing them a favour. I'm right, aren't I?'

For a moment Alzac's fine narrow features began to turn foxy again. Then he recovered and tried a faint smile as he said, 'Aren't you the clever one? All right, Mr Faber, there's an obligation. I don't deny it. So let's get it over with, shall we? Then we can both get back to our proper business.'

'Oh no,' said George. 'I'm not rushing into this. That's what you wanted me to do, wasn't it, you sly bastard? First time you offered to help, if I'd said something flip, like yes, you can close the door as you leave, that would have been it, wouldn't it? Favour done, you completely free. But I reckon this is worth a bit more than that, Mr Alzac. Quite a bit more. Just how far do your powers go anyway?'

'Far enough to turn you into a toad if you don't stop standing there croaking!' snarled the young man.

'Oh yes? And how would I be able to ask you a favour then?' mocked George, feeling very much on top of the game now. 'No, I reckon you can do a lot, a hell of a lot, if you'll pardon the expression. So how about it?'

Alzac's shoulders sagged in defeat.

'All right,' he said. 'You win. I admit it all. And yes, I can do a hell of a lot. I can get rid of your wife's body, for example. No trace. The police can dig and search for a hundred years and they'll never find her. How about that?'

For a second George was tempted.

45

Then he shook his head.

'No,' he said. 'Getting rid of the body's not enough. There's still the suspicion, the enquiries . . . and the guilt. I'm not sure I can live with that.'

Alzac said, 'Well, I'm sorry, guilt's one thing we're not allowed to touch. Tell you what, if you feel so guilty, how about I bring her back to life? That's a real connoisseur's trick, believe me. You'd really be getting value for money there.'

'Back to life?' exclaimed George. 'I'm not sure . . . back to life . . . you know, I don't think I really want that either . . .'

'I wish you'd make up your mind!' cried Alzac. 'This has always been the trouble with you lot. You know what you want, only you can't stand the heat getting it. It's this guilt thing, isn't it? Without that, we'd be masters of the universe by now! All right, here's my final offer. I bring her back to life then I give her a swift heart attack. I know that's really two for the price of one, but what the hell? Today's my rebirthday. I'm feeling generous.'

George was shaking his head.

'No good, I'm afraid,' he said. 'The thing is, I'd still know that it happened because I'd wished it to happen. Are you with me? What I really want is a life without Phyllis, I mean, without her from the start. I was young, I was naive, I just slipped into marriage before I had enough sense to realize what I was letting myself in for. I don't want to harm her, I just don't want to get tied up with her at an age when neither of us knew any better . . .'

He paused, took a deep breath, and said, 'That's it. That's what I want. I want to live my life again, but with the knowledge that I've got now from the very start.'

He looked at Alzac expectantly but the demon was shaking his head. 'Sorry, no can do,' he said. 'The trouble is, if you live your life again, your present life won't have happened, and you can't have knowledge of something that doesn't exist, can you?'

George could see the logic of this, but he said desperately, 'All right, let's forget precise knowledge, let's think about . . . wisdom.

46

That's different, isn't it? The accumulated wisdom of my forty-six years. Couldn't I have that from the start?'

Alzac considered, then nodded slowly.

'Yes, that might be possible, I suppose. You'd live your life again, but be as wise from the start as you are now. That's what you want, is it? You're quite sure?'

'Absolutely,' said George. 'Only . . . it would be nice to know about it too, about its being a second time around, I mean. But from what you said that wouldn't be possible, would it?'

Alzac looked dubious, then his expression brightened like marsh light on a lonely moor.

'It might be done,' he said. 'But not until you reach the same age you are now. You see, you'll have moved through the same time twice, and it's not until both paths converge at this point of time that you'll be able to see the two of them together.'

'But I'll be able to make a comparison then?'

'Oh yes,' said Alzac.

'Then that's what I want. Definitely. That's the little favour you can do me, my friend.'

'You've got it,' said Alzac. 'Hold tight. Here we go.'

He grinned maliciously, showing more teeth than a human ought to have, raised his left hand, made a circle with his fore-finger and thumb, then snapped it open with a fearsome cry.

The air trembled and became full of dust again. George closed his eyes. A current of boiling heat followed by another of crip-pling cold surged round his veins. He felt the agony of death and the ecstasy of orgasm at the same time.

And then it was past. He felt quite normal again.

He opened his eyes.

He was still standing on the patio with the same flowers in the same tubs, the same black clouds in the same turbulent sky. He was wearing the same clothes. He felt the same twinge of arthritis in his left knee, the same sniffle of head cold in his nostrils.

The only thing different was that Alzac was gone.

Oh God, he thought, I'm going loopy. Nothing's changed. I've just started having delusions, that's all.

He turned to re-enter the kitchen and stopped in his tracks in the doorway.

Something had changed. Phyllis's body had vanished. There was no sign of it, nor of the Liberty tablecloth, though oddly most of the Tuscan tiles were covered by a large square of carpet.

George looked at his hands. There was no blood on them.

He stepped into the kitchen and looked down at the carpet. No bloodstains here either.

He needed air. He staggered to the door again, his mind struggling to make sense of all these things, or rather to make another sense than that which his powers of logic were printing out as truth.

But truth cannot be denied. He threw back his head and saw it written in the stormy sky.

'Is this it?' he cried in despair. 'Is this all the difference the accumulated wisdom of one lifetime can bring to another? Have I managed to live through another forty-six years without anything better to show for it than a piece of carpet where there was no carpet before? Oh God. What kind of pathetic excuse for a human being am I?'

There was a rage boiling up inside him which had to be released if it was not to be self-destructive. He let it out on the obvious target.

'Alzac! Where are you? Oh you cunning bastard. You knew, didn't you? You knew I'd do no better second time round and you didn't warn me! Wherever you are, damn you to . . . to . . .'

Even in his rage it occurred to him that damning a demon to hell was a touch tautological.

It also occurred to him that perhaps he knew exactly where Alzac was.

He ran into the kitchen, flung open the cellar door and snapped on the switch.

Light flooded down from the unbroken bulb to reveal stone flags, unmarked by pick or shovel, and strewn with household junk.

He began to laugh.

'I didn't kill her second time round so I didn't need to dig up the cellar!' he crowed. 'You're still down there, Alzac. Can you hear me? You're still down there, you stupid bloody demon, and that's where you're going to stay!'

There was a noise something like a groan and he quickly put off the light and slammed the door.

Then he turned and stood on the carpet looking down at the spot where Phyllis's body had lain, trying to work out whether he was sorry or glad that this time round he hadn't killed her.

But why hadn't he killed her? Could it be perhaps that this time he hadn't wanted to be rid of her? If he'd had a second chance, then she must have had one too. Perhaps she'd made better use of it, suppressing those wilful and domineering elements in her character which made her such a pain to live with. In fact, it came to him in a flash, if he wanted evidence of such a change, he was standing on it!

He recalled her fury when he'd suggested that the way to protect her beautiful tiles from his dirty feet was to put a bit of carpeting down. But this time round she must have given in. And not just a bit of carpet but a large square.

There was something else. The old Phyllis, even if she'd agreed to the carpet, would have chosen a piece of such quality and expense that he probably wouldn't have been allowed to walk on that either! She wouldn't have given houseroom to the kind of cheap, rubber-backed nylon-tufted merchandise he was standing on now. Even the colour was entirely wrong, a garish purple, screaming against the tiles' siennas and the units' olive green. The change this suggested went deeper than simple self-restraint. He racked his brain in an effort to recall what life was like with this new and altered Phyllis.

The new and altered Phyllis, coming up behind him, was pleased to find him so rapt in thought. She buried the hatchet in his skull with one powerful double-handed blow and stood back as he collapsed with scarcely a sound on to the centre of the carpet square specially laid to receive him.

Then she went to the door and softly called, 'Freddie.'

A stocky, gingery man came out of the garden shed. He was pale-faced and his brow was glistening with sweat.

'You've done it?' he said tremulously.

'Of course I've done it,' snapped Phyllis Faber. 'But I can't do everything myself.'

'I'm sorry,' he said as he followed her into the kitchen, 'I don't know what came over me . . . oh my God.'

Impatiently Phyllis threw a corner of the carpet over George's ruined head.

'Come on,' she said. 'No time to waste. I've got my Age Concern Committee in forty minutes.'

'Look,' said Freddie. 'I've got an idea. Why don't we just bury him in the cellar? There's a pickaxe in the shed, it'll take no time at all. That'd be best, wouldn't it? A nice grave in the cellar, far less risky . . .'

His face recovered its colour in a flush of enthusiasm as he went to the open cellar door and peered down into the depths.

But Phyllis was looking at him as if he'd just crawled out of the woodwork.

'For God's sake, Freddie, pull yourself together! That's the most stupid thing I ever heard. We'd need to be brain dead to put him in the first place even our noddy policemen are going to look. Now let's get this carpet folded up and out to your van, shall we?'

'I'm sorry, darling,' said Freddie in a bewildered tone. 'I don't know why . . . I just got this sudden urge . . .'

With a perceptible effort of will, he turned his back on the musty darkness of the cellar and came to kneel at her side.

Together they folded the carpet over George's body, then bound it round with cord. Next they half dragged, half carried it out of the kitchen, across the patio and round the side of the house to where a furniture van marked CORCORAN'S INTERIORS stood with its rear doors open and its hydraulic tailboard lowered.

Leaving her lover to manoeuvre the carpet into the van, Phyllis went back into the kitchen and checked the tiles to make sure there was no blood. As she'd anticipated, the rubber-backed carpet had prevented any seepage. Satisfied, she made for the door.

Then she paused. Was that a sound in the cellar?

She went to the open doorway and stood at the top of the steps and listened.

Nothing.

It had probably been a mouse. She shuddered. She was terrified of mice. But she was not a woman who cared to admit such a weakness.

'You just stay down there,' she called. 'Come up here and you'll regret it, believe me!'

Satisfied, she slammed the door shut and hurried out on to the patio.

The storm was just about to break. She didn't see it, but somewhere there must have been a flash of lightning, for as she got into her car and followed the furniture van out of the drive, a peal of thunder rumbled round the circling mountains, like laughter from the belly of a god.

The Perfect Murder Club

I switched on the news.

Starvation in Africa. Earthquake in Asia. War in Central Europe. Bombs in Belfast. And so many murders only the most gutting merited a soundbite.

Life was cheap.

One of the bodies lying by a roadside looked a bit like my bank manager. No way it could be. Nothing to do with him ever came cheap.

But it got me thinking. All these dead people and I didn't know any of them. What a waste!

I found a sheet of paper and started making a list of everyone I wouldn't mind seeing dead. I drew three columns; the first for the name, the second for the offence, the third . . . I wasn't yet sure what the third was for.

It turned out to be a surprisingly long list even though I limited myself to those I knew personally. Once start admitting people I didn't know, like those neanderthal yobs rampaging round the Arndale, or this horse-faced telly-hag now droning on about the Health Service, and the list could have gone on forever.

Finished, I read through it slowly, excising one name (gone to live in Provence, which surely must be regarded as some sort of sanctuary for the unspeakable) and adding two more.

On the box a weather forecaster was being brightly facetious. I studied her vacuous smile and was tempted. But no. Rules are rules.

So I turned to the problem of the third column. No problem! It was obvious what it was for. Mode of dying.

I had a lot of fun with this, making the death fit the life. Thus *he* whose halitosis had nauseated me these many years should choke on a pickled onion, while *she* whose voice had cut through my sensibility like a buzz saw should swallow her tongue.

But eventually the game palled. It was more interesting than TV but just as empty. What I needed was a strong shot of reality. I took another look at column three and soon saw where I'd gone wrong.

It wasn't for mode of dying, it was for method of killing.

Now fancies fled away. Now there was only one real consideration. How to do it and get away with it.

I had to devise the perfect murder.

An hour later I was still staring at a blank column. Perfection, I'd discovered, was surprisingly difficult. Or perhaps what was surprising was that I should have been surprised. After all, I'd never come close to achieving it, not even in the things I used to do every day. Perhaps if I had I might still be doing them. But it was no use brooding over what had gone forever. What I needed was expert assistance. But there was no government retraining scheme in this field, and it was pointless turning to the Yellow Pages. One obvious condition of the perfect murder is that you don't advertise.

I let my mind go blank in the hope of enticing inspiration, and suddenly I found it being invaded by that most ephemeral of messages, a Radio 4 *Thought for Today*. It had been uttered by one of those bouncy bishops who like to be known as Huggable Henry or something equally execratory. After the

usual mega-maunderings, he had cast the following already soggy
crumb of philosophy upon the morning waters.

*Sometimes what looks like an insurmountable barrier can turn
out to be an open door.*

On the whole, you'd be better off pulling Christmas crackers.
But this time, in this one respect, it struck me that Bishop Henry
might unawares have come within hugging distance of a truth.

Think about it. If you've committed a perfect murder, the last
thing you do is go around shouting about it. But what's the point
in perfection without appreciation? It must be like running a
mile in under three minutes, and no one knowing about it. Of
course, some people would probably be content to hug such
knowledge to themselves. But if even a small fraction of the
probable total of perfect murderers were as eager to talk about
it as I was to listen, then all we had here was the classic marketing
problem of how to match supply and demand.

Now this was something I *was* quite good at. I'd already
established that *they* couldn't advertise. But there was nothing
to stop *me*.

The next morning I went down to my local newspaper office.
The young man I spoke to first proved singularly stupid and I
found myself wishing I knew him well enough to put him on
my list. But finally the advertising manager appeared, and after
I explained to him that I wanted to place the ad in connection
with a TV programme I was researching, all went smoothly. You
could persuade people to show their arses in public if they thought
it was for the telly. In fact, I believe if you're tuned to the right
satellite, you can see it happening already.

My advertisement appeared that very same evening. I read it
with a certain complacent pride.

HAVE YOU COMMITTED THE PERFECT MURDER?
If so, you've probably felt the frustration of not being able
to tell anyone about it. But relax! Your troubles are over.

A new organization has been formed to exchange information on method and technique. To complete your job satisfaction and enjoy at last the applause which is your due, contact:

THE PERFECT MURDER CLUB

Confidentiality guaranteed. Ring now.

You won't regret it!

After some debate I'd given my home number. It was pointless running the ad unless people could get in touch. I knew it also opened access to undesirables like the police and the usual pranksters and cranks. But not having committed any crime myself (yet!) I had nothing to fear from the law. And as for the rest, I was pretty sure I could sort out the wheat from the chaff with a few pertinent questions.

The first call came within half an hour of the evening edition hitting the streets.

The caller was male, slightly adenoidal, and, I soon deduced, not very bright.

'Hello,' I said.

'Hello.' Pause. 'Is that the . . . er . . . Perfect Murder Club?'

'Depends,' I said. 'How can I help you?'

'I dunno.' Another pause. 'Look, I saw your advert . . . What's it all about?'

'It's about what it says it's about.'

'Yeah . . . well . . .'

I could almost smell his desire to strut his stuff.

'Are you interested in becoming a member?' I asked, very businesslike.

'Yeah . . . well, maybe . . . it depends . . .'

'It does indeed,' I said. 'It depends on whether you are qualified. You're not a time-waster, I hope? Ringing up out of curiosity or for a giggle?'

'No!' he replied indignantly.

'OK. How about a few facts then, just to establish you qualify for membership. No names, of course. Nothing to give yourself away. Just an outline.'

'Yeah? Well, all right. It was my wife. She fell down a cliff. Everyone thought it was an accident. It wasn't. I pushed her.'

'I see. And where was this?'

'Scar . . . on holiday!'

What a twit!

'And that's it, is it?' I said.

'Yeah. Why? What's wrong with it?'

'It's not exactly perfect, is it?'

'What do you mean? She's dead. I'm married to a woman I really love. I got a hundred thou insurance. If that's not perfect, what is?'

'I'm glad things worked out so well for you,' I said patiently. 'But there was no guarantee she was going to die when you pushed her, was there?'

'It was a hundred-foot drop on to rocks!'

'So? There was a Yank fell five thousand feet when his parachute didn't open. Landed on a hypermarket roof in Detroit. Only injury was he sprained his ankle climbing down the fire escape. No, your wife could easily have survived to give evidence against you. Was it daylight? Good weather?'

'Of course. You don't go walking along that path in the dark when it's raining!'

'Right. Then suppose a birdwatcher had spotted you through his binoculars? Or another walker? Or maybe a farmer? Where would you have been then?'

'But that's the point! Nobody did!'

He was getting very agitated. Time to close.

'No,' I said. 'The point is this, Mr . . . sorry, I didn't catch your name?'

'Jenkinson . . . oh shit!'

'Precisely, Mr Jenkinson,' I said. 'You are clearly not a perfect murderer, merely an extremely lucky murderer. Word of advice, Mr Jenkinson. Use some of that insurance money to have a mouth bypass or you could end up in real trouble. Bye now.'

I chuckled as I replaced the receiver. Poor sod. Preening himself on being the undetected Maxwell of murder when all the time he was merely its John Major, in the right place at the right time and probably too wimpish for anyone to suspect he could have given the monstrous woman in his life a fatal shove.

I settled down to wait for more calls.

They came steadily over the next couple of hours. There were two clear cranks, one confessing to the murder of Marilyn Monroe, the other claiming to be Lord Lucan, plus a few pranksters, sadly unimaginative in their tall stories. I was entertained by an indignant lady who told me I was a symbol of the moral corruption of our society and invited me to repent at a charismatic pray-in she was holding in her house later that evening. I excused myself, but compensated a little later by sending along a couple of men who'd mistaken my advert for a coded signal for the next meeting of their sadomasochist group.

And as anticipated I heard from the police. Of course the mastermind who called didn't say he was police but pretended to be a punter. It was like listening to some village thespian stumbling through *Hamlet*. I let him ramble on, till finally, thinking he'd got me fooled, he said, 'Look, I'm sure I've got something that would interest you, but I'd rather not discuss it on the phone.'

'Perfectly understandable,' I said. 'Do drop in any time you like. I'm sure you've traced my address by now.'

Pity we don't have video phones. I would have liked to see the expression on his face as I rang off.

Now all this was good fun, but as yet there'd been nothing to help me in my serious research. Then finally, just as I was giving up hope, I got a call which sounded like it might be genuinely useful.

It was a woman's voice, youngish, rather nervous, but with an underpinning of determination that made me feel this wasn't just a time-waster.

Not that she gave anything away. I liked her caution. The urge to share a triumph is one thing, the kind of stupid gabbiness displayed by the idiot Jenkinson quite another.

For a long time we just walked around the subject, but I soon became aware that I wasn't doing all the leading. In the end I felt myself being steered into the first steps to openness.

I said, 'So what is it I can do for you, Miss . . . er . . . ?'

Not even acknowledging this clumsy attempt to get her name, she said, 'I would like to be able to talk in safety.'

'The Samaritans are said to be very discreet,' I said, trying to regain the initiative. 'And sympathetic.'

She fell silent for a while, then said softly, 'It's not sympathy I want. It's empathy. And appreciation.'

Gotcha! I thought.

'I think the Club can guarantee both of those,' I said in my strong, serious voice. 'If you could perhaps just give a flavour of what you would be bringing . . .'

Another silence. Then speaking very carefully she said, 'It's to do with a person who had the power to injure me. I was not able to continue under this threat. So I worked out a method for disposing of this person without leaving any clue to link the death to myself.'

'A method?' I said, perhaps too eagerly. 'Poison? Accident? Can't you give a hint?'

'I think I've said enough,' she said, her nervousness returning. 'Perhaps too much. The compulsion to talk is strong, but the instinct of self-preservation is stronger.'

I was terrified I'd lost her. This was the genuine article, there was no doubt in my mind. This was someone who had the brains to work out what had to be done and the will to do it.

I said, 'I understand, believe me. You who have already had to extricate yourself from someone's power will be more reluctant than any of us to risk recreating that situation. This is precisely why the Club has been formed. Nobody will hear your story who has not a similar story to tell in return. When secrets are exchanged, their power is cancelled. Believe me, any confession made here is as safe as any ever heard by a priest in the confessional.'

I stopped myself from saying more. I could feel her being tempted, but it was her own desire which would bring her to me, not anything further I could say.

She said, 'I would need to see you face to face before I could decide whether to trust you.'

'No problem,' I said. I could still sense her hesitancy. This was no time for making rendezvous with copies of *The Times* and white carnations. To bring her into the open I had to put myself there first.

'My name,' I said, 'is Hulbert. I live at Bullivant House, Flat 36. I shall be here all evening.'

'Alone?' she said, suspicious still.

'I promise. And of course you may check before you as much as open your mouth.'

'I will, be assured. If I come.'

The phone went dead.

After that it was a case of sitting and waiting and hoping. The phone rang again a couple of times. One was a pushy young fellow who said he hadn't committed a murder but would really like to try. I told him it was like a good golf club, you needed an official handicap before you could join. The other was my ex-wife, one of whose ferrety friends had recognized my number in the ad and passed the information on. She pretended concern for my mental health, but I knew that all she was really worried about was whether I'd hit upon some money-making scheme I wasn't revealing to her solicitor.

I knew better than to offer a simple denial but told her, yes,

I was collecting material for a book and all I needed to get lift-off was a little financial backing to help me hire a top PR firm and could she see her way . . .

She'd rung off by now, so I turned to my list and promoted her from number four to number three, above my ex-mistress. Equal first remained my ex-accountant who'd mishandled my finances and run off with my ex-wife, and my ex-boss who'd made me redundant and shacked up with my ex-mistress.

I was debating further revision when the doorbell rang. She'd come! I dropped the list on to the coffee table and hurried to let her in before she could change her mind.

A man stood there, square jawed, red-haired, and built like a rugby-league forward. I'd never seen him before but I recognized his voice as soon as he spoke.

'Evening, Mr Hulbert. You were right. No problem tracing your address.'

It was the cop I'd spoken to earlier. With my nervous murderess on the way, this was a nuisance.

Deciding the quickest way to get rid of him was to cut through the crap, I said, 'Good evening, Inspector.'

'Sergeant, actually,' he said, producing his warrant card. 'Sergeant Peacock. All right if I come in?'

He pushed by me as he spoke. Hamlet he might not be, but when it came to acting the heavy, he was clearly well rehearsed.

He said, 'It's about this advert of yours, sir. We found it . . . intriguing.'

'But not illegal,' I said confidently.

'Not in itself maybe. But it could be a channel to illegality.'

'I'm sorry?'

'Taken at its face value, this ad invited people who've committed murder to confide in you. If anyone did confess murder to you and you didn't pass on the information to us, that might be an offence. If after making that confession, this person or any persons privy to the confession went on to commit a similar offence, that too might make your advert an offence. Or if . . .'

'All right,' I said impatiently. 'I get the picture. All I can do is assure you that I placed the ad on a frivolous impulse, nothing more. It's a joke, a mere squib. Naturally, if any of those replying should rouse my suspicions in any way, which I much doubt, I would of course immediately contact the police.'

He wasn't so easily satisfied.

He said, 'So you've had replies?'

'A few. Cranks, mostly. Nutters. Nothing to worry you with.'

'We worry quite a lot about nutters, sir,' he said significantly, his gaze drifting down to the coffee table.

Too late I recalled that my death list lay upon it, difficult but not impossible to read upside down. This put paid to any immediate implementation. Even if my nervous murderess did turn up with the perfect method, I'd be mad to start knocking off people whose names might have registered on Peacock's suspicious mind.

I said, 'There we are then, Sergeant. Now unless there's anything else, I have a heavy day tomorrow and would really like an early night.'

'Of course, sir,' he said. 'Work, is it?'

'Indirectly,' I said. 'Looking for it. I'm one of the three million, I'm afraid.'

He didn't look surprised. He probably knew already. Once he'd got my name and address from the telephone company, it must have been easy to check everything else, from my health record to my credit rating. I could feel all my exes getting safer by the second.

'Good luck, sir,' he said. 'A job's important. I've seen what not having one can do to the most sensible of people. Leads them into all kinds of stupidities. Like putting silly ads in the paper.'

'Yes, I'm sorry. And if anything in the least suspicious turns up . . .'

The doorbell rang.

I suppose in that brief moment my expression must have flickered from faintly-embarrassed-honest-citizen to guilty-thing-surprised and back, for he was on to me like a claims clerk.

'Expecting someone, sir?'

'No . . . well, not exactly . . .'

'Wouldn't be someone who answered your ad, would it, sir?'

I could only shrug helplessly. I mean, I was sorry for my nervous murderess, if that's who it was, but after all, I had still committed no crime.

Peacock said, 'I think maybe I should deal with this. What's through that door?'

'The kitchen,' I said.

'Right. You duck in there and don't come out till I tell you,' he said.

What could I do but obey? I went through, leaving the door just a fraction open behind me so I could hear what was going on.

I heard his footsteps cross the tiny hall, then the front door open.

'Yes?'

'Mr Hulbert?'

I recognized the voice instantly as belonging to my nervous murderess.

'Yes.'

'We spoke on the phone earlier.'

'Oh yes.'

He really was a terrible actor. He couldn't hope to get by on monosyllables forever!

'You are the Mr Hulbert who spoke to me on the phone?' insisted the woman. 'About the Club?'

'Yes I am,' declared Peacock, at last getting some conviction into his voice. 'And what might your name be?'

I strained my ears for her reply, but all I heard was a noise like a kitchen knife cutting through an iceberg lettuce followed by a sort of bubbly sigh and a gentle thud.

Then silence. Broken by a man's voice – not Peacock's – saying thickly, 'Oh my God.'

'Shut that door,' said the woman. 'You want everyone looking in?'

'No. Let's get out of here! What are you doing?' The voice was spiralling into panic.

'Just checking in case he made any notes.'

The woman's voice was unexpectedly close. She must have moved silently into the living room. Fortunately when startled I tend to freeze rather than jump. I held my breath as I listened to her rustling through the pad on the telephone table and searching through its single drawer.

'Nothing,' she said.

'Sylvie, please hurry,' pleaded the man in vaguely familiar tones. 'God knows who else he's got coming round here!'

'You reckon the world's full of idiots like you who want to shoot their mouths off to strangers?'

Her tone was tinged with affectionate exasperation rather than real scorn and her words triggered the memory which the man's voice had primed. This was Jenkinson, who'd pushed his wife off a cliff at Scarborough. Sylvie must be the lover he'd referred to. And perhaps his accomplice? No. That wasn't likely. In the first place, from what he'd said, the murder sounded more like a sudden impulse than a thought-out plan, and in the second place, if he'd confided in Sylvie even after the event, he wouldn't have felt the urge to ring the Perfect Murder Club.

Her next words confirmed this.

'If only you'd told me what happened, there'd have been no need for this.'

'It didn't seem right to tell you somehow,' said Jenkinson unhappily.

I could see his point. When proposing marriage it can't

strengthen your case to reveal that you pushed your last wife off a cliff. But once it dawned on him that he'd been stupid enough to give a complete stranger the means to identify him, he'd gone running to her.

How marvellous to have a woman whose reaction to such a revelation was neither outrage nor recrimination, but direct action to clear up the mess. I felt quite envious. Dim wimp he might be, but Jenkinson must have something I didn't to inspire such loyalty, even if it was only a hundred thousand quids' worth of insurance money!

'Right,' said Sylvie. 'Nothing here. You haven't touched anything? OK. Let's go.'

I stood with my ear pinned to the kitchen door till I was sure they had left. Then I waited another five minutes to be absolutely certain.

My relief at not being discovered had been so great that it didn't leave much of my mind to speculate on the possible connection between Sergeant Peacock and the noise of a kitchen knife slicing through a lettuce, so when at last I peeped through the door into the hallway, I could still pretend I wasn't sure what I was going to find.

I saw at once that I'd been right about the kitchen knife but wrong about Peacock not getting away with monosyllables forever. They'd seen him into eternity, no bother. He looked quite peaceful slumped against the wall with the knife sticking out of his throat. His eyes were still open and seemed to be staring straight at me. Suddenly I felt a surge of hope that perhaps after all he wasn't dead. I stooped over him, took the knife handle in my fingers, and with infinite care drew it out of the wound.

That was how his driver, coming up to tell the sergeant he was wanted on the car radio, found me.

At my trial he testified he'd seen no one either entering or leaving the building after Peacock went in. But of course he wouldn't have been able to see the side door I'm sure my careful little murderess used. Naturally I told both the police and my lawyer about the man called Jenkinson who'd pushed his wife off a cliff at Scarborough. They both checked independently and both discovered there was no record of anyone of that name dying of any cause in that area in the past ten years.

Only later did it occur to me that I'd deduced Scarborough from a single syllable. It might have been Scafell in the Lakes, or the Isle of Scarba in the Inner Hebrides, or Mount Scaraben in Caithness, or simply Scar in the Orkneys.

But by then it was all over. I was sure that once Sylvie Jenkinson realized what had happened, she had set about covering their tracks too deep for pursuit. Besides, I found I didn't really want to pursue them. If a perfect murder is one you get away with, they've managed one each. That's a record you've got to respect. If they have kids, we may yet see something really spectacular.

And really spectacular is what it will have to be to make the headlines. I still watch the news every night. Life in here isn't all that different from life outside, not if you've been unemployed for a year or two. And life out there hasn't changed much either.

Starvation in Africa. Floods in Asia. War in Central Europe. And queues for hospital beds in Britain.

Now they've gone over to *Today in Parliament* where they are all bawling and yelling and bickering about whether kids today spell better or worse than kids twenty years ago. Suddenly as I watch this spectacle I get a surprising revelation, like Huggable Henry's *Thought for Today*.

A man who sets his sights too low can't win even if he hits his bull.

The headline round-up running across the screen confirms it.

The EEC are making farmers pour milk away because they have exceeded their quota.

Fifty kids an hour are dying of starvation in Somalia.

Some prat of a politician may have to resign because he's been humping his secretary.

Twenty thousand Bosnian women may have been raped in the past six months.

An England striker has been flown home from Italy for treatment to a strained tendon.

In Sarajevo they're so short of medical supplies, they are amputating limbs without anaesthetic.

Suddenly everything's clear to me. No wonder I ended up in here. I was fighting out of my league. I set up business in competition with the multinationals. Westminster, Brussels, Washington, the UN – God is always on the side of the big guns. And now it's too late even to join, as they tell me convicted criminals aren't eligible for election to Parliament.

I suppose it's only fair really. They've got to be choosy.

I mean, innocent or guilty, if you've been stupid enough to get caught, how can you possibly hope to qualify for membership in the Perfect Murder Club?

The Thaw

He had stayed behind knowing he must be there when the snow melted.

The snow which had fallen so heavily at Christmas was still there in March.

Twice the temperature rose and the streams off the fellside began to swell, and twice Carpenter had laid out his gear in readiness. But each time the wind had turned back into the North and West, whipping old snow and new into another savage blizzard.

The second of these came early in March and set the local farmers complaining loudly of huge lamb losses. Carpenter listened to them in the village pub, nodding in sympathy and noting every word of local weather lore.

He said little himself but kept up a front of conviviality, partly for the sake of his fellow drinkers but partly also because the very effort of pretence helped stave off the depression which could grip him as numbingly as the nightly frost gripped the snow-pleated hills.

For their part the farmers were used to his presence now, as one gets used to a crowned tooth, hardly giving it a thought yet still aware somehow of its strangeness. Their greeting this night was the same as always, guardedly welcoming.

'Evening, Mr Carpenter. How are you?'

'Fine, fine,' said Carpenter, warming his hands at the fire and stamping his feet.

'You chose a bad winter to stay on.'

'Ay,' interjected George Thwaite, who had sold Carpenter the tumbledown cottage on the eastern boundary of his land four years earlier and glumly watched prices rise ever since. 'You'd have done best to go home after Christmas.'

His tone was light, but the chorus of assent which went up round the bar had a knowledgeable ring, as though the assembled drinkers were in no doubt whose fault it was that the winter had been so hard.

Carpenter walked the three miles to the pub almost every night, except Wednesday. Wednesday nights, he sat and waited for Mary to telephone. At first the calls had been more frequent, gone on longer.

Night after night Carpenter had found himself repeating the same assurances that it would soon be over and that it was best that he remained alone in the cottage, till finally constant use bleached all colour and texture out of the words.

But by then the calls were down to one a week and soon there was as much silence as conversation. After replacing the receiver. Carpenter would sit perfectly still for a while, trying to conjure up a picture of Mary.

But at best all he got was a vague shadowy outline which soon faded away into a white vacancy like driven snow.

There were other calls. His agent rang occasionally to ask how the work was going. He had thoroughly approved Carpenter's sudden decision not to return to London after Christmas but to stay in Cumberland and finish his new book. But now he was faintly suspicious.

He had cause to be. Carpenter had not written a word for over two months.

Friends rang from time to time, asking when he was returning to London and filling him in on all the current gossip. He heard several versions of the split between Mary and Jack, all full of circumstantial detail. It should have pleased him, but it took all his time to pretend surprise and interest.

Some of the callers fished for weekend invitations, formerly very plentiful. Carpenter pleaded pressure of work, but he was always conscious that he was acting out of character, though soon he began to find it almost as hard to remember his 'normal' behaviour patterns as to recreate an image of Mary.

The old Carpenter seemed like a childhood friend, once close, but now through time and circumstances drifted almost beyond recall.

He glanced at the pub clock. The 'new' Carpenter usually left about nine, and it was a quarter past already. The lonely cottage three miles up the valley seemed even less attractive than usual, but he did not feel part of the circle of noisy merriment round the huge open fire. He finished his drink, said goodnight, and left.

He had only gone a few hundred yards up the dark narrow road when the roar of an engine fragmented the deep snow-silence and he saw his shadow cast before him by headlights. He stood aside and the vehicle came to a halt beside him.

It was the police minivan which Dave Wilkinson, the local sergeant drove. He had met Wilkinson a couple of times and quite liked him. They shared a common 'foreignness' as the sergeant came from the distant shores of Cheshire.

More important, he had an open and informed mind and was good company in a conversation on matters other than lambing and the cost of silage.

'Like a lift?' called Wilkinson.

'Thanks,' said Carpenter, climbing in.

'Grand night.' said Wilkinson as the van moved forward. 'I don't think the frost's as hard.'

'No,' said Carpenter, his eyes watching the dark line of road unfurl before them. Its surface had been cleared of snow and the frost lay on it like a reflection of the stars in the hard black sky.

On either side rose ramparts of snow-sweepings, higher than the hedgerow in places, and in the fields the smooth expanse of white picked out by the headlights sent the eye racing forward, seeking a break, till suddenly the fields were behind and the moonlit fells crowded the sky, their equal whiteness broken only by the sheer outcrops of rock where no snow could cling.

'I wanted a word with you,' said Wilkinson. 'I meant to call earlier, but there was a bit of a panic. The Mountain Rescue was alerted. Some kids were late coming back. You'd think people'd have more sense than to let them loose on the fells in this.'

'No trouble, I hope,' said Carpenter.

'No. They landed back at the hostel all right; I had a good talk with the man in charge,' he added grimly.

The road surface got more slippery as they climbed up the valley and the sergeant concentrated on his driving till the minivan had bumped up the frozen-rutted path which led to Carpenter's cottage.

'Come on in,' said Carpenter.

'You've got it nice,' said Wilkinson, looking round the cosy living room.

On a table in a corner, the phone began to ring, an alien startling noise in the snow-silence which seemed to have penetrated even here.

Carpenter started stirring the dormant fire, willing the noise to stop.

'I'll do that,' said Wilkinson, taking the poker. 'You take your call.'

Turning his back on the policeman, Carpenter lifted the receiver and pressed it tight to his ear. He had no doubt who it was and it must mean trouble.

'Carpenter here,' he said.

'Where've you been? I've been trying to get you all night.' She sounded hysterically querulous.

'I'm just back from the pub,' he said lightly. 'You're lucky to find me in now. I would have still been on the road if I hadn't got a lift.'

There was a pause.

'Is there still someone with you?'

'That's right.'

'Some strapping peasant lass warming herself on the hearthrug, I suppose?'

'Nothing like that.'

'No matter. You enjoy yourself while you can. The police have started asking questions.'

'Is that so? Nothing serious, I hope.'

'Serious? Of course it's serious!'

'I shouldn't worry,' said Carpenter soothingly.

'That's fine for you! All you have to do is hang around up there enjoying yourself. But I think you ought to know that your name came up. So just think about that while you're sampling your rustic pleasures!'

The phone was slammed down viciously.

'Bye,' said Carpenter gently and replaced his receiver.

'Damn nuisance, phones,' said Wilkinson. 'There now, I've fixed the fire. We'll soon be warm. Outside at least.'

He straightened up and stirred the fire with his boot.

'There's some Scotch on the dresser,' said Carpenter. 'Help yourself. And tell me what this is all about.'

He sat down by the fire and stared into the flames. Talking to Mary had dulled his mind when it needed to be at its most alert. Even her voice seemed changed and foreign now.

'It's about a Mr John Yates,' said Wilkinson. 'I believe he was staying with you at Christmas?'

'That's right. And Mary. Mrs Yates. Nothing's the matter, I hope?'

71

It was surprisingly difficult to act out one's own estimated reactions, Carpenter had discovered. His words sounded stilted, unmistakably false, like the opening lines in an amateur play spoken by someone you know intimately.

'Have you heard from Mr Yates since you last saw him?'

'Why yes, he rang me to say they'd reached home safely. And I got a . . . no, I'm, sorry. It was Mary who wrote it. They sent me a thank-you note, but it was Mrs Yates who wrote it.'

'So you haven't heard from or seen Mr Yates since, when was it, sir?'

'Let me see; they left on the twenty-eighth, I think. Two days after Boxing Day, that was it. No, I haven't heard from Jack since he rang that night.'

'And Mrs Yates?'

'Well, no. Apart from the thank-you letter, only indirectly.'

'Could I ask you what you heard indirectly?'

Carpenter hesitated, only half-acting now. He was remembering that this sergeant was a lot more astute than a rustic policeman had a right to be.

'I heard from mutual friends that Mr and Mrs Yates had split up. Or, to be more precise, that Jack had packed his bags and left. I wrote to Mary saying how sorry I was to hear this.'

'I see. You wrote to Mrs Yates, you say?'

'Yes.'

'You didn't write to Mr Yates as well?'

'Well no,' said Carpenter, slightly taken aback. 'I didn't know where he was, did I? But I heard that Mary was still living in their old home.'

'Otherwise you might have written to him?'

'Yes, of course. I don't see—'

'I was just trying to establish which of the two, Mr and Mrs Yates, was your point of contact, sir. Normally, with a married couple, a man knows the husband best.'

'In this case, there was absolute parity of affection,' insisted

Carpenter, wondering whether he ought to show offence at the possible overtones of Wilkinson's last comment. 'I was deeply distressed to hear they had separated.'

'But not distressed that Mr Yates seemed to disappear completely thereafter?'

Now Carpenter felt able to let himself go.

'What do you mean, disappeared? As far as I was concerned, I just hadn't heard from him for a few weeks. Sometimes months, as much as a whole year could pass without my hearing from him, and that's with us both living in London.'

Wilkinson seemed quite unperturbed by Carpenter's small outburst.

'Yes, your permanent address is London, isn't it? But this year you decided to stay on here after Christmas?'

'That's right. I've told you before, I wanted some peace and quiet to finish a book.'

'You picked the right place,' commented Wilkinson, carefully pocketing the small pad on which he had been making notes. He looked approvingly round the room.

'You've got it nice,' he said again, rather sadly. He now looked ready to leave. Carpenter felt relieved but also felt that something more would be expected of him.

'What's this all about, Sergeant? I don't want to distress Mrs Yates by ringing her to find out. Do you really believe something's happened to Jack?'

'All I know, sir,' said Wilkinson from the door, 'is that early in the New Year, Mr Yates left his wife. No one has seen him since.'

'He does move around a lot. He's a freelance photographer,' offered Carpenter.

'I gather so. That's probably why it's taken so long for his absence to be noted. In the end it was some of his business associates who started getting worried when he didn't make contact.

'Evidently he'd made arrangements for money to be paid to his wife, so she just assumed he was keeping out of her way for personal reasons.'

'I hope he's all right,' said Carpenter fervently.

They stood together outside the cottage, staring, as one always did in these parts, up at the heights. A stiff breeze had started up from somewhere, blowing across the snow-smooth slopes, drawing plumes of white into the black sky.

'They got on OK when they were here, did they?'

'Why, yes, I think so. The usual marital friction, but no sign of anything deeper.'

'You're not married, Mr Carpenter?'

'No. Why?'

'It was just what you said: *The usual marital friction.*'

'I'm a writer, I observe things,' said Carpenter drily. 'Lots of married friends take pity on me for meals and weekends, so I'm quite expert. I try to return hospitality by inviting them here. Like the Yateses at Christmas.'

'Of course, sir. Very nice too. But no one since then.'

It was a statement, not a question.

'I've been busy.'

'Well, I'll keep you no longer. If you do see or hear from Mr Yates, would you mind letting us know? Once we know he's alive and well, our interest ends, of course. Goodbye, Mr Carpenter.'

He climbed into his van, wound down the window after starting the engine, and stared expertly into the sky.

'I wouldn't be surprised if we see a thaw soon,' he said. 'Cheerio.'

The thaw began two days later. Suddenly in the valley everything was wet. Water dribbled off the roofs, out of the trees, under the hedgerows. The ditches which followed the hedges along the lower roads were water while the fields began to rise again from the snow.

But the lines of stone ran deep into the snow again not far up the fellside and Carpenter saw that the mountain streams, though swollen, had not yet become the hectic brown torrents of the full thaw. It would depend on the night.

The spirits of the high hills were still capable of throwing a savage frost over the landscape and binding everything in its grip for a few more days. Or even weeks. He gathered his gear all the same. The rope. The rubber groundsheet. The ice axe. The short-handled spade. Everything necessary for survival.

The phone rang that night. It was Wednesday again, Mary's regular night. He had rung her back after Wilkinson's departure but got no reply. Nor the next night. And he had resolved furiously that he would not try again.

Now he seized the phone quickly from its rest.

'Mary,' he said.

'No. Mr Carpenter,' said a man's voice apologetically. 'This is Sergeant Wilkinson.'

'I'm sorry. What can I do for you?'

His voice sounded perfectly normal as far as he himself could judge. But insanely he felt tempted to press the mouthpiece to his chest so that his racing heartbeat could be heard along the line.

'If you're expecting a call, I could ring back later,' offered Wilkinson.

'No, that's all right.'

'Well, I'm sorry to trouble you, Mr Carpenter, but a thought occurred to me after I left you the other day.'

'Yes.' His tongue felt dry, a foul obstruction to his breathing.

'It's my wife really.' The man's mad, thought Carpenter. 'She's secretary of the local Women's Institute. And when I mentioned you being a writer, she wondered if you would be willing to give a talk at one of their meetings. If you were going to be in the district for a little while longer, that is.'

Carpenter held his hand over the mouthpiece while he let out a long sigh that was almost a sob.

75

'That's very flattering,' he said. 'But I think I may be going back to London quite soon.'

'Oh. She'll be very disappointed,' said Wilkinson, adding as though it were a powerful extra argument, 'She's read some of your books.'

'Well, I'm sorry,' began Carpenter, but there was an interruption at the other end. It sounded like a radio crackling in the background and Wilkinson excused himself abruptly.

He was gone a couple of minutes and Carpenter was on the point of hanging up when the sergeant's voice resumed.

'Sorry about that, sir. Another youngster's got himself into trouble and they're calling out the Mountain Rescue. Twice in a week! I'll have to take a look at things. Perhaps I could ring you in the morning to see if we can't sort something out. Goodbye now.'

He rang off before Carpenter could reinforce his refusal. Carpenter stared down at the silent phone for a few moments, wondering if Mary would ring now.

He shook his head and went about his business. It did not matter if she rang or not. It did not matter if he never saw her again. There was still work to be done.

It took him a long time to go to sleep that night. He lay awake listening to the steady drip of water from the roof and the perceptibly growing spate of the brook which ran down the valley beyond the cottage. The thaw was continuing.

It was still half dark when he set out the following morning. He would have started off even earlier, but it was foolish to risk a broken ankle a quarter mile from home just for the sake of an extra half hour.

He walked steadily, following the line of the valley, not stopping till the misty sun had cleared the fells to the east and his cottage was the merest blob of grey paint in a romantic landscape.

Here, resting on a flat rock above the leaping, wrestling torrent of the swollen brook, he was surprised to discover how tired he was. It was a long time since he had done any steep walking.

Not since the twenty-sixth of December to be precise.

This was the way they had come. With the kind of contrived irony the subconscious mind loves, he was sitting on the very same rock they had all rested on that day.

He had not been lying to Wilkinson when he described his relationship with the two of them as being based on a parity of affection. Though he had slept with Mary two or three times during some of Jack's long absences, he felt no sense of disloyalty.

There had been no sense of incongruity in having them to stay for Christmas, and the holiday had seemed to pass very well. Mary had done the cooking and they had wined and dined in grand style.

And on Boxing Day as they laboured up the fellside on the stiff walk which Carpenter insisted was a necessary counter to their celebratory excesses, they seemed joined together in a bond of friendship which Mary's adultery only made the stronger.

By early afternoon they had had enough and he left them exhausted to eat roast goose sandwiches washed down with whisky, while he vaingloriously climbed the remaining two hundred feet to add a stone to the cairn on the summit.

It had taken him longer than he anticipated and as he descended the afternoon light was fading fast, helped on its way by the dark grey clouds of a lowering sky. He began to hurry, glad of the help of the homemade alpenstock he always carried on the fells, much to his friends' amusement.

They were not at the place he had left them. For a moment he thought they must have started the descent without him. Then he saw them far over to the right, dangerously near the edge of one of the deep clefts which radiated from beneath the crest of the mountain.

They were close together: embracing, he thought with a pang of jealousy which surprised him. But their movements were too violent for a mere embrace. They were struggling.

He ran toward them, calling. For a moment they paused.

'Tom!' screamed Mary. 'Help me!'

Her cry was desperate and it was cut short by Jack's fingers at her throat. He had the look of a man beyond all rational control. His eyes were dilated and his face was stretched taut and bloodless, except where Mary's fingernails had drawn livid lines down his cheeks.

She seemed to have lost all strength now and without thinking Carpenter raised his alpenstock and thrust at Jack with all his might. The steel ferrule caught him high on the temple, opening up a three-inch gash. Releasing his wife, he turned to face Carpenter and seized the shaft of the alpenstock.

His mouth worked as though he were trying to say something. Then with a sudden convulsive gesture, he wrenched the implement from Carpenter's unresisting hands, staggered back with the impetus of his own success, and as though by a trick with a cine camera, he was gone.

'He was trying to push me over,' sobbed Mary. 'He knew about us. He was trying to kill me.'

Jack's body lay about forty feet down, wedged deep between two jagged rocks. In his hand he still clutched the alpenstock. To scramble down within ten feet of him was relatively easy; to get further without a rope, impossible.

But from this range the ruin of his head was clear enough for no closer diagnosis to be considered.

In any case, there was no time. Mary was in a state of near collapse and the last remnants of light were being squeezed out between the grey skies and the grey rock.

Even with Carpenter's local knowledge, to be caught on the fellside in darkness could be fatal, given the kind of weather he felt in the air. Taking Mary's arm, he set off down.

At first she was a burden, sobbing and protesting, but something of his urgency finally communicated itself to her and by the time the first snowflakes began to fall, they were following the line of the valley which ran down past the cottage.

Even then it was a close call, and they were both exhausted and sodden by the time they staggered together through the black oak door.

Why he had not rung the police straightaway, he could not now precisely remember. Mary had pleaded, begged, wept, collapsed, recovered, and finally, most devastatingly, submitted. He had replaced the phone and left it till morning. With the weather as it was, there was nothing to be done that night anyway, he told himself.

Even then he had a sense of glacier-like inevitability. He could find no voice to protest when Mary came to him in the night, nor to argue when in the snow-light of morning she outlined her plan.

Jack had tried to kill her, she told him calmly. She felt no regrets at what had happened. Nor should Carpenter.

But the police might not fully understand if they found the body with its head split open, and an easily identifiable weapon in its hands. It could mean a lot of trouble for Carpenter.

Her plan was gruesomely simple. They would recover the body together and bury it. A shallow grave somewhere remote and inaccessible, well strewn with rocks, should remain undiscovered forever.

She would then return to London and establish Jack's presence there – not difficult as he had been writing a couple of business letters to be sent off on his return – and it would be fairly easy to give their circle of acquaintances the impression that Jack was around.

Carpenter himself could claim to have heard from him if necessary. After a couple of weeks, she would announce they had split up and Jack had walked out on her. And as he was a man of such irregular working habits, it might take months till his disappearance caused concern.

'It's impossible!' Carpenter had told her.

'Why?' she demanded. Carpenter looked at her. Her eyes were frightened. She looked defenceless, vulnerable, her red hair falling loose. So instead of saying it was impossible because he could not bring himself to do it, he pointed out of the window.

'The snow. We couldn't possibly get back up there in these conditions.'

She thought for a moment.

'That's all right,' she had said finally. 'No one else will be able to either. If necessary, I'll go back to London alone. You can stay up here and wait for the thaw. It will work very nicely.'

She ended on a triumphant note and produced such rational counters to his practical objections that in the end he was reduced to a silence which she clearly took for agreement.

Carpenter blamed himself. He had somehow let himself be cast in an unsuitable role in an absurd plot. He in no way loved Mary enough to kill for her, and he thought far too much of Jack to have caused him harm.

Gradually a kind of moral catalepsy set in so that he was able to contemplate his situation with a mere numb bewilderment and behave with apparent normality in an existence which had the kind of strange otherness that snow gives to the natural world.

Now the snow was going, though it had by no means all gone. He was climbing steadily up a long ridge whose sloping sides were crossed by a series of sharp undulations.

The sun had not yet been able to touch the bottoms of these hollows and the snow still lay there in long thin streaks, like ribs running out from the ridge's spine.

Something caught Carpenter's eyes in one of these depressions and when he turned aside to examine it, he found himself looking at the slight, pathetic skeleton of a small animal, almost certainly a lamb.

How or why its mother should have strayed so high to give birth was beyond reasoning. But its misfortune must have been a welcome relief to other ravening animals. The bones had been picked clean.

The scavengers would go no higher, Carpenter assured himself. Their natural tendency must be to make for the lower ground in such weather. The very cold itself would act as both deterrent and preservative.

Even so, for a moment he felt within a breath of turning round and going back down the mountain to whatever might ultimately await him there. But the moment passed.

With a savage thrust of his foot he scattered the small skeleton down the hillside and pressed on up the ridge at a fast pace, not pausing for another hour till he found himself approaching the spot at which he had left the Yateses on Boxing Day.

Here he slowed down, finally coming to a halt at the flat boulder on which they had sat and eaten their lunch. Something gleamed among the rocks.

It was a small whisky bottle, stripped of its label by the retreating snow. Absurdly Carpenter felt guilty at the thought that this was their litter, left three months earlier.

But even such feelings were mere procrastination. He turned toward the cleft in the rocky slope which lay about thirty yards to his left. Slowly he began to walk forward. It was as if he had stepped into a new dimension.

Rocks, sky, wind: the sliding stones underfoot, the cold air on his face: sounds, sights, smells: all combined in a new inimical way, opening his mind wide and telling him that what lay over the edge of that stony cleft was going to rise up to meet him and cling to him for ever.

There was no way of burying it here on the mountain, not really burying it. He would take it with him always as he played out his allotted role. Mary's lover. Mary's husband, perhaps. Why not? In fact, what else could happen? They were bound together now.

He came to a halt.

Here they had been struggling. Here he had stood, thrusting with his alpenstock, held lance-like.

And here Jack had stepped backwards.

He looked down.

Nothing.

Black rock, grey boulders. Snow in the crevices still. But apart from that, nothing.

He walked up and down the edge, convinced he had merely mistaken the spot. But after a few minutes he returned. There was no doubt. This was where it had happened. Right here.

Unless it had all happened only in his mind. Unless this strange frozen state he had entered during the past few weeks was merely a type of insanity producing an illusion of guilt more terrible than guilt itself.

The new dimension was still here. Sky was pressing hard down on him, trying to force him over the edge into the cleft.

Carefully he squatted down on his heels and, rocking gently to and fro, tried to work things out. It was important to do so. He knew that without doing this, there was no way for him to leave the mountainside. No way except one.

'Poor devil,' said the doctor looking down at the body. It was the only epitaph which had been uttered so far. The climbers of the Mountain Rescue team had borne their burdened stretcher down the fellside in the exhausted, despairing silence which always accompanies the returning dead.

The men waiting by the ambulance needed only a distant sighting of the party to know that there would be no breakneck drive along the valley roads to the hospital.

Now the husk of the man lay on a marble slab, his eyes still open as though trying desperately to glimpse some possible answer to an insoluble question.

With a shake of his head, the doctor began his examination.

*

Sergeant Wilkinson shivered as he stood in the cold living room of Carpenter's cottage.

The fire had not been lit that day and the chilling damp of the outside air had quickly established itself here.

The sergeant was a big man but he moved lightly round the room, as though unwilling to disturb that silence that can fall on a house as palpably as dust. There was little sense of purpose in his movements.

He lifted an ornament from the mantelshelf, opened a door of the ancient dresser which filled most of one wall, riffled through some papers which lay on the bureau.

'What are you doing?' said a voice behind him.

He turned. Standing in the door was a tall red-haired woman.

'Who are you?' she asked.

He glanced at the stripes on his tunic sleeve.

'Sergeant Wilkinson,' he said. 'May I ask who *you* are, please?'

'I'm Mary Yates,' said the woman. 'I'm a friend of Mr Carpenter's. Where is he?'

'Why do you want to see him, Mrs Yates?'

'Why . . . I'm a friend. I just happen to be in the neighbourhood, so I thought . . . Nothing's happened, has it?'

'Did Mr Carpenter know you were coming, Mrs Yates?'

'No. I did try to ring earlier, but there was no reply. What's going on?'

'Please sit down, Mrs Yates,' said Wilkinson gently. He waited till the woman had seated herself by the cold fire.

'Mr Carpenter went out on the fells today,' he continued. 'Not a wise thing to do by yourself at this time of year.'

'Has something happened?' demanded the woman, her voice strained.

'Have you any idea what might have made him do this?' asked Wilkinson, ignoring her.

'No. Why should I? He likes walking, that's why he has a cottage up here.'

'Yes. You all went walking together at Christmas, didn't you? You and your husband and Mr Carpenter, I mean.'

There was a long silence.

'How do you know that?' she asked finally.

'How? It's no secret, is it, Mrs Yates? Didn't you tell my colleagues that when they were questioning you about your husband's disappearance?'

'Yes, probably. It's of no consequence, though. I find it odd that you . . . Sergeant, tell me, has Mr Carpenter had an accident?'

She sounded very urgent, but Wilkinson was slow to respond all the same.

'Accident?' he repeated. 'When you bring a body down off the fells, that's the thing most people assume. Accident. I suppose that's what you could call it.'

'Oh! Is he badly hurt?' she demanded.

'Hurt? I said "a body", Mrs Yates. I'm sorry.'

She bent forward so that her long red hair screened her face.

'Where did you find him?' she asked almost inaudibly.

'I don't know. I expect the rescue team will have the spot pinpointed. Are you all right?'

'I'll be fine. It's just the shock.'

'Of course,' said Wilkinson sympathetically. 'And the strain of not knowing.'

'Not knowing what?' she asked warily.

'Not knowing if Mr Carpenter managed to bury your husband or not.'

She let out a long sigh, but said nothing. She opened her handbag and took out a packet of cigarettes.

'Well, you know now,' said Wilkinson. 'Is there anything you'd like to say? I must warn you that anything you do say . . .'

She lit a cigarette and stood up. 'I don't know what this is all about. Are you trying to say that something's happened to my husband as well? Just forget the circumlocutions and tell me what's on your mind.'

'All right,' said Wilkinson. 'A working theory would be that you and Mr Carpenter were lovers and decided to get Mr Yates out of the way. So you pushed him over a cliff at Christmas.'

'Absurd,' she retorted quickly. 'Firstly, my husband returned to London with me after the Christmas holidays. There must be ways of checking this. He wrote letters, made phone calls, that sort of thing.

'So if he did come back to see Tom and something happened, it's nothing to do with me. And secondly, Tom and I are not lovers.'

'Difficult to prove,' suggested Wilkinson.

'I suppose so, but there's circumstantial evidence. I'm in love with somebody else, that's true, and I have been for almost a year now. We intend getting married eventually.

'So Tom would hardly have joined me in a plot to get rid of Jack, would he?' she concluded triumphantly.

'Right,' said Wilkinson. 'If there were such a man.'

The woman thought a second, then scribbled a name and address on a page torn from her diary.

'There is,' she said. 'You can check with him, I don't mind.'

'Most cooperative,' said Wilkinson approvingly. 'So if Carpenter did harm your husband, it had nothing at all to do with you?'

'Nothing,' she said firmly. 'Absolutely nothing.'

'And the converse would be true,' pursued Wilkinson. 'I mean, if something did happen at Christmas, then Carpenter would have no motive to be involved?'

'A pointless question,' she said. 'May I go now, please?'

'Why, yes,' said Wilkinson, glancing at the door. 'I think we're all ready now.'

She turned and jerked convulsively as though she had walked into an invisible electrified barrier.

In the door, holding a large suitcase in his hand, was Carpenter.

'All packed then?' asked Wilkinson cheerfully. 'Good. Then there's nothing to keep us.'

'You told me he was dead,' whispered the woman.

'Never in this world!' denied the sergeant. 'I said they brought a body down off the fells. They did. But it was your husband's, Mrs Yates. The Mountain Rescue were looking for someone quite different when they found him, but they brought him back all the same.

'Mr Carpenter must have just missed them. It was a bit of a shock for him, I dare say, finding the cupboard bare. But fortunately he managed to work it out.'

'It doesn't make any difference,' she answered, staring fixedly at Carpenter. 'It's nothing to do with me.'

'That's not for me to decide,' said Wilkinson. 'But I think you'll need a better story, Mrs Yates. You see, the body was very well preserved. Refrigerated, you might say. And the doctor found some very interesting marks on Mr Yate's face.

'But more interesting still were the stomach contents. Roast goose sandwiches, he reckoned. Very Christmassy. And most interesting of all, there was evidence that he had recently imbibed a large quantity of sleeping pills, probably dissolved in some form of alcohol.

'A dangerous combination for a man on a mountain walk. Did you think it best to get him a bit groggy before you pushed him over?'

His voice was gentle, sympathetic even. The woman did not answer and Carpenter took up the thread of speech.

'But it didn't work fast enough, Mary.' he said, equally gently. 'You knew I would be back soon, so you had to go ahead. And Jack was still awake enough to make a fight of it.

'No wonder you didn't want it reported as an accident! A simple broken neck might have been accepted without much fuss, but you couldn't risk the kind of post-mortem they would probably give when they saw the evidence of a fight.'

'You and Jack were two of a kind,' she said scornfully. 'I could have divorced him and cited you as co-respondent!'

'Why didn't you just divorce him?' murmured Wilkinson hopefully. 'Insurance?'

'Jack was alive when you came back. I didn't have to push him over after all, did I?'

'No. And I won't forget that. But I can live with it,' said Carpenter. 'I can live with it now.'

But she was gone through the door and she didn't hear. Wilkinson went after her, in close formation.

Carpenter looked round the living room. He *had* got it nice, there was no doubt about it. But he doubted if he would be back. What lay ahead was not pleasant and Mary's story might still drag him down. But it could be no worse than the three snow-filled months he had just endured.

On the front step, after he had locked the big black door, he looked up at the darkening sky and listened attentively. It was good. The thaw continued. The valley was full of the sound of rushing waters.

Brass Monkey

'By the cringe!' said DCI Peter Pascoe, his teeth chattering together like tiny icebergs. 'It must be twenty below.'

'Aye. Grand weather for tracking a brass monkey,' said Andy Dalziel gleefully, adjusting his binoculars.

He stood there, bulky as a polar bear and apparently as impervious to cold, peering down the tree-scattered slope to the house below. Is he human? wondered Pascoe, stamping his rapidly numbing feet in the snow.

More importantly, is he right?

The windows of Hollybush Grange glowed gold, and before it the tall shapely tree, which presumably provided its name, was festooned with fairy lights and topped with a gossamer-winged angel poised for flight. It looked more like a traditional Christmas card than a villain's lair.

'Sure this is the right place, sir?' he asked.

'Sure as if I'd been led by a star,' said the Fat Man.

In fact, the light which led them to this frozen rendezvous had been lit by an exploding lasagne rather than a helpful deity.

Two weeks earlier a woman in the cafeteria at Mid-Yorkshire's famous Helm Museum in scenic Narrowdale had complained her snack wasn't properly defrosted. The overworked waitress replaced the dish in the microwave. A minute later, the oven exploded in flames.

The fire spread rapidly, or at least its smoke did, filling the building and setting off the state-of-the-art fire alarm whose fearful screech made it physically impossible for any human being to stay inside.

Except, that is, for a burly man in a Russian fur hat fitted with what must have been industrial-strength ear muffs, who had been admiring the Helm's most treasured possession, the Cellini Monkey.

This was a figure, about ten inches high, of an ape of indeterminate species, exquisitely wrought in gold and adorned with precious stones, which the great Florentine artist had wrought for a daughter of the Medici. Its value was said to exceed all of the other exhibits put together.

Once alone, the man stepped across the velvet rope separating him from the display area, lit a cook's blowtorch, and directed the flame at a sensor in the wall which, at a temperature of 200 degrees Celsius, released the electronic locks on the display cabinets.

A moment later, with the monkey in a poacher's pocket inside his capacious overcoat, he was pursuing his fellow punters to the exit.

Naturally all this activity triggered other alarms, but they were no match for the screaming siren, and it wasn't till the fire was brought under control that the theft was discovered.

Andy Dalziel was just getting his teeth into the case when news came through that the NCS were taking it over.

'NC bloody S!' snarled Dalziel. 'You know what that stands for?'

'The National Crime Squad?' suggested Pascoe.

'No. *Never Caught Short*. They gobble up all the glory, but if things go wrong, they walk away and leave the locals to clean up the mess. Flash bastards!'

The formation of the NCS a few years earlier had been aimed

at providing a law-enforcement agency whose remit was to deal with major crime and whose authority wasn't limited by the boundaries of local police forces. The fact that its officers were recruited from the Criminal Investigation Departments of these same local forces was meant to have prevented the kind of rivalries and antagonisms existing between cops and the FBI in the States, but inevitably, to many of the older denizens of CID who'd seen everything and got scars to prove it, NCS officers either got the job because they were born flash bastards or they became flash bastards as a condition of doing the job.

The flash bastard in this instance was DCI Dai Davison, who looked about eighteen, sported a Welsh Rugby Union tie, and wore trousers so tight they made Dalziel's eyes water just to look at them. 'Jesus!' he muttered to Pascoe. 'Here's me trying to do a man's work and they've sent us the Boyo David!' before putting on his village-idiot face to greet the new arrival.

The Boyo, speaking very slowly, explained that the NCS's theory was that the Cellini figure had been stolen for use in the international drugs market. 'Big money leaves a big trail,' he said. 'So the major traffickers are into barter. To them, all the Cellini Monkey represents is a million-dollar marker.'

'You mean they'll use it as brass!' exclaimed Dalziel, his look of rustic astonishment terrible to behold. 'D'you hear that, Pete? This is really a brass monkey they stole.'

And so the Cellini figure was christened.

The Boyo's team hung around Mid-Yorkshire for several days, during which time the Fat Man overwhelmed them with cooperation. Requested to provide an officer with detailed local knowledge, he immediately asked Uniformed if they could spare PC Hector for plainclothes duties. They gave him up with tears of gratitude and mirth.

Pascoe was horrified.

'Last time they let him out on patrol, an old lady had to show him the way back to the station!' he reminded Dalziel.

'Aye, he'll really test their commitment,' said the Fat Man, looking with delight on Hector who, with his expression of haunted vacancy and a shiny black suit a size too small, could have been a Victorian undertaker's mute. 'I give 'em two days.'

It took only one for the Boyo David to decide the monkey was by now probably several continents away. He took his leave, pursued by smiling reassurances that if anything relevant came up in Mid-Yorkshire, he would be the first to know.

But as the Boyo's gleaming BMW vanished from sight, the smiles faded, too.

'Right,' said Dalziel. 'Now we can get started.'

He was convinced the monkey was still on his patch, and quickly spread the word among his snouts that if they brought glad tidings before Christmas, their reward would be a choice of gold or frankincense, but if they withheld even the scrappiest scrap of information, they'd better stock up on myrrh.

Pascoe watched all this with some uneasiness, having strong suspicions that the Boyo's ears had more chance of being pleasured by Madonna's tongue than by the entry of any information thus garnered.

On the morning of December twentieth, Dalziel got a phone call and left the office alone. Some time later he returned, whistling a merry tune. For the next couple of days he was hard to find. But on the third day he reappeared again after lunch.

Pascoe went to see him, but paused at the closed door as he heard a strange voice within. It was saying in a hoarse, very broad Scots accent, 'Aye, Hollytree or bush maybe, in Borrowdale, that's what I said. Aye, Borrowdale, Cumbria, is there anither? And it's this selfsame nicht, definite!'

Pascoe went back to his desk. When he returned to Dalziel's room later, he found the door ajar. The Fat Man was alone, studying a folder. Pascoe glimpsed the name *Palliser Estates* before it was slid out of sight.

'Thinking of moving, sir?' he said lightly.

'Somewhere I can get a bit of privacy, mebbe,' growled Dalziel. 'What do you want?'

Before Pascoe could reply, the phone rang. Dalziel picked it up, listened, then banged it down.

'Snout,' he said. 'Reckons he might have something on the brass monkey.'

Pascoe stood up and said, 'Let's go.'

When interviewing registered informants, two officers were required.

Dalziel said indifferently, 'No. Probably a waste of time. I'll take Novello. Show her how it's done.'

But when he returned, he was much more excited.

He said, 'Ivor 'ull tell you the tale. I need to ring the Boyo.'

The tale WPC 'Ivor' Novello told was of a meeting with a snout who'd passed on the information that the gang who'd stolen the monkey were possibly hiding out at Hollybush Hall on the edge of Narrowdale, not twenty miles from the museum.

She'd been impressed by her boss's surprisingly subtle technique.

'This guy was really nervous. But Mr Dalziel put him at his ease with a glance, got the info, and sent him on his way. That's the way to handle snouts, I thought.'

Pascoe didn't like the feel of this. In his experience, the Fat Man's handling of informants involved fistfuls of shirt and hurricanes of hot breath. Also the memory of the Scotsman he'd overheard talking about a house called Holly something in Borrowdale, Cumbria, kept coming back. Surely there had to be a connection . . . ?

But the Fat Man, on his return, made no mention of this.

'They say the Boyo's off on some urgent case. Probably broken up for the Christmas hols already, idle buggers. Any road, I've left a message. And I've had a word with the chief. He agreed we should set up a discreet observation. Ten bodies should do it.'

'Ten?' exclaimed Pascoe. 'For observation? What is this place? Some kind of palace?'

'Better safe than sorry. See if Uniformed can lend us a few. I want 'em in plainclothes. Don't want to draw attention. Go on, Pete. Chop-chop!'

The duty uniformed inspector was unenthusiastic, but offered three men, as long as one of them was Hector, who'd been boring them all with tales of his exciting NCS attachment. Dalziel groaned and said, 'Needs must when the devil drives!' But he still didn't mention the Scotsman.

It was already dark when the little convoy finally set off, led by Pascoe driving Dalziel, who sat nursing his mobile phone.

'Expecting a call, sir?' he said.

'You wha'?' said Dalziel, looking at the phone as if it had emerged from his fly. 'No. Why should I be?'

The phone rang.

He put it to his ear, listened, said, 'You're sure? Thanks.'

To Pascoe he said, 'New info. My snout reckons there could be some kind of exchange fixed for tonight.'

'Exchange? What kind of exchange?'

'Drugs, he's heard. Some Krauts. All right, don't look like you've sucked a lemon, Germans, I mean.'

But it wasn't political correctness that was causing Pascoe to look unhappy. It was his growing sense of performance, which deepened as the Fat Man now rang NCS, expressed histrionic exasperation on learning Davison was still unavailable, and left another message for him to get in touch urgently.

'Shouldn't you have mentioned where we're going?' he said.

'He can always ask a policeman,' said the Fat Man, pulling out the Palliser Estates folder, which Pascoe was not surprised to see contained details of Hollybush, including a map of the grounds, copies of which Dalziel passed on to Sergeant Wield to aid him in the disposition of his troops when they rendez-voused in the woods flanking the approach to the house.

Pascoe didn't bother asking how these useful bits of literature happened to be in the Fat Man's possession. The whole thing stank, and the less he knew, the better.

But as he stood there freezing in the snow, he decided that the risk of losing his toes as well as the risk of Dalziel losing his job required one more effort to get the Fat Man to abandon this dubious operation.

'Sir,' he began.

'Hush!' said the Fat Man.

'What?'

'Did you not hear summat?'

Pascoe strained his ears. There was something . . . a long way away . . . rising . . . fading . . .

'Carol singers,' he said. 'Must be from the village. Sound really travels in the cold.'

'Aye. Too bloody far sometimes.'

Pascoe looked at him curiously.

'How do you mean?' he said.

'I were just recalling my great-uncle Hamish,' said Dalziel. 'He often stayed with us at Christmas, and one frosty night much like this him and me were coming back from a walk in the park when he stopped and stared up at this line of trees like he were listening. I said, "What is it, Uncle Hamish?" and he said, "D'ye no hear it, laddie?" And he began to croon this carol. 'Silent Night' it was, only the words he were singing were in German. *Stille Nacht, heilige Nacht,* that's what he sang. He'd served in the Great War, didn't talk about it much, but one thing he did talk about was Christmas 1914 – how the Germans sang carols, and the Tommies sang back, and then they all came out of the trenches, carrying bottles of booze, and they played football together, and got drunk together. And I'll tell you a strange thing, Pete. When he said, "D'ye no hear it, laddie?" and I strained my ears, blow me if after a bit I didn't hear it, and in German, too! Like the man said to Horace, there's more things in heaven and earth, eh?'

'Oh, yes,' said Pascoe, deeply affected, not so much by the story as the Scots accent Dalziel had put on when quoting his uncle.

Either the ghost of Great-Uncle Hamish had been in the Fat Man's office that afternoon or – his mind rapidly supplied the more likely explanation – or Dalziel had been on the phone to Davison, making sure he was well out of the way on a wild-goose chase up in Cumbria when the carefully staged delivery of this 'new' information he'd probably got from his snout at least three days ago came through!

If any of this ever came out, Dalziel would be lucky to save his pension, let alone his job. Only complete success – drugs confiscated, bodies in the cells, and the brass monkey recovered – could keep him secure.

He opened his mouth to remonstrate, but the Fat Man said excitedly, 'Hey, look there. This could be it.'

Pascoe looked. Distantly he could see the line of the road picked out by the headlights of a car.

Dalziel was on his radio, talking urgently.

Pascoe said, 'They're turning into the lane.'

'Yes . . . yes . . . Wieldy's on to it. It's a Merc, four passengers.'

'And how many in the house?' wondered Pascoe. 'We could be outgunned.'

'Only two inside,' said Dalziel confidently. 'And no guns with this lot, guaranteed.'

'What about this other lot?' said Pascoe.

A second set of headlights had appeared, slowed, then turned out of sight into the wooded lane.

'Who the hell's that?' exclaimed Dalziel angrily. 'Hello, hello! Wieldy, have you died down there?'

Sergeant Wield's voice came crackling back.

'It's a minibus, sir. Crowded . . . there's kids in it . . . and women . . . they've got lanterns . . .'

'It's them sodding carol singers!' exclaimed Dalziel. 'Stop them! Do you hear me? Stop them! Don't let them past!'

And that was when things started going seriously wrong.

*

Down below, Detective Sergeant Edgar Wield had disposed his officers according to Dalziel's instructions. When it came to PC Hector, the instruction had been simple. 'Put the bugger out of harm's way!' Hector, once more in his old black suit, looked so completely frozen that Wield had taken pity on him and put him in a tumbledown outhouse with the strict command, 'Stay in here unless Mr Dalziel himself orders you out!'

Hector had spent the next hour studying the instruction sheet on how to use his portable radio. Finally, triumphantly, he managed to switch it on.

And the first thing his frost-numbed brain heard was his master's unmistakable voice screaming, 'Stop them! Don't let them past!'

He rushed to the outhouse door and saw a golden glow of headlights pouring down the lane which led to the house.

And he obeyed.

From his vantage point up the slope Pascoe watched in horror.

The Merc came speeding down the snow-covered track to the house. Into its path floundered the cadaverous figure of Hector, waving and shouting. The terrified driver hauled the wheel over, the car skidded in the snow and rammed the festive holly tree. The fairy lights went into spasm and the angel's angle of flight changed from take-off to nosedive. Steam jetted out of the Merc's bonnet. The doors opened. Four men fell out. Two were clutching suitcases, and one of the others was clutching something Pascoe didn't want to believe in. They all started running towards the house.

Hector tried to grapple with the unencumbered one, a tall athletic-looking figure who with practised ease caught him in a wrist-lock and twisted his arm up behind his back.

Edgar Wield appeared from the lane, yelling.

And the man with the something Pascoe now had to acknowledge was a shotgun swung it in his direction and fired.

There was a high-pitched agonized shriek and Wield went face-down in the snow.

The house door had opened. The men with the cases vanished inside, closely followed by the tall man dragging Hector with him, and finally, after one last defiant flourish, the man with the shotgun.

Then all was still below and the only noise Pascoe could hear was his own heavy breathing as he floundered down the snow-covered hillside in his master's steps while his thoughts too floundered through drifts of dreadful speculation.

An unauthorized operation, NCS deceived, a policeman taken hostage, a shot fired, Wieldy lying wounded in the snow . . . or worse . . .

Mother of God! After a career signposted by burnt bridges and downtrodden enemies, was this at last the end of Andy Dalziel?

The good news was that it wasn't the end of Edgar Wield.

As they reached the bottom of the slope, a figure like the Abominable Snowman rose before them. They each seized an arm and kept on going till they reached the shelter of Hector's outbuilding.

'Right, Wieldy,' gasped Pascoe. 'Lie down. Where are you hit?'

'I'm not bloody hit,' said the sergeant with some irritation. 'I just took a dive when I heard that gun.'

'So why did you squeal like a stuffed pig?' demanded Dalziel.

'That weren't me, that was some poor sodding owl,' said Wield. 'I hope it were just scared.'

'With my luck, I'll likely get done by the RSPB,' said Dalziel gloomily. 'Right, sitrep: what's happened with them sodding singers?'

'Well, they've not showed up down here, so I presume they're safe up the lane.'

'Thank God. What idiot let their coach turn in?'

'That 'ud be you, sir,' said Wield. 'You said, no interference with any vehicle approaching the house.'

Dalziel glowered into the sergeant's famously ugly face and said, 'You want to watch it, Wieldy, else I might buy you a mirror for Christmas.'

But the insult lacked its usual force.

Reassured about his friend's condition, Pascoe now took stock of their situation. It wasn't good. Moonlight spilled through the fractured roof of the tumbledown outhouse to put its other-worldly touch on rusty garden tools, broken deck chairs, a slightly deflated red and yellow football. And there was something deflated about Andy Dalziel, too. After his crack at Wield, he relapsed into a sullen silence, staring down at the rubbish-strewn floor as if he saw there some image of his own future.

Pascoe said urgently, 'Sir, we can't just stand here doing nothing. We need to let NCS know what's happened, and we need to get an armed response team deployed as soon as possible. As for the carol singers, we should get them moved back to the village, then set up a one-mile exclusion zone, traffic diversions, the lot.'

Each point seemed to punch another hole in the Fat Man's casing. He continued standing there, head down, for another long minute.

Finally he took a deep breath, as if trying to restore his old bulk, and said, 'You're right. No use freezing here like three brass monkeys. Wieldy, tell the lads to hold their positions but do nowt without my say-so. We don't want dead heroes.'

'You think they might make a break for it?' said Pascoe, who'd already been examining the possibility.

'Doubt it. They'd need to go cross-country on foot. Their car's knackered, and all the Penders have got is a sporty two-seater.'

'Who the hell are the Penders?' asked Pascoe.

'Couple who rent Hollybush. You'll have seen 'em on the Helm security video. Homework, that's the secret of success, lad,' said Dalziel. 'Have I learned you nowt?'

The thought of asking the Fat Man what particular success

he believed this bit of homework was the secret of flashed across Pascoe's mind, but kicking Andy Dalziel when he was down was likely to break your toe.

'Very good, sir,' he said. 'But they're armed and have a hostage. What if they threaten to cut up Hector unless we supply transport?'

'Tell them to start with his brain,' said Dalziel. 'That should take time to find. Ivor, that you skulking out there?'

WDC Shirley Novello, who'd been lurking in the doorway observing the discomfiture of the Holy Trinity not without a little schadenfreude, stepped into the moonlight.

'Get yourself up the lane to them carol singers,' commanded the Fat Man. 'Tell them there's nowt to worry about, bit of trouble with poachers in case they heard the shotgun. Oh, and while you're at it, give them this' – he took a couple of notes out of his wallet and handed them over – 'and ask them if they'd sing us a carol afore they go. "Silent Night" 'ud be nice. My favourite.'

He's gone mad, thought Pascoe. Uncle Hamish has come to haunt him.

Novello looked at Pascoe, who nodded. She left. Then he turned his attention to Dalziel, who gave him what looked like an approving wink.

'Andy,' he said pleadingly. 'Shouldn't you be ringing the Squad? We're running out of time.'

For answer, the Fat Man picked up the brightly coloured football and started bouncing it off the wall. It can't have been punctured, and as the air inside got warmer, it began to recover its old shape and resilience.

Like Dalziel in the past, thought Pascoe. Hit him hard and he reinflates! But there was no way he could bounce back from this situation.

'Sir,' he said in a harsh formal tone, 'I've got to warn you, if you won't ring the Squad, I will.'

He hadn't wanted to utter the threat, but it had to be spoken. The *Titanic* was going down. Unless something was done, they could all be sucked under by the turbulence.

'Well, thank you kindly, Mr Christian,' said Dalziel. 'You follow your conscience, Pete. Me, I've got other things to do.'

'What, for God's sake!' demanded Pascoe.

There was a second of confrontational silence. Then distantly, eerily, a sound came floating through the air.

Silent night . . . holy night . . .

'How about a little game of footie for starters?' said Dalziel.

And before they could stop him, he stepped out of the outhouse, booted the ball towards Hollybush, and trotted after it.

'What the hell's he doing?' demanded Wield.

'Oh God,' groaned Pascoe. 'He thinks he can declare a truce like they did in the Great War!'

'You going to ring the Squad, Pete?'

Pascoe knew he should. But he knew he couldn't. Not yet, not with that pathetic figure out there, trying to keep the ball in the air.

'Anything else happens, you ring them, Wieldy.'

'What'll you be doing?'

'Showing the terror of Twickers how to play a real ball game.'

And with the deep sigh of a man who knows he's doing something unbelievably stupid, Pascoe trotted slowly forward.

'This ball's the wrong sodding shape,' complained the Fat Man, who was a rugger man through and through.

'Give it here,' ordered Pascoe.

Dalziel threw it to him. He caught it on his thigh, bounced it on his right knee a couple of times, and then, as the skills of his youth gradually creaked back into life, he lofted it high and got in three headers before it dropped into the snow.

'By God, I'd love to have seen you in *Swan Lake*,' mocked Dalziel, taking out a hip flask and putting it to his lips.

'Belt up,' said Pascoe. 'We've got company.'

The house door had opened and a man stepped out. It was the tall athletic man who'd seized Hector. He was in his thirties and dressed in black trousers and a rather sharp black jacket over a black turtleneck. He held his arms wide, probably to show he was unarmed, but Pascoe took it as an invitation for a pass and lobbed the ball to him. He took it on his head, nodded it down, and volleyed it with great force straight at Dalziel. The Fat Man didn't flinch but caught it one-handed in front of his face.

Now the three of them stood still while high above them through the cold bright air floated the lyrics of 'Silent Night'.

'Gentlemen, please introduce yourselves,' said the man in a faintly Germanic accent.

'I'm Detective Superintendent Dalziel of Mid-Yorkshire CID,' said the Fat Man. 'This is Chief Inspector Pascoe, and the man you've kidnapped is Police Constable Hector, and I'd like him back.'

'Good Lord,' said the tall man. 'Is the man who attacked us really a policeman? He keeps on claiming so, but I found it hard to believe.'

Dalziel laughed. 'Me too, sometimes. Is he OK?'

'A little incoherent. He keeps telling us we are surrounded by cruise missiles and the SAS. But I think he has the wrong war. With the snow and the football and the carols, this is more like Christmas in no man's land in 1914, eh?'

'A historian, are you?' said Dalziel.

'I try to learn from history,' said the man. 'So tell me what you want, Superintendent. It's very cold.'

'Aye, what we call brass-monkey weather,' said Dalziel, taking a swig from his flask. 'In fact, it's so cold, my brain's half frozen, which is why I've got to think aloud. And what I'm thinking is this. What are we all doing here? I can tell you why I'm here. A tip-off. We get 'em all the time. Most of 'em are a waste of time, but we've got to follow them up. So I'm here 'cos I got told I might see summat to my advantage. All I've seen so far is four men turning up with suitcases. Question is, why are they here? Could be they've come to spend Christmas with friends. Could be they're hoping to do a bit of rough shooting, which 'ud explain why they brought a shotgun.'

He paused to take another drink.

'Thirsty work, thinking aloud,' he said, proffering the flask.

'And listening, too,' said the man, taking it. 'Go on.'

'So what have we got?' resumed Dalziel. 'Gents turn up for a Christmas break and suddenly there's a lot of shouting and people jumping out of the bushes. If that happened to me, I wouldn't ask questions, I'd reckon I were being mugged and head for cover. Gun goes off in self-defence, someone makes a citizen's arrest on one of the attackers, that would be perfectly understandable, too.'

Pascoe couldn't believe this. He stepped forward to speak but the Fat Man's elbow in his ribs silenced him.

The man in black nodded emphatically. 'Precisely what happened to me and my friends,' he said. 'But the police I think would still want to ask questions, make searches?'

'Oh aye. Cops ask, lawyers answer, everyone goes home,' said Dalziel. 'It's the way of the world. As for searches, you can't find what's not there. God, but it's chill! Goes right to your bladder, this air. I expect after a long drive you and your friends will be all queuing up for the bog.'

'The bog?' echoed the man.

'Bathroom. Lavatory. Loo. I daresay you'd need to use it quite a bit to make yourselves feel comfortable afore we go off to meet your lawyer. No need to rush.'

The man in black was regarding him speculatively. 'You are local police, you say?'

'What else would we be?'

'I am a foreign national, Mr Dalziel, a totally innocent foreign national, of course, but I have read somewhere that here in

England serious crimes, especially those with an international dimension, have been taken out of the hands of local forces and are now dealt with by what I think is called your National Crime Squad.'

'You're certainly well informed, sir,' said Dalziel admiringly. 'But I don't see any reason for the National Crime Squad to be involved in a little local mix-up, do you? Getting them down here flexing their muscles wouldn't do either of us much good, would it?'

Suddenly the man smiled as if everything had become clear.

'*Prosit*,' he said, taking another swig from the flask before handing it back. 'Yes, fifteen minutes should be fine.'

Then he turned on his heel and went back inside.

'Sir!' exploded Pascoe.

'Not in front of the servants, lad,' said Dalziel, striding back to the outhouse.

Once inside he said, 'All right, spit it out afore you choke on it.'

'You can't do this, sir. It's just plain wrong.'

'Wrong? They've got Hector in there, remember?'

'Come off it! This isn't about Hector. This is about saving your skin! There's a gang of drug dealers in there flushing the evidence down the pan on your instructions so you can keep your job!'

'Nobody's perfect,' said Dalziel.

'It won't even work!' said Pascoe desperately. 'Not for you, anyway. Yes, some sharp brief will probably get them clear, but everyone in the job will know the truth. You don't imagine Davison and his masters are going to let you get away scot-free? Screwing up is bad, but there's some dignity in putting up your hand for it. Trying to cover up by letting these scumbags walk free is unforgivable.'

'You'll not be contributing to my going-away prezzie then?' said Dalziel.

For a moment the two old colleagues stood toe to toe like a pair of bare-knuckle pugilists.

Then Wield, who'd stepped outside when the row began, called, 'The door's opening. He's chucked the shotgun out. He's waving us over.'

Inside the warm house, Pascoe's feet began to thaw, but that was the least of his pains.

They were met by the tenants of Hollybush, the Penders, a handsome young couple with cut-glass accents whose reaction to events was a carefully judged mixture of righteous indignation and noblesse oblige. They confirmed that the Germans were old friends and honoured guests, come to enjoy an English Christmas and do a bit of rough shooting over the holiday. Pascoe tried to spot some usable resemblance between them and the couple on the Helm security video, but found none. Not even the remarkable sight of Fat Andy grovelling in apology could divert his mind from its growing sense of angry frustration.

As expected, the suitcases contained nothing but clothing. Hector was no help whatsoever. He couldn't recall anything incriminating being said in his presence, but he did report that there'd been a great deal of toilet flushing during the last fifteen minutes of his ordeal. 'Thought they must be getting worried because of what I told them about the penalties for kidnapping a police officer,' he concluded proudly.

The Germans, meanwhile, sat at their ease in front of a roaring fire, drinking brandy and chatting away about football.

'So how much of your money's gone down the drain then?' interrupted Pascoe, desperate to score some kind of hit. 'Half a mil? More?'

The man in black laughed and said, 'Don't know what you mean, but in any case, what's money? What is it you English say? Money doesn't grow on trees? I have news for you. In some parts of the world, it really does!'

He had to translate his bon mot to one of his compatriots whose English wasn't so good, and the four of them fell about laughing.

Their self-possession remained undented even when Dalziel apologetically invited them to let themselves be taken down to police headquarters to tie up some loose ends. The man in black smilingly replied that in anticipation of this he'd already arranged for his lawyer to rendezvous with them there.

Assuring their hosts they'd be back soon, they departed.

Pascoe, without consulting the Fat Man, had requested the Penders' permission to search the house. They gave it without a moment's hesitation, which didn't fill him with much hope of a successful outcome.

He left Wield to supervise the search. He wanted to stick close to Dalziel, who'd sunk into a big chair by the roaring fire. At the moment, he didn't trust him not to offer the Penders some sort of deal. Not that they seemed in the mood for negotiation. In fact, everything about their manner suggested they were completely unworried.

'What on earth are you looking for, anyway?' enquired the woman. 'Or is that an official secret?'

'You'll laugh,' said Dalziel. 'It's a monkey. The brass monkey, we call it.'

'A monkey? Good lord, you don't mean the Cellini Monkey that was stolen from the Helm? And you think it might be hidden here? How bizarre!'

'Aye, well, I get these daft ideas. Time of life, I reckon,' said Dalziel. 'I could murder a cup of tea.'

'Certainly. Earl Grey all right?'

'Why not? Drop of this brandy in it 'ull give it a bit of body.'

Some time later Wield appeared at the door shaking his head. Dalziel finished his tea noisily and stood up.

'Sorry to have disturbed your evening, folks,' he said. 'We'd best be off to make sure your friends get back to you as soon as possible.'

The Penders saw them to the door, showing graciousness in victory.

Outside in the snow Dalziel said, 'Make sure we've got everything. Don't want to disturb these good folks again. Who's got that shotgun?'

Novello held up the bag into which it had been placed.

'Let's have a look,' said Dalziel.

And to Pascoe's horror he reached in and took the weapon out of the bag. The old sod was determined to contaminate even what little evidence they had.

'Nice balance,' said the Fat Man, hefting the weapon. 'Even with the short barrel. Used to be a dab hand at the old clay pigeons myself.'

So saying, he raised it to his shoulder. Above him towered the holly tree. Its lights had settled down, but the angel still hung precariously. It reminded Pascoe of a photo he'd seen of the shell-blasted Basilica at Albert with its Golden Virgin leaning parallel to the ground from the ruined tower. The night seemed full of images of the First World War.

And he recalled that on the Front, popular mythology had said the war would end when the statue fell.

Perhaps Dalziel felt the same.

'Put it out of its misery, shall we?' he said, squeezing the trigger.

They heard the shot ripping up through the foliage. Snow melted. Fairy lights exploded. And the angel, separated from its supporting branch, nose-dived to the ground, which it hit with a most unangelic thud.

Everyone stood stock-still till the thunderous echoes of the gunshot had rolled to silence across the frosty sky.

Then Wield moved forward and stooped to pick the fairy up.

He let out a grunt of surprise at its weight, then turned to Dalziel, cradling the ornament in his arms like a child.

'Sir,' he said. 'It's the monkey.'

But Pascoe did not need his words. He'd been watching the faces of the Penders in the doorway, and the truth was written clearly there. No wonder they hadn't been worried by a house search!

'Bit of damage, I'm afraid,' said Wield, stripping off the angelic gauze. 'Reckon you might have some explaining to do to the insurers.'

The shotgun pellets and the impact with the ground certainly hadn't done Cellini's masterpiece any favours, but Dalziel only laughed.

'Not to worry, lad,' he said, turning to the couple in the doorway. 'Don't think it will help your defence, but you've been done. You see, Mr and Mrs Pender, it really is a brass monkey and all them lovely gems are nowt but paste. The insurers insist the real one's kept safe in a bank vault. I should have thought a couple of clever crooks like you would have known that. Now wrap up warm. Don't want you catching cold on your drive to the station, do we?'

As they stood in front of Hollybush Hall watching the cars vanish up the lane, Pascoe said, 'You knew all along the real monkey was safe?'

'Aye, but I made sure I were the only one. They've got big gobs at NCS. If word got out it were a worthless copy that had been stolen, there'd have been no incentive for the Germans to come, would there? But I'd no idea where it were hid till yon car hit the tree and I noticed how it leaned over. Good old Hector did us a favour. I may not kill him after all!'

He sounded so pleased with himself that Pascoe found it hard to point out what should have been obvious. But it had to be said.

'Look, sir, it's great that we've got the Penders, but they're not going to make things worse for themselves by admitting to a drugs deal, are they? And with all the evidence gone down the bog, we've no chance of making anything stick against the Germans.'

'In other words, you still think it's going-away prezzie time?'

'Without the drugs, it's still going to look like a real cock-up,' said Pascoe sadly. 'There'll be an enquiry, and NCS will be out for your blood.'

'You reckon? Here, let me show you something.'

He took the Palliser Estates folder out of his inside pocket, opened it at the sketch map of the house and its grounds, and led the way along the side of the building and down the garden at the back. Once more Pascoe found himself treading in his master's steps.

Finally the Fat Man came to a halt.

'Here we are,' he said, kicking at the snow. 'Get ahold of that and pull.'

That was a manhole cover.

With some difficulty Pascoe raised one end.

'Hell's bells,' he said, averting his face.

'Aye, pungent, ain't it?' said the Fat Man, breathing in deeply like an oenophile sampling the bouquet of a fine old wine. 'No mains drainage, see? This is Hollybush's septic tank. Everything comes here, and with the overflow frozen solid, everything stays here, too. Them Krauts wouldn't have thought for one moment a place like this might not have modern plumbing with everything being swished away out to sea. We'll need to get all this lot down to the lab, of course, to separate the wheat from the chaff, so to speak. Might leave that to the Boyo David, let the *Never Caught Short* mob clean up the mess for a change.'

Pascoe let the cover fall back into place with a clang.

'You knew about this when you conned that German with all that Christmas truce stuff, didn't you?'

'He conned himself. You heard him say he'd learned the lesson of history. Mebbe he didn't learn enough.'

'Meaning?' said Pascoe.

Dalziel chuckled richly, like bubbles passing through a poteen still.

He said, 'Another thing Great-Uncle Hamish told me on our way home from the park that night was that while they were boozing and singing carols and playing football with the Germans at Christmas, him and his mates took a careful note of their strength and disposition. Day after Boxing Day, they launched a surprise attack and knocked hell out of them.'

He laughed at the thought. Pascoe didn't join in, and the Fat Man's laughter faded and he looked at his colleague speculatively.

'Tell me, Pete, you said you were going to ring the Squad yourself and break the bad news. You had the chance. Why'd you not do it?'

'Don't know,' said Pascoe. 'Maybe I really have learned the lesson of history. Listen!'

'What?'

Pascoe cupped his ear and strained his eyes up to the line of trees running along the crest of the snowy slope where they'd kept watch at the start of the evening.

'Thought I heard someone singing a carol, sir. Yes, there it is . . . *"Stille Nacht, heilige Nacht"* . . . do you not hear it?'

For a moment Dalziel listened, then he swung his fist and punched Pascoe on the arm.

'Bog off, buggerlugs!' he exclaimed. 'You had me going for a moment there.'

'Thought I had you going forever half an hour back,' said Pascoe, grinning through his pain. 'Shall we head somewhere a bit warmer? I think I can make it back to the house with a bit of help.'

'Glad to hear it. There's a brandy bottle there I don't think we searched thoroughly. Merry Christmas, lad.'

And arm in arm the two men made their way back to Hollybush through the bitter weather.

True Thomas

It was mirk, mirk night, there was nae starlight.
They waded thro' red blude to the knee;
For a' the blude that's shed on earth
Rins through the springs o' that countrie.

'Not guilty!'

Disbelief. Shock. Anger. The need for a drink.

DI Tom Tyler was heading for the court exit before the judge had pronounced the dismissal. But quick as he was, Chuck Orgill was even quicker, bounding out of the dock to ignore Miss bloody Morphet QC's congratulatory hand and crush her instead in a joyous bear-hug.

Over the lawyer's skewed wig, his gaze met Tom's. For a second his lips pursed in a derisive moue. Then, which was worse, they spread in an almost sympathetic smile and his left eyelid drooped knowingly, ironically, conspiratorially.

Scotch became essential to sanity. Tom shouldered his way to the exit till he met a body too solid to be shouldered.

'Lost it then, did you?' said Superintendent Missendon. 'I got here in time to see little Miss Muffet take you to the cleaners.'

'Sodding lawyers. I hate them!'

'We had one on our side too, remember?'

'That prancing ponce! If he pissed in a snowdrift, he'd miss.'

He tried to resume his progress but Missendon caught his arm.

'Smithson's here from the Prosecutor's office. He's got a spare hour and would like to go over the Bryden case with us. And Tom, do me a favour. Go easy on the prancing ponce line, eh?'

It was a quarter to two before Tom made it into the murk masquerading as afternoon in wintry Lancashire. On the law court steps Missendon said, 'Fancy a drink? We can make the Sailors before closing.'

Tom hesitated. The need was still strong, but not for the company of colleagues he'd find in the Sailors.

He said, 'I'll pass if you don't mind, sir. I ought to get down to South to check those points Smithson brought up.'

'Such devotion to duty. I'm impressed,' said Missendon unconvincingly. 'Catch you later then.'

He strode away. Tom watched him out of sight then headed over the road to the Green Tree.

The Tree had its disadvantages too. The nearest pub to the law courts, it was the traditional trough of sodding lawyers. Sodden lawyers, too. Despite the lateness of the hour, it was still crowded with the bastards, red in tooth and glass. Using his shoulder as a ram, Tom took a direct line to the bar, filling the air with protest and claret.

He was served quickly. Studying himself in the bar mirror, he understood why. A stocky, muscular thirty-year-old with a lowering, truculent expression, he looked the kind of trouble-maker the police warned the public against approaching.

He raised his drink in a mock toast. 'Long life,' he said. 'And up yours, Miss Muffet.'

He drank, and as if by magic, his image vanished to be replaced by a view of the woman he was so abusively toasting.

The door linking the saloon with the small bar serving the dining room had swung open. Miss Morphet, brandy balloon before her, was shaking hands with a man Tom recognized as Orgill's brief, Walter Lime, 'Harry' to his friends, 'Slime' to the constabulary. They'd probably just finished a celebratory lunch and Slime was oozing off to keep another of his crooked clients out of jail. Miss bloody Muffet, on the other hand, didn't need to rush her cognac. Crooks were dusted down and cleaned up before being ushered into her hygienic presence.

She was laughing now at some farewell pleasantry, probably some crack about how easy it was to stuff the police.

Tom turned from the bar with an abruptness which set the claret flying once more and headed purposefully for the dining room.

The brief had gone. Miss Morphet looked up at him with the expression of interested puzzlement she'd worn as she insinuated that most of the police evidence was pathetic forgery.

Tom said, 'I'd like a word.'

She said, 'I'm sorry, I know we've met, but I can't place you . . .'

'No? You don't look at people you call liars then?'

'Ah,' she said. 'Inspector Tyler, isn't it? I don't believe that in fact I used that term . . .'

'Of course you didn't. A bit too plain for a lawyer. What was it you said? Oh yes. My notes had clearly been composed so long after the event that, like Shakespeare's *Richard III*, they might be great entertainment, but they were hardly history.'

'Did I say that?' she said with amused complacency. 'Oh dear. Though I'm sure it sounds far worse with a strong masculine delivery. Now I really ought to get back to chambers, so perhaps if there were anything else . . .'

'I just wanted to know what it feels like to put a dangerous criminal back on the streets.'

She pursed her ripe cherry lips and said, 'I don't know, Inspector. Perhaps you can tell me. Keeping people on or off our streets is more in your line, I believe.'

'That's right,' he said. 'You just stand up in court, play with words, never give a damn for the consequences of what you're saying . . .'

She was gathering her bag from under her chair and her jacket from its back.

'I think it best if I didn't hear this, Inspector,' she said. 'And to tell the truth—'

'What the hell do you know about telling the truth?' he exploded. 'Before you rush off to make your official complaint, why don't you try it, just for once in your life. Is Orgill guilty? Yes or no?'

'The jury found him Not Guilty, don't you recall?'

'Sod the jury! That's a verdict, not a fact. In truth, in honest simple truth, is Orgill guilty? Did he do it? Yes or no?'

For a brief moment he thought he saw the professional mask of that narrow, fine-boned, Siamese-cat-like face fracture.

Then she said, 'Won't you sit down, Inspector?'

Tom's anger, though still strong, had lost its head of steam and he was aware that other eyes in the dining room were watching the encounter with undisguised interest. He sat.

She said, 'You clearly pride yourself on plain speaking, so why not say exactly what you've got on your mind.'

He took a deep breath and said, 'All right I will. I believe – I *know* there's a dangerous man roaming free because he didn't get sent down for a crime I *know* he committed. I reckon you're far too bright not to know that he did it too. But this didn't stop you asserting as true things you knew were lies, and smearing as lies things you knew were true. OK. I've heard all that garbage you people trot out about everyone being entitled under law to a defence. I just want to know how you as an individual human being can live with twisting the truth like this.'

He fell silent and sipped his whisky.

She toyed with her brandy balloon then said, 'My trouble is, I don't really know you, Inspector. I mean, I don't know enough about you to help me decide whether I should just tell you to go screw yourself, or whether I should simply get on the phone to the Chief.'

'And how much would you need to know to make you try to answer my question honestly?' he sneered.

'Oh, very little,' she said. 'I'd just need to be persuaded it was the question of an honest man. Are you that rare creature, Inspector?'

'I'm on the side of truth,' he growled, annoyed with himself now because it sounded pompous. 'And I don't believe you can get there through lies.'

'A real True Thomas,' she said, smiling as though at a secret joke.

'Sorry?'

'Thomas the Rhymer in the old ballad who went to Elfland and when he came back he could never tell a lie.'

'Look, I'm not saying I've never told a lie, but . . .'

'But they are not necessary for your way of life whereas they are for mine?'

'Something like that.'

'So you wouldn't find it difficult to manage, say, twenty-four hours telling nothing but the truth? What's up, Inspector? You look disconcerted. You want to condemn me for allegedly doing something you couldn't avoid yourself for a mere day? Surely not?'

'Of course I could but—'

'Then that's my best offer. You go twenty-four hours without telling a lie and I'm yours to do with as you wish.'

She saw his eyes widen slightly at her choice of phrase and gave a wicked smile.

'I mean, *morally*, of course, Inspector. So what do you say?'

He looked at her, trying to show his scorn for such a daft idea. She had green eyes, and those lips which in court had lured him into so many damning uncertainties and qualifications were full and moist. As he hesitated she picked a Cox's pippin from the bowl of fruit in front of her, polished it against her breast and offered it to him.

'What's this for?' he asked.

'In the ballad, the Queen of Elfland gives Thomas a magic apple which makes him incapable of telling a lie,' she said. 'I'm beginning to wonder if you don't need a bit of magic too, Inspector.'

The mockery stung. She'd done the same in court, provoking him into responses he knew were unwise. But even as he recalled his resolve never to be so provoked again, he heard himself saying, 'Not tell a lie for a day? No problem.'

'Oh good.' She nibbled a tiny wedge out of the apple, then offered it to him once more. 'A bargain, then?'

He took the fruit, said, 'A bargain,' and sank his teeth deep into the incision she'd made, filling his mouth with the crisp juicy flesh.

'That's fine. What's the time?' As if at command, the old wall clock above the kitchen door began to chime. 'Two o'clock. You've started. See you here in the Tree tomorrow. Or perhaps I should say under the Tree.'

The secret mocking smile again.

'Suits me,' he said, trying to sound indifferent as he watched her wriggle her supple, slender arms into the sleeves of her jacket.

She caught his eyes and suddenly looked serious.

'One thing more, Tom. I may call you Tom? And you must call me Sylvie. Tell me, Tom, are you happily married?'

'Yes,' he said. 'I mean, most of the time, we have our ups and downs but . . .'

He stopped, not just because of the tangles his search for the precise truthful answer was leading him on to, but also because she had brought her face so close that he could feel the warmth of her five-star-scented breath while under the table her long, red-nailed fingers gently caressed the inside of his thigh.

'But would you fancy sleeping with me, Tom?' she whispered.

'What?' He pushed back his chair in confusion.

She stood up, laughing.

'No need to answer, Tom. Dirty trick, you reckon? I think you may be surprised just how many dirty tricks twenty-fours can play on a man devoted to the truth. See you tomorrow. Or, if not, I'll know why.'

He watched her go then he picked up the whisky glass he had set on the table. He still needed a drink but it was no longer to feed his anger.

He spent the afternoon at his desk catching up with paperwork. Scrupulously, he applied as strict a regulation here as he knew he'd need when speaking, and the truth cost him frequent revisions and would probably cost him even more frequent rebukes when his reports were read.

But by six o'clock he felt satisfied he'd made an excellent start to his twenty-four hours. Now with a bit of luck he'd have till eight thirty the next morning, safe from the testing pressures of the job. Not that he doubted his ability to meet Miss bloody Muffet's challenge, but he knew that his working life offered all kinds of traps to the unwary.

One of them was coming along the corridor as he came out of his room.

'Tom, just off?' said Missendon. 'You got things sorted with South, did you?'

'Sorry?'

'You said you were heading off to South to tidy up some loose ends on the Bryden case.'

'That's right. I did.'

'Did sort things out, you mean?'

'Did say I was going,' said Tom.

'Ah.' Missendon was looking nonplussed. 'And did you go?'

'No,' said Tom.

'Oh,' said Missendon. 'Why not?'

'Because,' said Tom carefully, 'I'd already got everything sorted that needed sorting.'

He smiled in valediction as he spoke and started to move towards the stairs. Missendon fell into step beside him.

'So why did you say you were going?' he persisted.

Tom sighed inwardly and said, 'It was an excuse.'

'For what?'

'For not going to the Sailors with you, sir.'

'You mean you didn't fancy a drink? Why not say so?'

'That's not what I meant, sir.'

'What then?'

'I didn't fancy a drink with you, sir, at the Sailors.'

Missendon was looking at him very strangely.

'Are you feeling all right, Tom?' he asked. 'You've been acting a bit odd lately.'

'Yes, sir. I feel fine.'

'That's all right then. I'll see you in the morning. Good night.'

'Good night, sir,' said Tom.

He heaved a sigh of relief as he made it to his car without further encounters. This truth business wasn't quite as straightforward as he'd asserted. Of course, the kind of lie he'd told Missendon at the law court was pure white, a bit of that social mortar which holds the fabric of relationships together. But it made him aware that perhaps simply being away from his work wasn't going to give him the easy ride he'd hoped.

His fears were confirmed almost as soon as he entered his house.

Mavis appeared at the head of the stairs dressed only in her underwear, but not to offer him the soldier's welcome after a long campaign.

'Tom, there you are! Get a move on. We're due there at seven.'

It came to him instantly. It was a Very Special Day, to wit, his parents-in-law's wedding anniversary, and the whole Masterman family were going out to dinner.

'What kept you so late? You didn't forget, did you?'

This was a form of reproach rather than a serious accusation. Mavis didn't believe it was humanly possible for anyone to forget so important an occasion. The correct answer was something on the lines of, 'Of course not, darling. It was just that Missendon wanted to chat and with my promotion board coming up, you know I've got to keep on the right side of the old sod.'

Tonight was different.

He said, 'Yes. I forgot.'

Fortunately she hadn't stayed for an answer but turned back into the bedroom. He watched her heavy buttocks wobble away. He didn't mind that she had started putting on weight, in fact he found the extra pounds in most places a real turn-on. But he wished that she would acknowledge the change in her choice of clothes. The fact that her skimpy silk pants now almost disappeared into her rear cleavage affected only her own personal comfort, but when he came out of the shower and saw her struggling into the kind of figure-hugging dress she'd once looked so devastating in, his heart sank.

'There,' she said, pirouetting. 'What do you think?'

'Oh yes,' he said, nodding vigorously and smacking his lips. 'I'd better get a move on. Mustn't be late.'

'You mean, oh yes, you like it?' she said, unhappy as always with anything less than hyperbole.

He said, 'It's a very nice dress. Super. Shall I wear my plain blue shirt?'

He knew she hated the blue shirt because it looked like official police issue, but even this provocation only provided a temporary diversion.

As he buttoned up the pearl grey pinstripe which nipped him under the arms but which Mavis thought made him look distinguished (i.e. not like a policeman) she said, 'You don't like it, do you?'

He sought for further evasion, saw how close he was skirting

118

the boundaries of truth, and said, 'No, not really. The dress is all right but . . .'

'But not on me, you mean? Why? What's wrong with me?'

'It looks a bit tight, that's all. Perhaps you got the wrong size . . .'

'No, I didn't. I got the size I always get. What you mean is I'm fat, that's it, isn't it?'

She was glaring at him angrily, waiting for the reassurance, the explanation, the full-frontal flattery.

He sighed and said, 'Yes.'

Only the fact that her parents were waiting to be picked up and must on no account be kept waiting on this Very Special Day saved him. Nothing must be allowed to interfere with the smooth running of a Masterman VSD. He'd long since given up the attempt to count exactly how many VSDs Mavis's family celebrated per year, but he was pretty certain if they were all made public holidays, it would solve the unemployment problem at a stroke.

They drove to his in-laws' house in a frost of silence beyond the reach of the car's heating system. Mummy and Daddy's presence warmed things up superficially with Mavis exuding enough heat for two, but his in-laws' attempts to bring him into the conversation created more problems.

'So how's work, Tom?' asked Father Masterman in his hearty down-to-earth, am-I-right-or-am-I-right, self-made Northerner's voice.

'Much the same.'

'And your promotion board, is that looking hopeful?'

'There's always hope,' said Tom.

'Well, don't forget our little agreement. The moment you feel things have stopped moving for you in the police, there's that nice comfortable seat waiting for you at Masterman's.'

Father Masterman was a builder, one of the biggest in Lancashire, and for years now he and his daughter had been urging Tom to take charge of the firm's security. So long as Tom could imply that he was moving steadily onwards and upwards towards the socially acceptable level of Chief Constable, he could fend them off. But somehow a purely unilateral 'agreement' had evolved whereby they understood that any hiatus in his upward progress meant he would resign and join the firm.

Tom grunted unintelligibly.

From the rear seat Mother Masterman piped up, 'I dare say Tom's secretly hoping he doesn't get his promotion so's he can leave and join Father. Isn't that right, Tom?'

He didn't reply.

Mavis said sweetly, 'Tom, Mummy asked you a question, didn't you hear?'

'Yes, I heard,' said Tom.

'So why don't you answer? Polite people reply when they're asked civil questions.'

'What was the civil question again?' asked Tom.

'Wouldn't you rather give up this awful trying police work and take a nice nine-to-five job with Father?' said his mother-in-law, choosing a bad moment for one of her rare excursions into precision.

Tom considered, then said, 'No. I think I'd rather pick cotton.'

There was a long silence, ended when his father-in-law began to laugh.

'*Pick cotton!* That's a good 'un, Mother. Pick cotton! They're too sharp for us, these youngsters. *I'd rather pick cotton.* I'll have to remember that one.'

That got them over that hurdle without much immediate pain. But as they got out of the car and he gave Mavis a ruefully apologetic smile, all he got in return was a cold stare which promised payment deferred with interest.

He sighed deeply. He hadn't been lying to Miss Muffet when he said his marriage was generally speaking a happy one. He and Mavis shared far more than they were divided by. Unhappily,

Mavis's family was one of the divisors, and various guilt feelings of her own meant that no compromises were permitted here.

The rest of the family were already waiting in the restaurant. There was his brother-in-law, Trevor, weak son of a strong father who tried to compensate by eschewing charm and embracing fascism. With him was his wife, Joanna, whose alcoholism might be either a cause or an effect of her husband's growing impotence. Tom quite liked her, but he had never been able to grow fond of his sister-in-law, Trudi, who spoke as rarely as she bathed, which was not often. And to make up the party there was Trudi's husband, Fred, shambling and uncoordinated, who had finally been found a job in Accounts to keep him away from machinery and sharp edges.

The meal followed much the usual pattern.

As their orders were being taken, Joanna announced with the piercing clarity of the chronically pissed, 'Spinach. My husband will have spinach. They say it helps with erections.'

At the same time Fred, who despite his utter lack of physical coordination, loved sport, was describing to Mavis how he'd built a break of six in his last game of snooker. Drawing his right arm back to illustrate the shot, he drove his elbow into the crotch of the wine waiter who was uncorking the mandatory champagne. The man doubled up with a strangulated scream, the cork blew off like a bullet and hit a woman at the next table plumb between the eyes, while the jet of wine caught her dining companion on the back of his head with such force it removed his toupee.

What puzzled Tom on these occasions was the fact that no matter what outrageous observations Joanna made, no matter how much of the infrastructure Fred destroyed, their behaviour never drew more than a resigned chuckle from his father-in-law, while he, Tom Tyler, who stayed stone-cold sober and could eat his prawn cocktail without breaking the dish, was clearly regarded as the disruptive member of the family.

121

Tonight, however, he at last caught up with his reputation.

He kept out of trouble till well into the main course. Then: 'How's crime, Tom?' asked Trevor.

'There's a lot of it about.'

'You're telling me. It's the courts I blame. Too much wrist slapping. It's time the legislature got its act together. Right?'

After his experience in court that morning, Tom couldn't disagree.

'Right,' he said.

'Slap their wrists with a sharp axe if they're caught thieving, that's what they need,' continued Trevor, warming to his thesis. 'The stuff we lose off our sites, you wouldn't believe it. It's the Irish, too many bloody Irish, why we let them in I can't fathom. And if we do catch them red-handed, what happens? Nothing! They're off robbing some other poor devil the next day. We need to make a few examples, encourage the others. Am I right, Tom?'

Tom said judiciously, 'As a general principle, even-handedly applied, I think a rational man might make a rational case for that approach, Trev.'

It was, he felt, in the circumstances a rather good answer. But the trouble with the Mastermans was, they didn't just want a polite nod in the general direction of the family faith, they needed you inside the temple, flat on your belly, kissing the idol's big toe.

'So why don't you join us, Tom?' said Father. 'Or if you're not yet ready to do that, at least give us the benefit of your expertise. Sort of consultant.'

'That's right, Tom,' said Trevor. 'Family's got to stick together, eh? So as an expert law man, where would you start to clean up Mastermans?'

At the top, was the answer that rose in Tom's throat, but he let it stick there.

'Look,' he said, 'the kind of petty thieving on the job you're talking about, it sounds to me like it all comes down to how much supervision you want to pay for.'

'Private security, you mean?' said Trevor. 'That's a bit rich, coming from you.'

'Sorry?'

'Well, haven't I heard you going on about the evils of private education? And private medicine? And private everything else? Why's it all right all of a sudden for your own family to be expected to pay for private security? What's happened to the forces of law and order, then? I mean, just because we're not the undeserving poor, aren't we entitled to the law's protection too? After all, it's people like us who pay for it, isn't it? We're not on state benefits. We're paying our taxes. So shouldn't whoever pays the piper call the tune?'

'Depends.'

'On what?'

'On all kinds of things. Whether the piper's getting paid full whack, for instance. Fred, could you pass me the horseradish?'

His attempt at diversion failed. Fred performed the minor miracle of passing the dish without dropping it or knocking anything over with it. He looked hopefully at Joanna, but she seemed to have relapsed into a state of catatonia.

Father Masterman said slowly, 'Now I'm not sure I understand you, Tom. Let's get this straight. First off, the police force is a public service right?'

'Right.'

'That means it's funded from the public purse, right?'

'Right.'

'Which means taxes. And we pay our taxes, right?'

Tom didn't answer.

'Right, Tom?' insisted Father.

'To a certain extent,' said Tom.

'To a hell of an extent!' exploded Father. 'Have you ever seen our tax bill? Fred, you tell him. You know the figures. How much did we pay last year?'

For a moment panic pitted Fred's face like smallpox. Then he took a deep breath, let his lips move as though totting up columns of figures and said, 'A hell of a lot.'

'That's right,' said Father. 'A hell of a lot. So where's the problem, Tom?'

Time for evasion. Time to duck and weave. Time to kick Joanna under the table and hope she'd wake from some dream of Trevor's sexual inadequacy which she wished to share with the company.

But a vision of Miss bloody Muffet rose into his mind, the green-eyed Queen of Elfland offering him the apple with juice oozing out of the nick she'd made with those wicked white teeth.

He said, 'The problem's what you want those taxes to be spent on. The problem's the kind of people you vote into power to spend those taxes. The problem's that you might pay a hell of a lot, but you slide out of paying a hell of a lot too.'

'Tom!' exclaimed Mavis in outrage.

'No, let him speak,' said Father. 'What are you saying, Tom? That we cheat? Is that it?'

'Yes,' sighed Tom, thinking with regret of the sherry trifle. They did a very nice sherry trifle here and he'd been looking forward to it. But he had the feeling that he would be heading for bed without any pudding tonight.

'You'd better explain yourself, I think, Tom,' said Trevor in his best senior management voice.

Tom pushed his plate away, saying goodbye to the rest of his roast beef too.

'All right,' he said. 'Take this dinner. You've got an arrangement with this restaurant, haven't you? They advertise Masterman's on the back of their menu. And the annual cost of that advert just happens to be whatever you spend on entertaining people here over the year. I've heard you boasting about the arrangement, Trev. So the cost of this meal will go down on your books as a tax-deductible advertising expense.'

'Aye, that's right,' said Father Masterman. 'I thought that one

124

up myself when they stopped business entertainment except for foreigners. Nothing wrong with keeping one step ahead of the game, is there, Tom?'

He smiled proudly as he spoke, and lowered his left eyelid in a man of the world's knowing, conspiratorial wink.

'Oh no, nothing wrong,' said Tom. 'Except that it's a tax fiddle! No. Hear me out. Let's take those building workers you're always complaining of, the ones who are robbing you rotten. How many of them are working on the lump through so-called subcontractors that in fact you run yourselves? That way, there's no records to keep, no National Insurance to pay, and you can get away with paying them under the odds, 'cos you know they need the work and they won't be filling in tax returns anyway. In other words, you and others like you chicane your way out of paying millions of pounds to the Revenue every year, then you have the cheek to squeal, "We're paying our taxes, aren't we?" The truth is, no, you're bloody well not! And until you do, you're not entitled to make cracks about an underfunded, overworked public service like the police!'

It must have been building up for some time, the way it gushed out in a swift unstoppable flow.

Some similar process must have been taking place inside Joanna, for suddenly she awoke, opened her eyes and her mouth very wide, said, 'Oh dear,' then her half-digested dinner gushed out in a swift unstoppable flow also.

Surely this would divert attention, if only temporarily, from his own disruptive outburst!

But no. Not even when Fred's attempt to dodge his sister-in-law's regurgitations sent him tumbling backwards in an explosion of splintering chair did the spotlight move from Tom.

'Now see what you've done!' cried Mavis. 'You've ruined everything!'

And Father said, 'You must hate us all very much, Tom, to go out of your way to destroy such a happy family occasion.'

It was his pulpiteeringly self-righteous tone that finished Tom off.

'Happy family?' he cried. 'Take a look at them. A limp dick, a fall-about drunk, a shambling wreck, a smelly mute, and a Michelin tyre advert! Charles Manson had a happier family than this!'

He headed for the door.

Mavis caught up with him as he paused to take in a deep breath of car park air.

He was already regretting the Michelin tyre crack. Nothing else, not yet. But that had been unforgivable.

He was right. She wasn't about to forgive him.

She said, 'You bastard. That's it. I won't be home tonight. And when I do come, I don't want to find you there. I want you out, do you understand? Out! Or I'll get Daddy's solicitor to throw you out!'

She could do it too. The house, a Masterman 'Georgian' villa, had been her father's wedding present and it was registered in her sole name.

He should have held out at the start, insisting that he didn't want a house he hadn't paid for. But he'd loved her too much then to believe it could be a problem. Loved her too much now to believe she meant what she was saying.

He said, 'Mavis, I'm—' but was prevented from further explanation or apology by a round-arm blow that sent him reeling.

She really was putting on weight. Last time she'd hit him she hadn't got punching power like this!

He wiped the blood off his lip and drove home.

There he sat and slowly worked his way down a bottle of Scotch which seemed to have lost its anaesthetizing power. Eventually the bottom came in sight, but he was still cold sober.

He knew this because when the phone rang he had no difficulty in getting up and going to answer it.

'Hello?'

'Tom? Missendon here. Listen, I was just driving home from a speaking engagement when I caught a shout on my car radio that there was a barney at the Dog and Duck. It sounded serious.'

Tom glanced at his watch. It was after midnight. It must have sounded very serious for the Chief Super to let a pub brawl keep him from his pit.

'You still there, Tom?'

'Yes, sir.'

'Well, listen, you'll love this. You know what was going on at the Dog? A private party to celebrate the release from custody of your old chum, Chuck Orgill. There's been a ruckus. And there's been some serious injuries, maybe worse. I'm on my way there now, and I thought, seeing who it is, you might like to join me.'

Orgill. Where all this had started.

'Yes, sir,' said Tom. 'Thank you, sir.'

He climbed into his car and found he was still carrying the whisky bottle. Carefully he laid it on the passenger seat. Was he fit to drive? Legally, of course not. But he felt he could have walked a high wire with no problem. He started up.

There were lots of police cars round the Dog and Duck. Lots of people too, despite the hour. An ambulance came belling out of the forecourt and there was another one gently pulsating by the main door.

'Tom. There you are.'

Missendon came towards him, smiling. He was still wearing his dinner jacket and looked like a head waiter welcoming a high-tipping diner.

Tom said, 'Hello, sir. What's the score?'

'One dead, two critical, four or five badly cut, a lot more gently bleeding. About par for the course when you let a mob like this loose among the bubbly.'

'And Orgill?'

'The guest of honour? He's inside getting a couple of stitches

127

in his face. He keeps shouting he wants to get off to the hospital, but there's no way he's going out of my reach till I'm done with him.'

'So who's dead?'

'Orgill's cousin, Jeff.'

Tom whistled and said, 'Someone's done us a favour, then. What happened?'

'Power struggle, from the sound of it. You know Jeff's been the heir apparent in the Orgill family for a long time. And when it looked like Chuck was going down for a stretch, he must have reckoned his hour had come. But little Miss Muffet changed all that. My reading is that once the booze loosened him up, he couldn't hide that he was less than happy to be welcoming Chuck back. Perhaps he even suggested that it was time for a change in the pecking order. Only he got pecked.'

'By Chuck, you reckon? Now that would be nice. Got any witnesses?'

'Don't be silly, Tom,' said Missendon. 'In the first excitement, the barman rattled on about the two cousins having a bit of a barney, then all hell breaking loose. But once he had a chance to remember who he was talking about, he went amnesiac. The rest'll be the same, no matter whose side they were fighting on. There's only one boss now, and no one's going to risk crossing him.'

As he spoke, he led the way into the pub. Through the saloon door Tom saw a mixed bunch of men and women, most of them walking wounded, accompanied by half a dozen policemen noting names and addresses. Then Missendon ushered him into the public bar and he didn't need to ask where the fight had taken place. There was literally blood on the walls and the room was in such a state of chaos that amidst the confusion of broken glass and shattered furniture it took the eye a few moments to pick out the one piece of human wreckage.

'Stabbed?' said Tom, approaching carefully to avoid treading on the blood which had gushed copiously out of the dead man's wounds.

'Three times by the look of it, maybe more. I just let the doc close enough to confirm death. I don't want anything moved in here till Forensic have gone over it with a fine-tooth comb.'

'What're you hoping for?'

'Anything that will put Orgill in the dock for murder. He slipped away this morning, Tom. He's not going to do it again.'

'It's going to be hard without witnesses,' said Tom. 'The kind of ruck that obviously went on here, it could have been anyone.'

'You sound like Miss bloody Muffet. Look, there's a knife over there. Obviously got chucked when the first of our boys arrived. Could be the weapon. It'd be handy if it had Chuck's dabs on it. There's blood on Jeff's hand. With luck it'll match Chuck's that spurted out when Jeff shoved a glass in his face. And I've got Chuck's shirt. Covered in blood. I bet it'll turn out to be Jeff's group.'

It was an empty optimism, thought Tom, because even if justified, what did it prove? For a start Chuck Orgill was blood group O – the commonest. He knew this because he knew everything about the man. And chances were that Jeff was O or A like 90 per cent of the population. He could hear Sylvie Morphet's insidiously persuasive voice.

'How many people received injuries during this fracas, Inspector? Fifteen? Twenty? More? So there was a lot of blood around. And how many of those bleeding were groups A or O? *That* many? In which case how can you be certain . . .'

And so on.

'What's up, son? You don't look happy,' said Missendon sharply. 'Spit it out. What's on your mind?'

'I was thinking you're clutching at straws, sir,' said Tom baldly. 'If the blood's all you've got to pin this on Orgill, Miss Muffet will have us dancing the polka. You'll need something a lot stronger than that to make this a runner.'

'You think so, do you?' exclaimed Missendon angrily. 'What's up, Tom? Miss Muffet got you scared?'

'You'd better believe it,' said Tom. 'Hello. What have we here?' He squatted down close to the body and peered at the floor.

'What's up? You got something?'

'That shirt of Orgill's. Is there a button missing?'

Missendon joined him and peered down. About eighteen inches from the corpse's outstretched hand was a small mother-of-pearl button with thread and some fragments of cloth still attached, as though it had been forcibly ripped from its place.

'Hold on,' said Missendon excitedly. 'I'll take a look.'

He left the room and returned a few seconds later with a sealed plastic evidence bag. Carefully, without opening the bag, he shook out the bloodstained shirt it contained.

'Tom, you're a genius,' he said squatting down and displaying the garment.

The buttons were mother-of-pearl and the third one down in the shirt front had been ripped off.

'Now that could be the clincher,' said Missendon. 'Happy now?'

'It'll help,' agreed Tom, rising. 'But it's just another pointer. How many more buttons and bits of cloth do you think Forensic will find in this lot when they start looking? Now if it had been in Jeff's hand . . .'

'But it was,' said Missendon in a surprised tone. 'Don't you remember? Look.'

He too stood up and stepped aside. Tom looked down at the corpse.

Almost concealed in the curled fingers of the outstretched right hand was the mother-of-pearl button.

'Grabbed the shirt as Orgill stabbed him, fell back and tore the button loose,' said Missendon. 'Even Forensic can't miss that.'

'No, it was on the floor,' said Tom stupidly.

'That's right. Jeff was on the floor and the button was in his hand,' said Missendon. 'You remember now, don't you?'

He was smiling, and as Tom met his gaze one eyelid dropped in a knowing, conspiratorial wink.

'You do remember, Tom, don't you?' repeated Missendon.

Tom didn't reply.

He thought of Orgill who, if there were justice in the world, should tonight have been starting a ten-stretch.

He thought of Sylvie Morphet's secret smile, mocking his claim to be able to exist in a world of complete truthfulness.

He thought of the Mastermans' dinner and his ruined marriage.

He said, 'No.'

'Sorry?'

'No. I can't do that. I can't go along with a lie.'

Missendon's face set hard as iron.

'What are you saying, Inspector?'

'I'm saying that, if asked, I'll tell the truth about where I found the button.'

'Then it's just as well you never found it, isn't it? It's just as well you've no standing here. It's just as well you're going home now and your name's going to appear nowhere in this investigation. You've been working too hard, Tom. You've managed to cock up one case today from not being up to scratch . . .'

'That's bloody rubbish and you know it!' snarled Tom.

'Rubbish?' Missendon stepped up close to Tom and sniffed. 'You've been drinking. Thought you must have had something to make you speak to me like that. How much have you had?'

'A bottle, but I'm not . . .'

'A bottle!' Missendon was genuinely amazed. 'And you drove out here? Have you gone off your trolley or what? No wonder you don't know what you're doing. Now listen to this. You go near your car and I'll have you arrested, so help me God. I'll get someone to drive you home. And you can stay at home. Sick leave, till further notice, you understand me, Inspector?'

'Oh yes,' said Tom. 'I understand. But you'd better understand me, sir. If I'm asked . . .'

'If you're asked?' yelled Missendon. 'Who the bloody hell's going to ask you anything?'

'I am!' cried Tom. 'I am.'

It was ten to two by the old wall clock when Tom walked into the dining room of the Green Tree.

Sylvie Morphet was at the same table, talking earnestly with Slime. Tom had no trouble guessing what they were talking about.

He approached and stood by the table till they looked up at him – the solicitor in surprise, the woman with that expression of secret amusement which was both irritating and beguiling.

'Inspector Tyler, you look tired,' she said. 'Burning the midnight oil in pursuit of justice, perhaps?'

'Something like that.'

'But not very like it,' she chided. 'Mr Lime's been telling me you've got poor Mr Orgill banged up again. You don't waste time, do you?'

'Don't I?' he said. 'Look, sorry to interrupt, but you did say two o'clock.'

She looked puzzled, then smiled and said, 'Of course. Excuse us, Mr Lime, a little private wager. No, no need to go. It won't take a minute. Well, Inspector, how did it go? Have you come to tell me you've won and want to claim your prize?'

In fact, he didn't know why he had come, except that when he woke up, out of all the confusion of a life which seemed as complete a wreck as that bloodstained room in the Dog and Duck, only this appointment at two o'clock had remained as something solid to cling on to.

She was looking up at him expectantly, green eyes glinting like raindrops on spring foliage. Little white teeth gleaming behind soft red lips parted in a sympathetic smile, one blue-veined eyelid dropping in a knowing, conspiratorial wink . . .

It came to him then that he had seen that expression before. So Orgill had looked in his triumph at beating the rap. So Masterman had looked as he boasted of his tax fiddle. So Missendon had looked as he invited complicity in fixing the evidence.

Now here it was again, the same look, the same wink, on the face of the Queen of Elfland . . .

That was it! It came as no surprise. He'd known it all his adult life. These three – and God knows how many more like them – actually belonged together, not in the ordinary workaday human world, but in another shadowy country of hazy boundaries and shifting sands and swirling mists above rivers that ran red with blood . . .

And what did that make him?

Simple. He was a stranger in Elfland, and if he spoke out of turn, he might stay here for ever.

'Well?' she urged. 'Did you win?'

He laughed and shook his head. He didn't know much, but he knew there was no way a mere human won bets with the Queen of Elfland.

'Don't be silly,' he said easily. 'Of course I didn't win. No chance. You always knew that. Now if you'll excuse me, I've got to go and meet my wife.'

Oddly, that wasn't a lie. At least he hoped it wasn't.

The way he saw it was that by now Mavis would have had an evening of Tom-bashing with the whole family, carried on the good work over breakfast with her parents, sunk into soul-searching soliloquy during morning coffee with her silent sister, and was probably at this very moment having her future spelled out during the course of a long lunch with Trevor – on the firm, of course.

Now that, by the most conservative estimate, ought to be exposure enough. For Tom Tyler knew his wife's darkest secret.

Too much contact with her family got right up her nose. This was why the VSDs had to be so very perfect, to ease her guilt at neglecting them the rest of the time!

She would never admit it, of course, at least not more than the odd hint in those confidentially languorous moments which followed their lovemaking. But Tom felt sure that by the time lunch was over, Mavis would have had enough, and she'd make an excuse about needing to collect something, and head for home to get some time to herself.

Well, she was going to be out of luck. Or in it, depending how you looked at things. He would go a long way towards mending his bridges with the family. Not as far as working for them, no way! But a long way. And if she wanted evidence that he still loved her and found her irresistibly attractive, he didn't doubt he could supply testimony that would stand up to any examination.

As he reached the door, the clock began to strike two.

It occurred to him that this meant his lie about losing had fallen within the twenty-four hours, which meant he really had lost . . .

Except if he really had lost, then it wasn't a lie . . .

Which meant . . .

He shook his head ferociously. This was Elfland logic. He had done with all that.

Boldly he stepped out of the shadows of the Green Tree into the bright winter sunlight which had replaced yesterday's mists, and headed homeward to start reassembling the fragments of his truth-wrecked life.

Castles

After the funeral I leave as soon as decently possible.

Maybe a little sooner.

'What are you doing in Mum's bedroom?' demands Harry.

I point to the bedside phone.

'Wanted a taxi,' I say. 'Didn't want attention.'

'You going already?' he asks incredulously.

When I arrived, he'd said, 'So you came, then?' in exactly the same tone.

I say, 'Harry, most of the people here are your mother's friends and family. I think they'll be glad to see the back of me.'

'Can you blame them?' he demands. 'When they know you're responsible for killing her.'

That's a real chiller till I realize it isn't specific.

'A heart attack killed her,' I say.

'Because she was living alone, and we all know whose fault that was,' he spits out.

From the door, Emily says, 'This where you've got to. What's going on?'

'He's ringing for a taxi. He's leaving,' says Harry.

'You off then, Dad?'

'Yes. Sorry. Need to be back in town this evening.'

'Keeping busy, eh? That's good. Not too busy to come again soon, I hope.'

Doesn't quite get it right, but at least she tries. Harry just glowers.

It's funny, I always favoured Harry over Emily, but when the split came, it was Emily who kept her cool, Harry who threw shit.

I don't bother with any other farewells. York was where Donna came from and York was where she returned. Far as I can make out, she was greeted like a returning prodigal. Me, I feel as welcome as Ian Paisley at a Sinn Fein wake.

Out in the street I use my mobile to raise a taxi. In fact, I've no real reason to hurry back, but even less to hang about in this chilly city. I've got a seat booked on a train in half an hour, but when I reach the station and find a delayed train to London just leaving, I jump aboard.

Everyone else seems to have the same idea and the train is crowded. I get an aisle seat on a table for four with my back to the engine. Never used to bother me, but as I get older I like to see the landscape sliding away rather than rushing towards me as I travel.

Very soon the train rocks me into a waking sleep in which it's not landscape but the past I see sliding by.

I met Donna at my first job. Hers too. She was in the typing pool, prototype provincial lass, starry-eyed and a bit intimidated at her first sight of the Big City. I was the office boy, just as unsure of myself, but coming from Walthamstow, I could put on the airs of a native.

So she made me feel sophisticated, and I made her feel safe.

Not a bad basis for a teenage relationship. Not, maybe, such a great one for marriage.

We got engaged at seventeen. Her parents objected, mine didn't give a damn. Her mother wanted to know if I'd convert to RC. Her father wanted to know if she was pregnant. I told her *why not?* and him *yes*. End of objections. My parents still didn't give a damn.

I felt triumphant. So did Donna. After all, we were getting our own way, and kids at that age don't have any real idea what they want, except their own way.

There was a moment, just before we left for our brief honeymoon, when I looked around for Donna and saw her in her mother's arms, both of them staring towards me like they'd found a stray dog crapping on their lawn. *What the hell am I doing?* I asked myself. Or rather, *What the hell have I done?*

But God, in His wisdom, deals out such moments of clarity very sparingly to the young.

Now my memory goes into fast forward, sending those early years racing by, which was how they seemed to go at the time. Two kids in quick succession, not a lot of money, me making my way, bustle bustle bustle. And if there was a pause, a brief space for us to look at each other, we didn't use it to take stock, but talked instead of the always mythical future, of some promised land which would make all this present slog worthwhile, of ships coming in, missions accomplished, sunlit uplands, castles in the air. Mine were, I think, the airier. I wanted to travel, to have new experiences, to learn how to sail, to ski, to fly, while Donna had her sights set on a lovely house in a nice area with the kids doing well, a car that didn't break down, an en-suite guest room for her mum to stay in. And so we talked excitedly without really listening to each other.

And then we reached stage two of our journey. My dad had a little greengrocer's shop in Walthamstow. I wanted no part of it, but when my mum died soon after Dad had been diagnosed with Addison's disease, I started lending a hand. Donna didn't mind. Family loyalties were big in her book. Then an old school chum of mine in the restaurant business asked my help in getting hold of some decent veg. I obliged. He was well pleased and offered me a contract as his regular supplier. And it occurred to me that while small-time retail was drudgery, there might be real money in wholesale.

Now Donna did object, as this meant investing most of our savings, but for once I won a major argument, and after a couple of glitches, we were up and running. In a year or two we were able to move to a bigger house in a better area, with much better schools. Things were looking up, and at last life seemed to be slowing down.

The train, too. We're coming into Doncaster. The two people in the window seats get up to leave. I start to shift across till I notice that both seats have reservation tags from Doncaster to King's Cross. I think of moving into one of the other window seats now available but don't bother. There's not much to look at between Yorkshire and London.

People are pouring in from the crowded platform, some narked at being kept waiting, others chuffed to be catching an earlier train than expected. There's a wedding party on the platform who look like they belong to the first group. All the usual time-honoured jollities seem to have gone limp with repetition, and though the guests manage to whip themselves into a final frenzy of confetti throwing, balloon bursting, and tear shedding, they can't altogether hide their relief at being shot of the happy couple.

It's not till said happy couple come down the aisle of my carriage that the significance of the reserved window seats strikes me and then it's too late. The only other empty seat visible is the one opposite me.

They can't be more than eighteen or nineteen. His pale, thin features are taut with embarrassment as he tries to brush the confetti off his shoulders. Her broader face, its edges softened with the remnants of adolescent puppy fat or the beginnings of mature obesity, is flushed with excitement and she doesn't seem at all averse to being a centre of attention.

I stand up. I expect him to opt to sit next to me, the kind of meaningless defensive gesture I'd have made at his age. But the girl says, 'I like to sit with my back to the engine else I spill my guts.'

This seems an unanswerable argument, and they take their seats accordingly.

I do what I can to give them privacy, heading for the buffet and checking for other available seats en route. There aren't any. I have a couple of large Scotches, standing up.

Finally I return to my seat, where I immerse myself in one of those magazines in which almost-famous people tell you how marvellous the railway is.

Beside me the bride is in full spate, bubbling through a critical analysis of what their wedding guests had said, worn, and given, ending in what sounds like inappropriately envious speculation about their plans for tonight.

'Lizzie . . .' (Lizzie, I gather, is her best friend) '. . . Lizzie said they'd likely be going down the Parrot, it's disco night down the Parrot tonight, and you get in half price if you get there between eight and half past, and there's a happy hour at the bar . . .'

I try to remember the last time Donna and I went to a disco. And fail. Try to remember happy hours. There were quite a lot of those, but they come up like scenes from an old movie, something I've seen rather than taken part in, with the cold night always waiting for me outside.

After a dozen or so years, the cold night seemed to have come inside too. I felt like I was on a lonely road to somewhere I didn't want to be. Guessing Donna probably felt the same, I tried to bring things out in the open. Faults on both sides, I said. Face it like adults. No need to turn a cold breeze into a blizzard. And even if the worst came to the worst, these days divorce was hassle-free, none of the stigma it had for our parents' generation . . .

Except, it seemed, if you'd married a nice Catholic girl.

Donna wasn't all that religious, but in this one respect she was as devout as the Pope. She'd listened quite calmly till I mentioned divorce, then I turned into Genghis Khan kicking down the door of a convent. I left her screaming and praying and went away to have a think.

It was a long think, nearly ten years long. Funny how quick time passes, even when you're not enjoying yourself. I accepted that divorce wasn't an option, and contemplated simple separation. But things got messy with the kids. I tried to hide the way things were, but I wasn't all that good at concealment and we had trouble with both of them. Possibly we'd have had trouble anyway. Most people do these days. Sometimes I get the impression that any family where the boys aren't delinquent druggies and the girls hysterical anorexics must have something seriously wrong with it.

Then, just to give us a full set of troubles, Donna got ill. Her heart sometimes went off at the gallop. Tachycardia, they call it. No one knew the cause, but top of the list of things to be avoided was stress, and Donna made bloody sure I knew that. Any comment which she interpreted as indicating I still had thoughts of breaking free had her clutching her chest and gasping for her medication. Naturally, I sometimes thought she might be faking, but when I hinted a suspicion to her doctor, she looked at me like I was a serial killer and assured me it was a very real condition which, not properly treated, could be fatal.

This girl next to me is a serial talker. She could gab for Ireland. Her husband tries to insert enough monosyllables to create the impression of a conversation, but it's like chucking pebbles in a millrace to hear the splash. She finishes with the wedding, disposes of their friends, and without pausing for breath starts rolling out their future like turf over a new grave.

Such certainty almost forces admiration. Nothing speculative here, no doubts or hesitations.

This girl's castles in the air have the solidity of bricks and mortar.

'. . . and we'll have an old-fashioned cobbled patio, not real cobbles, like, they get right greasy and you can turn your ankle specially in high heels, no, but you can get cobble effect, looks like cobbles but it's flat, and we'll have a barbecue area, gas is best, none of that charcoal stuff that keeps on going out and makes everything smell funny, and a double garage with a flat roof that's a balcony outside our bedroom, so's I can sunbathe without needing to go downstairs, like in that hotel in Ibiza, only a lot bigger, well, it would need to be being over a double garage, 'cos we'll need a car each . . .'

I bury my nose in my magazine, avoiding all eye contact with the young man. I know nothing about him, but I know young men and I'd lay odds his vision of the future is at the same time a lot more down to earth and a bit more grandiose.

Or maybe not. We all like to excuse our own guilt and failure by saying everyone's the same. I don't doubt the world's full of unhappy marriages but how can I be sure these kids are going to join the club?

And even if they do, being disappointed, miserable even, doesn't inevitably mean that either of them will end up wishing the other dead.

That's how low I got. I'm not proud of it, but to be fair, the downward spiral was long drawn out.

At first, I kept going by assuring myself that when the kids reached eighteen, I'd simply walk away.

Simply!

Last time things were simple as that, God was still a greengrocer and tailors hadn't been invented.

The kids, like kids usually do, had got through the worst of their teenage traumas without much help from their parents. Emily celebrated her eighteenth by getting married. I thought this was crazy, but I kept my mouth shut and did everything the father of the bride is supposed to do. It was a hollow act. Donna, on the other hand, played her role with utter conviction. That was her great strength. As long as things were going the way she wanted them, she was the perfect mother and wife, leaving no doubt who was the bluebottle in our family ointment.

Emily's husband worked in Harrogate (a Yorkshireman – Donna liked that) so naturally she moved up there. A year later, when Harry reached his eighteenth, he headed north too, to York University to do a degree in Art History. This was a blow. I'd always felt we were really close, and I had hopes he'd come into the business, but there's not much call for art historians in the fruit and veg trade.

Now we were alone again, Donna and me. I tried to talk sensibly to her but immediately she had one of her turns. A close-ish call, said the doctor gravely. Good job she had her medication handy. Recovered, she slipped back easily into her old role of contented wife, and I went along with it because you can't go around telling all and sundry, look, this is a sham, it's all over between us only she won't let me go.

So, a civilized split seemed out of the question. As for walking away, at a distance that had looked a real option, but close up I saw the flaws. To start with, Donna would almost certainly have a turn, and she'd pull in a huge sympathy vote. Plus, her family would come at me mob-handed, and their lawyers would be all over my accounts. Competition in the fruit and veg trade had always been keen but in recent years it had become vicious. I couldn't afford the slightest downward shift in either my finances or my personal standing. Being good old Tommy who'd been flogging top-notch produce for years might still tip the balance when some smart young spiv tried to undercut my prices; on the other hand, being rotten old Tommy who'd just dumped his sick wife could give the waverers the excuse they needed to drop me.

But something had to be done. It wasn't just the public pretence that got me down, it was the fact that Donna seemed to expect it in private also. I felt like a jaded actor in some long-running soap who knows there's an exciting life out there with new and demanding parts to be played but can't get out of his contract without getting out of his career.

There was only one solution. If I couldn't leave Donna, then Donna must leave me, which meant that Donna must leave everyone.

It wasn't a decision. I just realized one day that was how I felt. But even at my lowest, I couldn't bring myself to contemplate simply pushing her under a bus.

No, what I opted for was a scheme which had a smack of justice about it. At least, that's how it seemed to me. Here's how it came about. Increasingly, at the slightest sign of opposition to her will, Donna started gasping for breath and reached for the bottle which contained what she called her lifesavers, the pink and white capsules prescribed for her tachycardia. After a short while her heart slowed down to its normal pace and so continued as long as things went her way.

About this time my dad died. We'd never really got on – to the end he always referred accusingly to the wholesale business as if I'd cheated him out of his birthright – but as I cleared out the old house, it seemed to me that I'd been a happy kid there, and finally I shed the tears I hadn't been able to shed at either of their funerals, but maybe they were for my lost childhood as much as for my lost parents.

When I came to empty the bathroom cabinet, I found a supply of Dad's medication. I was about to tip it down the loo when the idea came to me. Over the years I'd come to understand quite a bit about Addison's disease. It's caused by adrenal insufficiency, which means basically that the adrenal glands don't produce enough adrenalin, and this has to be compensated for by use of one of the cortisone drugs. Now adrenalin, of course, is the hormone that prepares the body for moments of crisis; it sets the heart beating faster, the blood coursing more freely.

This was pretty well the opposite of what Donna was suffering from. The function of her medication, the pink and white 'lifesavers', was to bring her out-of-control heartbeat down to its normal pace.

It seemed to me that anything which did the job of adrenalin in sufferers from Addison's disease would probably accelerate a tachycardiac patient into heart failure.

It wasn't hard to open up one of Donna's 'lifesavers' and substitute a powdered-down cortisone tablet.

When I say it wasn't hard, I mean mentally as well as physically. I felt no qualms at all. My thinking was that if Donna kept herself on an even keel by accepting that other people were also entitled to opinions, hopes, fears, and a measure of independence, then she wouldn't be in any danger. And even if she did resort to her capsules, well, there were at least a couple of dozen in her bottle, and she always kept it well topped up, so that meant she had a better than twenty to one chance of not selecting the ringer. And in any case, I couldn't be absolutely sure that its effect would be fatal.

So easily do we distance ourselves from our morally suspect actions.

I wish I could distance myself as easily from this young bride sitting next to me. Having finally run out of steam on her TV commercial vision of their future, she's produced a selection of glossy magazines from which she's started reading aloud any extracts that interest her. As their subject matter seems to be mainly an assessment of those features of male physique and performance most pleasing to a young female readership, I squirm with vicarious embarrassment which I put down to my age and upbringing, till I glance at the husband and see that, whatever else has changed, young men haven't lost the capacity for squirming.

It would be nice to be able to offer advice and/or comfort, but what would my lifetime's wisdom amount to? *Son, you've made a big mistake – better you make an excuse at the next stop, leave the train, and run away to sea?* If some old fart had said that to me twenty years ago, I'd probably have decked him. As for comfort, I have none to give. How should I when I can find none?

A couple of weeks after my experiment with the capsules I came home to find the house empty and a letter for me propped up against the clock on the mantelpiece.

Dear Tommy,

I've been thinking, let's be honest, we're pretty well washed up and with Emily married and up in Harrogate, and Harry settled in at York University, it seems silly for me to carry on living down here in London which, to tell the truth, I've never really liked anyway. So I've decided to move back to York where all my real friends and family live, and I'll be within easy striking distance of the children. I'll give you a ring when I'm settled in and we can talk about financial arrangements. I reckon we've done our duty by the kids and by each other for the past twenty years and now we deserve to be able to please ourselves.

Yours affectionately,
Donna

I should have been jumping for joy. Here she was, presenting me with what I'd been wanting for years. Instead I spent the night like a conventionally distraught husband with a bottle of whisky and a generous measure of self-pity.

But next morning I awoke to sunshine and a proper perspective.

I was free! I'd got what I wanted and without any of the expected hassle. Without, above all, becoming a murderer!

The doctored capsule was, of course, still in her bottle. I started trying to plot ways of getting it out of her possession. Then, when we finally met to sort out the final details of the generally very amicable agreement we had reached about money and possessions, she gave me the ideal opportunity.

We were in our London house. She was in the hall talking on the phone and suddenly she called, 'Tommy, I've left my bag in the kitchen. Could you be an angel and dig out my diary, please?'

God, it seemed, was at last on my side. I went into the kitchen, found the bag, opened it, and removed the diary.

Then my jubilation faded.

No pill bottle.

After she finished on the phone she returned and started to replace the diary in the bag.

I said, 'You're looking very well, Donna. Couldn't help noticing, your bag's not like a portable medicine chest anymore.'

'That's right. I had a thorough check-up when I signed on with my new doctor and he gave me a clean bill of health. Isn't that marvellous?'

'Marvellous? Almost miraculous,' I said.

She looked at me in search of malicious irony, but there was none. After all, her recovered health solved my last remaining problem, and we parted, if not friends, at least not mortal enemies, and this new neutral zone even extended to include Emily.

But I still paid a large price. Harry.

He seemed to regard the separation as a huge tragedy and he placed the blame very firmly at my doorstep. You'd have thought I'd thrown his mother out into the snow without a stitch on her back. He refused to come back to London and spent the vacations with Donna. And naturally, despite me and Donna keeping things civilized, all her friends and relations in

146

the north took their cue from Harry and elected me bastard of the year.

And was I truly happy now I'd got what I had so long wanted?

After the first bout of exhilaration, no. The man who goes into prison is not the same man as comes out. OK, I can't have been easy to live with either, but when I looked at things with as much disinterest as I could manage, it seemed to me that in the end it had been Donna's castles in the air – financial security, a nice house, a couple of kids grown up and well settled – that had got themselves built, while mine, vaguer, I admit, but just as important to me – excitement, exotic travel, new experience, joy! – were chimeras still.

I feel an urge to try and explain this to the young man in the train, but easily resist. If I can't manage advice or comfort, explanation is definitely a no-no. Who wants to listen to some middle-aged nutter with whisky breath babbling sentimental pap about chasing your dream?

On the other hand, it could be he'd welcome the interruption, *any* interruption. The whole carriage has fallen silent as his bride entertains us with a dramatic reading of the highlights from an interesting correspondence on the ins and outs of oral sex. I can sense the young man's yearning for some diversionary topic. Then, glancing out of the window in search of inspiration, his gaze falls on the ruins of an ancient castle about fifty yards east of the railway line which I recall noticing on the way up.

He says brightly, 'Oh look.'

She says, 'What?'

He says, 'Out there. A castle.'

She looks, glimpses the ruins briefly before the train bears us out of sight, and says with great contempt, 'They're dead stupid, these lords.'

What does it mean? A political statement? I let my eyes flicker to the young man's face. He looks as baffled as I feel. More. I don't have a future of such bafflement to look forward to. But that's his problem. I quickly bow my head into my magazine once more, before he can feel intruded upon.

Yes, his problem is the future. Mine is the past. The future is something I don't care to, or dare to, contemplate.

For just as I was beginning to think there might be hope of turning my life around, the news came.

Donna was dead.

It was Emily who phoned me. It was the old heart trouble. She'd seemed so well. Then bang! an attack in the middle of the night. They'd found her in bed with her pill bottle open in her hand.

I couldn't speak for a while. Finally I managed to ask, 'Didn't she have time to take her medication, then?'

'I don't know. What does it matter? She's gone.'

It mattered to me.

Had Donna had the last laugh by turning me into a murderer when I'd got all I wanted without going to that extreme?

The answer was in my pocket. That's what I'd been doing in the bedroom when Harry came in. A few moments earlier and he'd have caught me pocketing the medicine bottle I'd removed from the bedside drawer.

It was the criminal's instinct to hide the evidence of his crime, I suppose. Except that in this case, if there was any evidence, there hadn't been a crime. And if there had been a crime, then the bottle contained no evidence.

No, there was more to it than just my attempt to cover my tracks.

I needed to know if she'd taken the doctored capsule or not.

But I wasn't sure yet if I'd ever have the nerve to find out.

The suspicion that I had killed her might taint the rest of my life, but the certainty would destroy it.

I hadn't realized this when I made my plan, or even when I pocketed the bottle, but I realized it now.

You can't end somebody's life without ending your own as well.

It's funny how the human mind can function on two levels, the trivial and the traumatic.

Or maybe it's not funny, maybe it's what makes human existence possible.

Anyway, at the same time as I'm wrestling with my guilt feelings about Donna, I'm also trying to make sense of the young bride's mysterious pronouncement, *They're dead stupid, these lords*.

What on earth did she mean?

I can see the groom is pondering this puzzle, too. If asked, I'd have told him it was probably best to leave well alone. But of course he doesn't ask, so I settle back and wait to have at least one of my problems solved.

It's worth waiting for.

'What do you mean, they're stupid, these lords?' he says finally.

'Well,' she replies dismissively. 'With all that money, building a castle so close to a railway line, that's really stupid, isn't it?'

I can't help it, my head comes up. The last thing I want is to embarrass him by catching his eye, so I pretend to be looking out of the window to check our progress. But for a brief moment in the mirror of the glass our eyes meet and something flickers between us.

Then our gazes separate, and pass through the grubby glass, and as the train clatters south towards a terminus neither of us has much cause to be impatient to reach, we sit there, twinned in regret, staring at the moving landscape, he seeing all his life rushing madly towards him, and me seeing mine drifting slowly away.

Fool of Myself

'And what will you tell him in this letter of yours?' asked my mother as she lay dying.

'Everything,' I said.

'Then, as usual, you will make a very great fool of yourself.'

Even in death she spoke with such certainty.

And she was nearly always right.

Not this time, Mother, I thought as I swung the wheel over. Not this time!

Then I saw the tractor coming round the bend.

And my last thought was, oh shit.

Perhaps Mother was going to be right after all!

Dear Detective Superintendent Dalziel,

You don't know me, but I know enough about you to know you're a man of independent mind, above fear or favour. That's what I want, someone to understand, someone to be my voice.

So who am I?

My name is William Appleby. I am, and will now remain forever, nineteen. I'm an only child, my father dying when I was barely a year old. His car skidded off the Greendale Pass road and plunged into the gorge. It was recorded as an accident, but lately I have begun to wonder if it might not have been his last independent act, his bid for freedom.

But I'm getting ahead of myself.

I suppose that a son brought up by his mother alone must run the risk of being a 'mummy's boy'. It's a title I didn't mind. True, Mother was fearsomely protective, but at the same time she inspired a natural admiration and respect, not just from me but from everyone in our small town, and Yorkshire people aren't easily fooled.

And yet, if you look closely, you could find she achieved her reputation at least in part by making unacceptable offers of help, such as proposing our pocket-handkerchief lawn as the site of the church fete or offering her wedding ring (which it would have taken amputation to remove from her finger) as prize in the restoration-appeal raffle. Instead of direct contributions to worthy causes, she would dangle before them the hope of generous legacies, though always with the rider, 'Of course, my boy's fragile health means I first have to make sure he is properly provided for.'

I reckon my 'fragile health' was a trump card that got her out of a lot of tight situations. In fact it didn't consist of more than a slight tendency to get over-excited in certain situations, easily controlled by some mildly sedative capsules. Physically I usually felt on top of the world.

Another area where reality blurred a little was our finances. It was generally accepted that Mother, while not perhaps 'stinking rich', was certainly 'not short of a bob or two'. If anyone was bold enough to make direct enquiry, she might reply, 'Well, there's the house . . .' (worth over a quarter million in the current market) . . . 'and I have a little invested in the funds', contriving to suggest by the archaism both sharp financial acumen and a broad portfolio. In one sense this was completely true. No one could live as comfortably as she did on a widow's pension without knowing how to manage money. As for the portfolio, it was certainly broad. Susceptible visitors were permitted to glimpse a selection of annual reports from top companies scattered across the dining-room table before Mother with many apologies tidied them up, and the big calendar in the kitchen was always boldly annotated with mementoes of shareholders' meetings.

These 'susceptible visitors' were invariably men. Mother was an attractive woman, and knew how to maximize her attractions by dress, make-up and demeanour. But, as I eventually realized, the prize she dangled before her admirers was not her person but her portfolio. Passionate romantics were of little interest to her. In fact, I believe my own devotion fed all her emotional needs. What she set out to attract was men with calculator hearts; men who would wine her and dine her and buy her reasonably expensive presents (exchangeable for cash refunds); men who would always err on the side of caution in their sexual demands for fear of scaring her off; above all, men who, if they became too demanding, could soon be sent running for cover by the simple disclosure of the real state of her finances.

Am I trying to paint her as a monster? Certainly not. She was a human being following the same imperative that drives us all – survival. We are not simply born into this world, we are shipwrecked on it. The survivors are those who make the right choices.

I think after Father's death, Mother got all her choices right.

Except one.

A wise man, or woman, never comes between a dog and its bone, or a young man and his mate.

Adolescence arrived. I changed in all the ways that boys change. My devotion to Mother kept me from the extreme forms of teenage rebellion, but it could not damp down the fire in the blood.

You, Mr Dalziel, I guess are a man of the world and will know what I'm talking about.

I discovered girls. You might have thought that being such a mummy's boy, I might have developed some kind of quasi-incestuous fixation on older women. Far from it. What I wanted were girls who were teenagers like me, girls who would laugh and drink and dance with me, and enjoy what naturally followed without regret or recrimination.

Perhaps my freedom from any Oedipal obsession was down to a growing intuition of what really made Mother tick, though it wasn't till later when I went to university that I really began to look at her objectively.

As a schoolboy I was too busy for analysis. If there'd been an EU subsidy for sowing wild oats, I'd have been a rich man. I never had any problem with getting girlfriends and I found Mother surprisingly unconcerned by my success. The few who lasted long enough to visit our house often told me how lucky I was to have such a compliant parent and wished they could swap her for their mothers-from-hell. When I passed this on, she smiled and said, 'You enjoy yourself, son. Just remember two things: don't get serious and don't get careless.'

But of course I did get serious. There was this girl in the sixth form, Gina Lovegrove, daughter of Dan Lovegrove, the brewer. Three months after we started, we were still going out, and my friends were regarding us as an item.

Then suddenly we were done. No big scene. She started backing off, went clubbing with her mates, let some other guy take her home, that was that. I had one of my little bouts of mental over-activity which the capsules soon put right. Back to normal and determined to show I was cool, I soon took up with another girl, Kelly Hall, who was as blonde as Gina had been dark, and had left school to work in the family hotel business, so no overlap there. And very soon I couldn't recall what I'd seen in Gina.

Then Kelly was gone too. She broke a date and, when I rang her, she said she was sorry but it wasn't working for her any more. My thoughts and my pulse went racing again, the capsules did their work, and very soon afterwards I had the welcome distraction of leaving school behind me and heading for university. I packed my bags and went off to find whatever solace this new experience could offer.

Now for the first time I began to see Mother differently. Hitherto I had accepted her on the same terms as everyone else, which is to say as an attractive widow of independent means, full of community spirit, universally admired for her charitable works, her compassion for the needy, and of course her devotion to her child. OK, so she had men friends, but there was no hint of scandal, just an acceptance that she was engaged in the impossible task of seeking a man worthy to be my stepfather.

During my teens I did begin to get the message that we weren't perhaps as well off as people thought. While I never wanted for anything essential, I got few of the little luxuries I yearned for, like a motorbike. One day, looking for evidence to support my argument that if we had money to burn, I might as well burn some of it through the exhaust of a Harley, I did a bit of snooping through her bank statements, but all I found were the day-to-day transactions of a woman making ends meet.

I salved my unease by concluding that all our money must be tied up in shares. But a little later when I got accepted at Mid-Yorkshire Uni, which seemed quite perfect for me – only forty miles away, far enough for independence, close enough for easy access to home cooking, laundry and cash top-ups – I was flabbergasted to hear Mother wondering whether it might not make economic sense for me to commute from home!

'You mean we can't afford it?' I demanded. She backed down instantly, said there was no problem, no need to get myself excited. And that was the end of the matter.

But it stayed in my mind, and once I got to university and opportunities to run up bills came crowding, I decided I had to know just how well off we really were. Alone in the house during the Christmas vacation, I went looking for the statements from her shareholdings. What I found came as a real shock. They were worth a couple of thousand in total, no more. What was more, the house was mortgaged up to the hilt.

One other thing the search turned up was a scrapbook full of cuttings about you, Mr Dalziel. Mother was a real fan. I read through it, fascinated, and that's how I came to be sure you're the man to read this letter.

To confront her about her finances seemed impossible. I loved her too much to be her accuser. But I needed to work out what my new knowledge could mean.

I had all the necessary data, of course. A child sees far more than a parent realizes. And gradually over the remainder of that vacation, as I matched memory with observation and analysis, I began to re-evaluate what I knew.

My conclusion was that the rumours of our wealth, the reputation for charitable open-handedness, the company AGMs and the share prospectuses, all were nothing but window dressing. Instead of taking one of the other routes open to a single mother – Social Security; menial work; remarriage; writing a bestselling novel! – she invited a certain type of man to subsidize our living style. Morally questionable? Perhaps. But she sold them nothing but their own greedy dream.

Of course it made me see her differently. I understood now just how ruthlessly single-minded she could be, but I felt just the same about her. Everything she'd done had been done for me.

So I resolved to watch my expenses for her sake, but no resolve could make me follow her advice about girls.

Once more I got serious. And this time I also got careless.

Michelle Powers was perfect for me. We shared so many interests and tastes it was unbelievable. She was gorgeous to look at and incredibly sexy. And she adored me as much as I adored her. I never met her family, who are reputed to own half of Mid-Yorkshire, but I didn't doubt I could win them round. As for mother, she and Mitch seemed to get on famously.

Once more I was on top of the world and this time I could see no reason why I should not remain there.

Then it happened again. This time much more dramatically.

Mitch vanished.

I hadn't seen her for a couple of days but we had a date on Saturday night. On Saturday morning, I got a text cancelling it, no reason given. Getting no reply to my return texts, I called at her flat. The girl she shared with, a media studies student called Donna who didn't much care for me, said she'd gone away for a few days. When I asked where, she answered, 'If Mitch had wanted you to know, I think she'd have told you,' and closed the door in my face.

I made enquiries among my friends. None of them could help, but one recollected seeing her a few days earlier, having lunch at a pub outside town with an older woman. From his description, I was certain it was Mother.

I decided to go and talk to Donna again.

I got on my bike (push-bike not a Harley, but a lot more use at the uni) and headed for the house where they had their flat. As I approached, I saw Donna unlocking her bike from the railings.

I pulled in behind a parked car and watched as she rode away. Wherever she was going it wasn't towards the media studies centre.

I followed.

Half an hour later, we were on the outskirts of town. Finally she turned into the drive of an imposing suburban mansion. A sign on the gate read, THE CEDARS CLINIC.

I rode up the drive and left my bike beside hers outside the main door.

There were some rose bushes blooming on either side of the doorway. I picked a small posy and went inside. Donna had vanished, but there was a woman sitting at a reception desk.

I smiled at her and said, 'Miss Powers?' and when she looked at me doubtfully, I flourished my posy and said, 'I'm her brother.'

'First floor, turn left, Room 14,' she said.

I think she regretted it almost as she was saying it, but I was off running up the stairs. I turned left down a long corridor, and when I reached No. 14, I didn't hesitate but pushed open the door and stepped inside.

Mitch, pale as death, lay on a bed with Donna sitting by her side. Two pairs of eyes rounded as they registered me. Neither registered welcome.

I said something like, 'Oh Jesus, Mitch, what's happened to you?'

Donna jammed her finger on to a bell-push and demanded, 'What the hell are you doing here?'

And Mitch turned her head away and began crying.

That was as much meaningful conversation as we had before a nurse arrived, followed by a security man, and I found myself bundled down the stairs and out of the door.

I had to wait nearly an hour before Donna appeared. When I rode up alongside her shoulder she glanced at me, then said flatly, 'Listen to what I say because this is the last time we'll talk. Your mother told Mitch about your father being some kind of nut and warned her the condition was hereditary and you needed medication from time to time to stop you going the same way. Not surprisingly Mitch doesn't want any part of this, so consider yourself dumped.'

This was so devastating that the air seemed to go dark and I've no recollection of the next several minutes. When I took notice of my surroundings again, we were almost back at the flat.

I said, 'But why is she in The Cedars? She looked really ill.'

Donna dismounted, chained her bike to the railings, went up the steps and opened the door.

'She had an abortion,' she said. 'There were complications, but she's OK now.'

She stepped inside, and slammed the door behind her.

I went back to my room and lay on my bed to think things through.

It didn't take long. Everything now became crystal clear. My mother had invested so much of her time and energy in binding me to her that she couldn't bear the thought that one day I must break free. As long as I was flitting from girl to girl, she didn't mind. But as soon as I started getting serious, she sat up and took notice.

It had never struck me before that love could be a destructive force, but now for the first time I wondered if it might have been some aspect of this same obsessive love that drove my father to plunge into Greendale Gorge. That was speculation. What I was now certain of was that she had told Gina and Kelly the same lies as she'd told to Mitch!

That early interference I could just about forgive. Only my pride had been hurt. But when it came to Mitch, not only had Mother ruined my hope of happiness, she had so terrified the poor girl that she had ended up in The Cedars, destroying our unborn child and almost losing her own life.

I felt my mind spinning out of control and I reached for my capsules. As I took them, I recalled my mother's reluctance in handing them over to me for self-administration when I left for the university. Now I understood that in her eyes the act must have symbolized a relinquishment of power. Even then she only gave me as many as she estimated I might need in half a term, keeping the rest of the six-month prescription 'safe at home' as she put it. Keeping *me* safe at home was what she meant! At this moment I hated her and never wanted to see her again.

Then my mobile rang.

It was Mother. I was so worked up, I didn't give her the chance to speak but launched into a tirade of abuse and accusation. When I finished there was silence at the other end. What else could there be? Justification? Defence? No, not even Mother, realizing she had been responsible for the death of her own grandchild, could try that.

I said, 'Mother, I'm coming home to pick up my things. Then I'm out of there forever. Don't try to stop me. I can never forgive you. We're done.'

And I rang off.

I had calmed down by the time I got home. I was sure she'd be waiting for me, ready to promise anything in her efforts to make me change my mind. But I was resolved. For once in my life I was going to be the controller, not the controlled.

But she, as always, was ahead of me.

The broken capsules (my capsules, of course! she wanted me to suffer) lay all around her chair; the glass was still held lightly by her almost lifeless hand. All my cold rationality fled. I could only think of everything she had been to me all these years. There was time for only a few words, of love and forgiveness. Then the glass fell to the floor and her eyes closed forever.

Perhaps I should have called for help, but I fell into a trancelike paralysis of grief. When I emerged from it, I found myself sitting at her bureau, writing this letter.

I had to talk to someone, Mr Dalziel, and I thought of you. By the time you read this, I will have joined Mother in a better world. I know how and where I shall make the transition, high up on Greendale Pass where my poor father ended his life all those years ago.

Like father, like son.

All I ask of you, Mr Dalziel, is that you tell it like it is.

Yours sincerely
William Appleby

I floated in a featureless world of light and shade, myself a part of the chiaroscuro, till a strange rumbling sound like distant thunder drew me upwards and gave me once more a sense of individual being.

I opened my eyes. Before me I saw a tremendous figure, menacing, judgemental, and I was filled with fear.

'Lord?' I croaked.

'Eh?' said the figure.

I blinked. And blinked again.

The figure slowly reduced to a grossly fat man overflowing a small chair by the bed on which I lay.

I whispered, 'Sorry. Thought you were God.'

'Common mistake,' said the man. 'Name's Dalziel. NURSE!'

A nurse came bustling in. She said sharply, 'We do have bells.'

'Like a bike, you mean? Which bit of you's it fixed on?'

She took my pulse and my temperature, gave me a glass of water, and said, 'I'll tell Mr Kali the consultant you're awake. Try to rest. No talking.'

With a glower at the fat man, she left.

'I love a bossy woman in uniform,' he said.

He shifted his huge buttocks in the chair and once more I heard the rumbling sound.

'Better out than in,' he said. 'Now, Mr Appleby, William, OK if I call thee Bill? Or mebbe Willy? You wrote me a letter.'

'Did I? Yes, I remember. Oh God!'

I closed my eyes and a sob rocked my body.

'Don't tek on, Willy,' he said. 'You're a very lucky boy. Airbag saved you. Plus you can't have been going fast enough to clear the undergrowth and get a straight drop into the gorge.'

'It doesn't feel lucky,' I murmured.

'Not to worry, you're still young, all your life to kill yourself in,' he said consolingly. 'So let's see. You say you wrote to me 'cos you wanted a man who'd not be scared of the truth.'

'Yes.'

161

'Well, you've come to the right shop. So let's have a look at this truth, shall we? And to start off, I've got to tell you there's one or two things you've got a bit wrong. Best get them out of the way first off.'

He pulled my letter out of the inside pocket of a jacket which could have doubled as a marquee at a small wedding, and stabbed his finger at one of the pages.

'This stuff about your dad's accident. Suicide you guess. Trouble is, there were three witnesses. Walkers. Saw him skid on a patch of ice. Straight over the edge, no airbags to save him. So definitely an accident.'

'Does it make a difference?' I asked dully.

'Likely not. Except it does relate to what your mam said to put your girlfriends off you . . .'

'Oh God,' I interrupted. 'How could she tell those dreadful lies?'

'Likely her being a woman helped,' he said. 'And your mam. Plus, they weren't exactly lies.'

'I'm sorry?'

He patted my shoulder, sympathetically I suppose, but it felt like being clubbed with a baseball bat.

'Something you need to know about your dad, Willy. He weren't a very nice man. I mean, he had lots of charm, no problem getting in a girl's knickers. Bit like you. But underneath it . . . well, you'd likely not know he'd been married before when he met your mam?'

This was news to me and I said so.

'Aye, over in Lancashire, young woman, bit of money she'd inherited from her parents, plus the family house. They got wed, he soon went through the money, mortgaged the house, went through that too. Then she died. Accident. Fell down the stairs. Luckily for him he'd taken out a hefty chunk of term insurance on her. There was talk. There always is.'

'What's this got to do with anything?' I demanded.

162

'Just thought you might be interested. Any road, nothing proved, talk died, he moved away. But there was this old uncle, ex-cop, he didn't forget, he kept on digging. Found a similar case, down in Cheshire. Different name, but the newspaper pics looked like the same guy. Now he tracked your dad across here to Yorkshire. And when he discovered he'd got married again, he alerted the local CID chief. That's me, in case you've forgotten.'

Suddenly I began to understand Dalziel's connection with Mother. I should have guessed there must have been something that kick-started her interest.

'And what steps did you take?' I demanded.

'Bloody careful ones! But when I found out that he'd taken out a big term insurance on your mam, well, I had to talk to her, didn't I? It were hard, mind you, what with her having a babbie. That 'ud be you. You were an ugly little bugger. At first your mam didn't want to believe me, but I think deep down she were already having doubts. The insurance policy came as a real shock. But afore we could decide what was best to do, your dad had his accident. The clincher came when the lawyers told her that he'd got through her own little bit of cash and most of what they'd got from mortgaging the house – it was your mam's house, did you know that?'

I shook my head.

'At least she didn't get pushed down the stairs. But she were left with a kid to bring up and not much money. In the circs I think she's done pretty well. A lot of what you say about the way she made ends meet is probably true, but after her experience, you can't blame her if she took advantage of a lot of greedy men, can you?'

'No, no,' I said faintly. 'I didn't blame her. I make that clear in my letter.'

'So you do. But this business of putting your girlfriends off, well, think about it. There's you, with all your dad's charm, girls at your beck and call, but somehow it's always the ones with a

163

bit of money behind them that you get really close up and cosy with. Gina's dad owns a brewery, Kelly's family's got a chain of hotels, and with Mitch, you were really farting through silk. Landowners, huntin', shootin', fishin', all that crap. When your mam saw that, no wonder alarm bells rang. You'd been diagnosed borderline psychotic early on. Big mood swings, low moral sense, all right if you kept taking the medicine. She tried to keep it from you just how serious your condition was, but I think you knew, didn't you?'

I ignored his question and protested, 'But what she made Mitch do, there's no justifying that!'

'Well, she certainly spoke to Mitch, like her friend Donna told you. Doesn't much like you, that lass, happy to see you squirm, I'd guess. Thing is, Mitch didn't need to be warned off. She was ready to dump you anyway.'

'But our baby . . .' I said disbelievingly.

'Hers, not yours. Seems she'd been having a thing with one of her tutors. Hairy bugger, ranting Red, drops his aitches, even less her family's type than you, plus he's already got a wife and five bairns so wasn't going to be much enthused at the thought of another in either class. Mitch chatted to your mam about the pros and cons of termination. Not hard to guess which side your mam came down on after her experience.'

I was completely knocked back by this. I felt that otherworldly light and shade beginning to swim around me once more.

'Please,' I murmured. 'I need the nurse . . .'

'In a sec,' he said. 'Just one last thing to get sorted. Was it because you really thought your mam had buggered things up between you and Mitch that you killed her? Or was it finding the insurance policy that made up your mind?'

Suddenly I was completely back in the stark clear world of the hospital room.

'I don't understand . . .' I said.

'Aye, you do. Must have come as a real surprise when you

164

found that policy for all that money with less than a year of its term to run. Your dad had taken it out for twenty years when he got married. He didn't want to attract suspicion by going for a really short term. And your daft, doting mam kept up the premiums all them years, even adding a bit to it when she could, all to keep you covered in case she should snuff it before you came of age. I can see how you must have thought it a shame to let all her sacrifice come to nowt. And you'd have been able to buy that motorbike at last!'

'This is outrageous!' I protested. 'You must be mad. Nurse! Nurse!'

'Don't shout, she doesn't like it, remember,' he said. 'So you went home, made her a nice strong cup of tea, laced with the contents of your capsules. I bet you'd checked out the drug in the uni library and knew exactly how much would be a fatal dose. Soon she got dozy, and while she slipped away, you cleared away the cups, put a glass in her hand and sat down to write this letter. Then off to Greendale Gorge, crash gently through the fence, jump out of the car at the last minute, and scramble down the gorge to lie beside the wreck till you were found. Except you suddenly had a witness, the farmer in his tractor, so you had to take the risk of really going over the edge.'

'You're crazy!' I cried. 'You don't have a shred of evidence and if you dare repeat this in front of witnesses I'll sue you for every penny you have!'

'You'd not get much,' he said quietly. 'As for witnesses, well, I do have one. You see, your doting mam worried herself sick about you being away from home, having to do things for yourself, so she had some placebos made up which she mixed in with the real capsules, just to lessen the chance of you overdosing by accident. So there were enough sedative in her drink to knock her cold, but you'd have needed a lot more to kill her.'

'I don't believe you,' I said, dry-mouthed.

But I was already following his gaze to the door.

It opened, and Mother came in.

She smiled at me sadly, forgivingly, even – God help me – lovingly.

But she didn't speak. What was there to say?

She'd warned me I'd make a fool of myself by writing to Dalziel.

I should have listened.

Mother is always right.

John Brown's Body

It's a great beach for bodies.

To the north towers the craggy height of Bale Head, the county's favourite spot for suicides whose battered corpses a decorous current lays neatly on the crescent of golden sand curving two miles south to the sharp point of Bodd Ness. Beyond this the incoming tide squeezes itself into the narrow estuary of the Bodd and rapidly becomes a bit of a bore. Most of those caught in that sudden rush (and, despite the warnings, each year brings half a dozen) are swept out on the ebb and left as testaments to folly on our sunny beach. Add to this a funnel of tides widening out into the Atlantic which, after a big storm, has brought us bodies from as far afield as the Scillies, and you've got yourself a boddicomber's dream.

What's a boddicomber? With a capital B, it's a native of Boddicombe, the village half a mile inland where I've been living for the past twenty years. But with a small b, it's a beachcomber who's found a body. Macabre? Not really, not if you live here. Here with our tides and currents, it's almost the norm, and all the regulars in the bar of the Drowned Sailor are boddicombers in both senses.

All except one, that is.

167

Me.

John Brown.

I suppose, having married a local lass and lived here for two decades, I can claim the capital **B** as an adopted son of the village. Certainly, after some initial caution, quite natural when an outsider sweeps a local heiress off her feet, the denizens of the Sailor took me to their hearts and treated me as one of their own. Only one thing was needed to put the seal on the deed of adoption. But so far it hasn't happened.

For twenty years now I've been walking the beach once, sometimes twice a day, and I've never found a body.

Don't misunderstand me. They're not a morbid lot down in the Sailor. Bodies on the beach aren't a staple of conversation. But whenever another corpse is washed up, naturally this sparks off reminiscences of past tragedies with comparisons and contrasts and significant anecdotes as each discoverer in turn recalls *his* body. That's how they're identified, not by their own names, but by the boddicomber's name, as *Dick's body* or *Ernie's body*, or where the man in question has been fortunate enough to come across more than one, *Tony's second* or *Andy's third*.

It's amazing how possessive a boddicomber becomes. Every detail that can be gleaned from police investigations, coroner's inquests, newspaper reports, and any other source, is hoarded up and treasured. Sometimes their depth of background knowledge makes me wonder if some of them don't employ private detectives. I listen in dumb admiration. For that's all I can do, listen, though they've always done their best to include me, and everyone was mightily pleased when the year before last Charley Trenfold's *seventh* gave them a hook to hang their kindness on. Now as soon as Charley's *seventh* is mentioned, someone will turn to me and urge me to make my pathetic contribution. And I always do, because a man shouldn't turn his back on kindness. But oh! how the words bring back the bitter taste of *proxime accessit*, as sharp and pungent as it was on that misty morning two years ago.

I'd got up early to take a walk. To tell the truth it had been one of those nights I'd spent uncomfortably in the spare room after yet another row with Lorna. God, that mattress! Once when friendly relations were resumed after an earlier exile, I'd joked that if we were going to make a habit of this, we really ought to think about getting a more user-friendly guest bed. To which she'd replied that, if I had the money to spare, that might not be a bad idea. Which rapidly led to a breach of our armistice and another bout of sleepless nights for me.

This particular morning as I strolled along the path to the beach, I wondered gloomily whether my marriage was in terminal decline. For ten years after our romantic start, things had only got better and better. Lorna had been so in love that she'd assured me there'd be no problem in leaving the lovely family house she'd inherited in Boddicombe to move into my flat in town ninety slow miles away. But I knew how much she loved that house and assured her in turn that there was no need. Modern technology meant I could do my job as easily from Boddicombe as I could in company HQ, and I'd get to walk the beach nearly every day. Funny thing, love. We nearly fell out each trying to make sacrifices for the other! But I won, and for the next ten years I worked from home and, as I'd forecast, there were no problems at all. Then the company fell on hard times and suddenly the flaw in my arrangement became apparent. When downsizing's in the air, it's easier to start with the faces you're not seeing every day in the executive dining room.

So I was out, but it didn't seem to matter. I'd made enough money when I was in to provide a reassuring cushion till I found a new job. Except there were no new jobs, not even when I cast my net well beyond the old ninety-mile limit.

No problem, I said. If you can't find someone to employ you, employ yourself! I already had a well-equipped home office. Now I invested what remained of my money in upgrading it to cutting-edge status, called in a few old favours, and suddenly I was an entrepreneur.

For a while it looked like it was going to work, but at best I was never more than holding my own. Slowly I ran out of favours and commissions. The emails fell to a trickle then dried up completely, the fax only chugged out advertising junk, the phone never rang and the postman brought nothing but bills.

Till finally I had to face up to it. I was an unemployment statistic living in his wife's house on his wife's money. Things might have been better if I hadn't felt so guilty about it. Looking back, I think I spent so much time telling Lorna what a liability I was that in the end she believed it.

But I did get a lot more time to walk the beach.

And that misty morning, as I stood on my usual high dune letting my gaze run north along the sand, I thought my luck might be on the change.

Each tide left its own signature on the beach and over the years I had grown expert at reading those scrawls of flotsam and jetsam and beached jellyfish and sea wrack, and like all the boddicombers, I was ultra-sensitive to anything whose configuration or bulk was out of the ordinary.

And this morning there was something there, right at the limit of my view, nothing more than a dark smudge in the bluey-pink wreaths the sun's warm rays were drawing off the damp sand, but definitely *something* . . .

I took a deep breath and was just about to descend from the dune when a voice called my name.

'John! Good morning to you!'

I turned in irritation to see Maisie Palliser climbing up towards me followed by her overweight and panting pug, Samson.

I forced my features into something as close to a smile as I could manage and said, 'Good morning.'

Maisie Palliser was one of those women who get a reputation for kindness by making unacceptable offers of help and who uses her much-vaunted sympathy as a tool for getting under the defences of the vulnerable to the secrets below. She was Lorna's cousin, a couple of years older and unmarried. Not that she was physically unattractive. Indeed, she and Lorna could almost have been twins. But Maisie, though devious in many ways, had no art to conceal her desire to dominate. There'd been a quarrel between their fathers, the two Palliser brothers, over their inheritance many years before and as they grew up, the two cousins hadn't had much to do with each other. A pity in some ways. There's nothing like a shared childhood for giving you a proper insight into character. Myself I never cared for her from the start. How Lorna felt I never enquired, but I got an impression she wasn't all that worried about the after-effects of their fathers' quarrel. But when illness and accident removed the last of the older generation a few years back, Maisie had been so assiduous in bringing about a rapprochement that Lorna's gentler nature was quite unable to resist. The big card Maisie played was that she and Lorna were the last of the Pallisers, so family feuds must give way to family solidarity. I gently mocked this non sequitur, but it was no contest. Lorna was a sucker for sentiment and, perhaps unjustly, I date the beginning of the deterioration in my marital relationship not so much from the day I lost my job as from the day I first found Maisie enjoying afternoon tea in our drawing room. After that she became a regular visitor and soon Lorna seemed happy to admit her as a confidante. She drew the line however, at welcoming Samson, the pug, who combined a delicate stomach with insatiable greed, eating anything he could get his thieving teeth on, then after just long enough for his inefficient digestive juices to render it revolting, vomiting it back up, preferably on a chair or a carpet. Lorna was usually pretty neutral about domestic animals, but in this case she made an exception. She really detested that dog, its very presence set her teeth on edge, and in her quiet way she made it absolutely clear that Samson was not welcome in her house. So whenever Maisie visited, the pug was locked in the kitchen porch where he could do no harm.

171

'Best part of the day this,' said Maisie now as she joined me. 'I don't see it often enough but I couldn't sleep last night. My old trouble.'

She smiled bravely. What her old trouble was nobody knew exactly, but that it was exceedingly painful and bravely borne no one could avoid knowing.

'Same with you, was it, John?' she went on.

'Doubt it, Maisie. I don't have your old trouble,' I replied.

It was birdshot against a tank.

'How lucky you are,' she sighed. 'But I meant something must have got you out of bed early too. I sincerely hope it wasn't anything causing you physical pain.'

'No. Just fancied a stroll, that's all.'

'And you managed to steal away without disturbing Lorna, I'm sure. How is the dear girl? I must call round and have a chat soon. Don't worry. I won't take up too much of her time. I know how hard the pair of you work to make your business a success. Don't forget my offer. Anything I can do to help – folding envelopes, addressing labels, even a bit of typing – I can still manage to get my fingers dancing over a keyboard even with my arthritis – all you have to do is ask, John.'

She knew damn well the business had given up the ghost just as she knew damn well Lorna and I spent more time sleeping apart than together, but how was I to tell her that without telling her that, if you see what I mean, opening the floodgates to a new torrent of useless advice and ersatz sympathy?

But I might have exploded if over her shoulder I hadn't seen the last thing I wanted to see, the familiar hunched figure of Charley Trenfold dropping down to the beach from the dunes between me and that distant mist-shrouded shape.

I muttered something to Maisie, I don't know what, and set out after him. I was the younger man and got plenty of exercise to keep me fit. But old Charley was no slouch either, and by the way he was striding out, he'd clearly his *seventh* firmly in

172

his sights. It was partly the fact that his cottage stood a little way out of the village and a lot closer to the beach that gave him his boddicombing pre-eminence, but you couldn't deny that he had a nose for it, and though the idea was never openly expressed, everyone in the Sailor knew it was his ambition to overtake the record of the greatest boddicomber (and Boddicomber) of them all, Jacob Palliser, my wife's and Maisie's grandfather, who during the course of a long and profitable life had found a round dozen.

Fast as I moved, even breaking into a trot when I got close enough to see that the shape on the beach was undoubtedly a corpse, I couldn't overtake Charley. I couldn't even claim a dead heat. He reached the body a full step ahead, turned to look at me with a little start of surprise as if he'd been unaware of my pursuit, and said, 'Is that you, John Brown? Well, here's a sad sight for a summer's morn. Another poor soul lured by Old Nick to leap off the Head.'

I didn't doubt for one moment he'd be right. Old Charley was so familiar with the general configuration of the tides and currents and the modifying effect of specific weather conditions that he could tell with amazing accuracy the likely point of entry of any body washed up on our beach.

I looked down at the face of the man at our feet. There was a dreadful gash across his brow with splintered bone showing through, confirming Charley's judgement. Those who jumped off the Head usually died on the rocks below and lay there till the height of the tide picked them up and carried them away. I didn't recognize the face. The Head's reputation lured people from far and wide. But I knew from experience that over the next few weeks, Charley would somehow research chapter and verse of his life and background and the circumstances which brought him to this sad end. All of which would have been my task if Maisie hadn't delayed me. The bitch! She was my bird of ill omen even in this.

'Why don't you stay with him and I'll head back to the cottage and ring the police?' said Charley.

Reporting was the next important stage after finding. It got you officially into the records, established your claim, so to speak.

'No need for that,' I said, 'I'll do it from here.'

And I took out my mobile phone and dialled.

And that was how I got my footnote in the boddicombers annals. Mobiles, already the common furniture of urban life, hadn't reached Boddicombe in any great numbers then. Now everyone in the Sailor has one. Rumour has it that Charley went out and bought one the next day. I smile whenever I see him use it, for I know it still rankles slightly that every time his seventh comes up in conversation, some kind soul, eager to bring me into things, will say, 'Aye, that's the one that John Brown reported on his mobile, isn't that right, John?' and I'll get my thirty seconds of fame.

Two years on and that was still all I could lay claim to, though I seemed to spend more time walking the beach and its environs than I did at home. *Home!* It was hardly that any more. It was simply the house where I lodged by the grudging permission of the woman who used to be my wife. Why didn't she throw me out and sue for divorce? There were several reasons, not least among them being the fact that she'd been brought up as a Boddicombe Baptist. I don't know if this term has any official standing in the religious world, but I do know that the attitude of the BBs to divorce made the Roman Catholic Church look like Club Méditerranée.

As for me, why didn't I call it a day and walk out?

Again several reasons, with large among them the fact that I had nowhere to walk to. The years of desperately seeking work had made me a man old acquaintance crossed the street to avoid. And the years of not having any work had made me a man who crossed the street to avoid old acquaintance. So I'd zig-zagged to a situation where the only place I felt at home and among friends was the bar of the Drowned Sailor. If I walked away from this, my probable destination was a cardboard box in a shop doorway. Or Bale Head. Which would at least have meant that I got my place permanently in the mythology of the Sailor. But when I thought of the satisfaction it would give Maisie Palliser, I knew it wasn't really an option.

At my blackest moments I sometimes thought that my only chance of a future better than this demeaning present lay in Lorna dying. We'd never made wills. With only the two of us to consider in those early loving days, it seemed to be tempting fate to pay someone to formalize what would happen anyway, which is to say if one of us died, the survivor would get all. Well, those loving days were long gone, though deep inside of me I still nursed a weak runt of a hope that a love as strong as ours had been couldn't altogether die. Perhaps it was our common memories rather than Lorna's religion and my fears that kept us together? Certainly I can honestly say that even in those blackest moments I stopped short of wishing her dead, and I never got close to fantasizing about killing her. But words have a life of their own, and one day not long after Christmas when some minor financial irritation had melted the cold courtesy between us to molten antagonism, I exploded, 'Money, money, money, that's all you think about, isn't it? Well, I didn't marry you for your money, and as far as I'm concerned you can grow old and ugly counting it. I don't want any part of it!'

To which she replied, equally incensed, 'That's just as well, because from now on you're not getting any more. You might make me miserable but you're not going to make me bankrupt.'

And I, God forgive me, cried, 'So you're rich and miserable and I'm broke and miserable. Why don't you take a dive off Bale Head – that would solve all our problems, wouldn't it?'

I saw the shock in her face and wished it unsaid instantly. I wanted to say I didn't mean it, that we shouldn't be surprised if two people who'd loved each other as much as we had were as extreme in their quarrels as they'd been in their passion. But the door was pushed open at that moment and Maisie was standing there, saying, 'Sorry, I rang the bell but no one answered so I just came in.' How much she'd heard, I couldn't say. Everything, I suspected. Whatever, there was nothing for me to do now but leave with my retraction unattempted, and over the next couple of days Lorna gave me neither opportunity nor encouragement to apologize and, as is the way in these matters, I soon began to feel the fault was as much hers as mine, so why should I be the one who grovelled?

Then a few days later, returning to the house after another unproductive stroll along the beach, I heard Lorna call my name from the drawing room.

The first person I saw when I entered was Maisie, drinking tea. She gave a thin smile, which had something unpleasantly gloating in it. Once she'd been at some pains to conceal her antagonism towards me. For several weeks in the run-up to Christmas, Maisie had been all sweetness and light, indeed almost likeable. I wondered if she'd found God or taken up marijuana. Then suddenly, over the holiday period, she'd done a Scrooge in reverse and emerged at the other side even more of a foul-tempered, man-hating termagant than she'd been before.

Lorna was sitting opposite her on a sofa with the lanky figure of Tim Edlington, the Palliser family solicitor by her side. He rose to shake my hand and said something conventional like 'Good to see you again, John'. But I detected a certain embarrassment in his tone which worried me. One thing I learned in business was when lawyers sound embarrassed you're really in trouble.

Lorna said brusquely, 'John, I need you to witness my signature.'

'Of course, dear,' I said. 'On what?'

'On my will.'

I tried to hide my surprise. I doubt if I was successful.

'Your will?' I said. 'I didn't realize . . . I mean, isn't it illegal, for a husband I mean, to witness . . . ?'

'Only if he is a beneficiary,' said Lorna coldly.

And now I felt real shock and I didn't even bother to try to hide it. I saw at once what was happening. She must have been deeply shocked by what I'd said. I guessed she'd confided in Maisie. Indeed, with Maisie having overheard my outburst, it would have been impossible for someone feeling as vulnerable as Lorna must have felt to resist her cousin's spurious sympathy and vicarious outrage. No doubt in her present anti-male mood she'd assured Lorna that all men were murdering rapists under the skin. And now I was being told loud and clear in front of witnesses that, whatever else Lorna's death might do for me, it wasn't going to make me rich.

Maisie was observing me with her face set in a mask of sympathy which she didn't mind me piercing to the malicious pleasure beneath. Tim Edlington's embarrassed sympathy, on the other hand, was very real and he rushed in to fill the silence that followed Lorna's remark with an attempt at explanation.

'What Lorna and Maisie want to do, John, is repair the damage done to the Palliser estate, not to mention the Palliser family, by old Jacob's will.'

He glanced up at the portrait of Jacob Palliser, founder of the family fortunes and grandfather to Maisie and Lorna. It was from him that Maisie inherited her need to dominate. From all accounts he had kept his sons under his thumb until he died, and even then he'd left a will cunningly constructed to leave both feeling cheated, dividing the property so that the younger son (Lorna's father) got the house and land which the elder son (Maisie's father) thought his due, while the elder got a controlling interest in the dairy products business which the younger had almost single-handedly built up. Some necessary concessions had been agreed, but effectively that malicious will had set the brothers at each other's throats for the rest of their lives.

'So,' concluded Tim, 'Lorna and Maisie have asked me to draw up mutually beneficial wills by which, when in the fullness of time one or the other of them passes on, the estate such as it now is will once more be joined together as a single entity.'

He tried to make it sound like a reasonable act of conciliation, but he knew that he was talking bollocks. This wasn't about old Jacob and the estate. It was about me. And it was also about Maisie, who was potentially by far the biggest beneficiary of this new arrangement. Neither brother had made much of his inheritance, but whereas Lorna's father had hung on to a good proportion of his, Maisie had seen her prospects dwindle to the small family cottage in which she lived, and a small income to go with it. Already, it seemed to me, she was looking around that handsome drawing room with a proprietary air.

I said, 'Where do I sign?'

I didn't even bother to read the wills, just countersigned the women's signatures. Tim acted as the other witness. I shook him by the hand again and left the room. As I closed the door quietly behind me, I glanced up at old Jacob's portrait.

I'd never met the old man, but now I read in those piercing black eyes the scorn of a self-made man for a failure and a weakling who had not only lost his wife's love and respect but couldn't even find a single body on our bountiful beach.

Which of course was where I headed now. To rage and brood and plot. And to look for bodies.

Does that sound crazily obsessive? I suppose it must. But somehow my failure to find a body had become a symbol of all my failures. No; it was more than a symbol. It was as if everything that had gone wrong in my life could somehow be tracked back to this one deficiency. It placed the blame fairly not on my own shoulders but on a malevolent fate or at best the vagaries of blind chance. It seemed to me that if only I could find my body and take my place as of right among the native boddicombers in the Drowned Sailor, all would be well. I could look the portrait of old Jacob straight in the eye, Lorna would regain her respect for me, her love, her energy, and her healthy bank balance would be put at my disposal, and thus armed I could renew my assault on the world of commerce, and this time I would win . . .

Yes, I continued to think like this even after the business of the will. At first it had seemed to me that for Lorna to let Maisie into the act had been a deliberate attempt to add insult to injury. She knew how much I disliked and distrusted her. But more mature consideration led me to the conclusion that, far from wanting to pile on the pain, Lorna had looked for a device which would give the whole business a patina of rationality. She could just have left everything to the Boddicombe Baptists. But that would have been undisguisable as anything but a wish to cause me pain. The business of reuniting the estate was the best way she could find of softening the blow, and her general demeanour in the days that followed made me think the whole affair was making her feel guilty and gave me hope that the embers of our love might still be warm enough to melt her heart which my stupid outburst had so hardened against me.

So I continued with my secret crazy dream that things could still be turned around if only I could find that elusive body. One corpse. That wasn't much to ask. Charley Trenfold had had a great couple of years and was up to eleven now, just one short of old Jacob's record. Surely the great and generous ocean could spare a single corpse for me?

Who was it who said, be careful what you pray for because you might get it?

A couple of weeks later I came home in the gloam of an overcast February evening, slightly out of breath as I'd been hurrying.

Happily, Lorna's principles which forbade her to divorce me also forbade her to starve me and she cooked our meal every night. A creature of habit, her menu was dictated by the day, without any reference to possible variation of appetite, and she set our meal on the table between seven and seven thirty, and started to eat regardless of whether I had arrived or not.

On nut cutlet night, I didn't much mind whether I got it hot or cold, but today was pork chop day, my favourite, so I hurried to be on time even though it meant leaving the beach half an hour before high tide. I went round to the kitchen entrance as usual. But as I kicked off my wellingtons in the covered porchway, I realized that something was missing – the mouth-watering smell of grilling pork.

Puzzled, I pushed open the kitchen door. On the table I could see assembled for cooking all the ingredients of dinner. Mushrooms, tomatoes, chipped potatoes, and a succulent chop with the kidney in, the way I liked it. But no Lorna.

I went through the house calling her name.

There was no reply.

I went out to the old barn which acted as a garage. I had declined from Jag through Mondeo to Daewoo, but finally even that had gone and now our only vehicle was the aged Land Rover which Lorna claimed was all that country dwellers needed.

It wasn't there.

Puzzled and just beginning to be worried, but not wanting to give the local gossips still more material by ringing around, I walked into the village and called at Maisie's house. There was no sign of the Land Rover, and no sign of Maisie either. Only Samson greeted me on the threshold. He looked so disconsolate that I started to bend to stroke him. Then he belched noisomely and brought up a disgusting bolus of gristle and bone which spread itself across Maisie's pristine doorstep.

I walked down the street, past the Drowned Sailor. No sign of the Land Rover in the car park. I thought of going inside, but all that that would have done was feed the local rumour machine. Increasingly anxious but still a long way from panic, I walked home by a route which took me past several outlying houses belonging to various friends of Lorna, hoping I'd see the

Land Rover parked outside one of them. No luck, but as I passed the last of these, its owner, a farmer called Tony Simkin (two bodies to his credit, one of them a local politician who'd solved his problem with a corruption scandal by stepping off Bale Head) spotted me as he came out of his lambing shed.

'Evening, John,' he said. 'Fed up with the beach then?'

Meaning it was a bit unusual for me to be taking my evening stroll along these lanes.

'Change is as good as a rest,' I said.

'Could do with one myself,' he said. 'These early lambs are a pain. Thought I saw you driving that old heap of yours down the coast road earlier and I said to myself, there go John and Lorna off to the movies in Lymton, lucky devils.'

The ancient cinema which had somehow contrived to survive in Lymton, twelve miles north, was our nearest source of public entertainment.

'Not me,' I said lightly.

'No?' He looked at me doubtfully. 'Could have sworn I recognized the hat. But never mind. Here you are now. Won't you step into the house for a dram? Say hello to Betsy?'

Four months earlier, Tony's wife, Betsy, had left him, taking their two children. Then at Christmas there'd been a reconciliation, and Tony was still in the honeymoon period, wanting everyone who came near to call in and see what a happy united family they were.

I wasn't in the mood for happy united families so I made an excuse, took my leave, and hastened home.

Still no sign of Lorna, but Tony's possible sighting of the Land Rover was encouraging a new and reassuring hypothesis. Probably it was as straightforward as that . . . Lorna had simply gone to the cinema . . . a last-minute decision . . . someone had reminded her there was a film she was keen to see . . .

But she wouldn't have gone without leaving a note . . .

I knew there was nothing on the kitchen table but I checked

181

as I passed through. Our other note-leaving place was against the clock on the mantelpiece in the drawing room. I'd pushed open the door and called Lorna's name into the darkened room when I'd first missed her, but I hadn't actually gone inside.

Now I stepped in and put the light on.

No note against the clock. Above it, old Jacob sneered down at me.

I was turning away when my eye caught sight of what looked like a piece of paper on the hearth beneath the mantel. Perhaps the note had slipped. I went forward and picked it up. There was some writing on it in a familiar hand, but not Lorna's.

Mine.

It was my signature preceded by the typed words *signed by the testatrix in the presence of* . . .

The fire basket was grey with paper ash.

And as I stopped to take a closer look I saw something else.

A dark brown stain on the sharp corner of the raised stone hearth.

I touched it. It was dry. I scraped at it with my fingernail, raised the resulting powdery flakes to the light, sniffed at them.

It was blood.

I sank to the floor and squatted there, letting all the fragmented thoughts whirling around my head settle slowly into a meaningful mosaic.

I recalled the single chop on the kitchen table where there should have been two. And I recalled the bony gristly mess that Samson had vomited up on Maisie's doorstep.

Suddenly it was like putting a video in the VCR and pressing the *play* button.

Maisie had been here. Lorna had told her she'd changed her mind about the will. Maisie had protested. Lorna had been adamant. And being a woman who thought that deeds spoke louder than words, she'd produced the will and put a match to it and stooped to hold it over the fire basket. Maisie had tried to wrest it from her. Lorna, off balance, had fallen forward, crashing heavily, fatally, against the edge of the hearth.

And then . . . ?

I knew how Maisie's mind worked. The burned will, signs of a struggle, her cousin's corpse . . . even if the inquest brought in a verdict of accidental death, there would be talk for ever more. She would judge others by herself and guess that in the eyes of many she would be marked as a murderess who'd got away with it for the rest of her life. That wouldn't bother her too much perhaps if she could claim the compensation of Lorna's house and money. But the will was in the fireplace, burned beyond retrieval.

Then slowly as she sat there reviewing her options, an idea formed in her devious mind . . . an idea which at worst would clear her of any suspicion of involvement in Lorna's death and at best might result in her claiming the Palliser inheritance after all . . .

The coast road to Lymton which Tony thought he'd seen me driving along was also the road to Bale Head.

Maisie had put the body in the Land Rover, driven to the Head, and tipped Lorna over the edge.

Suicide while the balance of her mind was disturbed. I could hear Maisie at the inquest reluctantly letting herself be bullied into admitting that the wreck of our marriage and my unreasonable behaviour had brought Lorna to the edge of despair.

As for the burned will, who had lit the flame? Who benefitted most from its destruction?

I could see all eyes in the coroner's court turning towards me. I'm sure Maisie's lawyer, especially if it wasn't Tim, could make a strong legal argument for reinstating the burned will.

But why take a chance on the uncertainties of the law when there was another more certain way?

Maisie wouldn't find it hard when talking to the police to refer 'inadvertently' to my threats against Lorna's life, threats which had included a mention of Bale Head. Indeed, for all I knew she'd already told everyone in the village about them. The police would start looking for other evidence, and eventually they'd come up with Tony Simkin and anyone else who'd seen the Land Rover heading along the coast road.

Why had Tony had been so sure he'd seen me in the driving seat? He'd said something about recognizing my hat . . .

I went back into the kitchen and looked at the clothes hooks behind the door.

An ancient and very distinctive old-fashioned floppy cap I often wore when driving in cold wintry conditions wasn't there. The bitch had already been thinking ahead to putting me in the frame!

I shook my head and asked myself, could even Maisie be as cunningly manipulative as that?

Of course she could! I answered. She'd know that once the police started looking closely at things, it wouldn't be long before the bloodstains in the drawing room were found, and then . . .

But even as I ran this frightening scenario through my mind, I knew that what I was really doing was attempting to block off my shock, my horror, my despair, at the prospect of admitting Lorna was dead.

Before I was finally going to lay myself open to that destructive knowledge, I would need to see her corpse.

And if my hypothesis was right, I knew exactly where I'd find it.

For the first time in many years, I headed down to the beach, praying that I wouldn't find a body.

Two hours or more had passed since I'd come away and headed home for dinner and the tide had long turned and it was its receding roar that I heard as I clambered up the dunes. The night was pitch-black, the air full of wind and sand and the smell of sea wrack and the intermittent cries of storm-disturbed birds which fell upon my ear like the desperate appeals of a lost soul.

The sea itself was nothing more than a vague far-off line of dim whiteness and I could make out no horizon, sky and water blending into a single bowl of blackness. No use to stand up here on the dunes and try to pick out shapes on the beach. I needed to be down there, and even then, without a torch, it was almost going to be a matter of feeling my way along the sand.

My heart sank at the grisly prospect. Then as if in answer to my prayers, I saw a beam of light wavering towards me up the dunes.

It shone full in my face and Charley Trenfold's voice said, 'Is that you, John? God, you're keen, on a night like this!'

You too, I thought. But I was glad to see him, both for his torch and his company.

Then I recalled Charley's famous nose for a body, and I didn't feel so glad.

I said nothing except, 'Come on then. Let's get down there.'

We descended and moved forward together in silence along the wavering high tide mark.

We both saw it at the same time. I suppose what went through Charley's mind was, this could be my twelfth! This could be the night I equal old Jacob's record!

What went through my mind I have no words to tell.

I let out a cry compounded of shock, of grief, of anger, of recognition, of farewell, and, shouldering Charley aside, I ran forward, stumbling in the soft sand till I fell on my knees by Lorna's body.

She lay on her face, as if asleep. I turned her over and my straining tearful eyes saw the deep wound on her brow which I knew probably came from the corner of the hearth rather than her fall from the Head.

My grief is impossible to describe. Not for a single moment did it occur to me how damning it was going to sound when Charley described the way I shoved him aside and went rushing forward. 'And how could you be so certain that you had found your wife's body, Mr Brown? Unless of course you knew exactly where it was going to be found . . .'

Then Charley arrived, saying grudgingly, 'So I suppose we'll have to call this your *first*, John Brown,' as he let the beam of his torch play full on the face cradled in my hands.

And I looked at those dear pallid features in the pool of light. And I thought what strange changes death brought about. And Charley exclaimed, 'My God! It's Maisie Palliser!'

It was like the breaking of a spell.

I blinked once, and what the darkness of the night, the tears in my eyes, and above all my fearful expectation had persuaded me was Lorna, instantly and unmistakably became Maisie.

And with equal speed the hypothesis I had programmed in my mind was reformatted. I guessed I'd been right in most particulars except one. It had been Maisie who, rushing forward in a fit of rage when she saw that Lorna really was destroying the will, had fallen and smashed her skull against the edge of the stone hearth. And it had been Lorna who, fearful of the consequences – the long-drawn-out legal enquiries, the rumours and gossip, the threat to her treasured privacy and her family reputation – had untypically panicked, packed the corpse into the Land Rover, and driven up to Bale Head. My hat she'd have put on merely to disguise herself, not to masquerade as me.

Where was she now?

My heart went out to her, wherever she was. This wasn't something she should have to bear alone. I needed to find her, let her know that whatever happened, I was steadfast.

Charley was busy phoning the emergency services. My role with his *seventh*.

Finished, he said, 'Well, poor old Maisie. Anyone could see her disappointment over Tony had hit her really hard, but I never thought she'd take it this bad. At least she looks at peace now.'

And she did. In fact death had taken ten years off her face, another reason why I'd confounded her with Lorna. But these thoughts were for later. At that moment I was just trying to puzzle out what Charley was talking about.

'Sorry?' I said. 'What disappointment?'

'Didn't you know?' He sounded genuinely surprised. 'I thought everyone knew. When Betsy left Tony, Maisie was right in there. You know how she was. Anything I can do to help? Washing, cleaning, ironing, shopping . . . and is there anything else, Tony? Anything a big strong handsome man like you is missing . . . ? Well, he wasn't going to say no, was he? Not when it's there on a plate. From all accounts, Maisie got to hoping this was going to turn into something permanent, but anyone could have told her, first sniff Tony got of Betsy coming back, and goodbye Maisie! Well, that happened at Christmas. You must have noticed Maisie wasn't exactly going round wishing everyone a happy New Year!'

I listened, amazed and delighted. Wrapped up in my own affairs, I'd been stone deaf to local gossip. It certainly explained why Maisie's mood had changed from one of relative benevolence for several weeks to one of more than normal malignancy! And best of all, it provided a motive for self-slaughter, which would never be allowed into the open but which would certainly be whispered in the ears of the police and the coroner.

I said, 'Charley, can I leave you to handle this by yourself? I'd like to get back and let Lorna know what's happened before someone else gets there with the story.'

'No problem,' said Charley. 'You're right. It'll be better coming from you. Poor Lorna. Last of the Pallisers now.'

'Indeed. Thanks, Charley. And by the way, sorry I rushed forward just now. No way to behave. This is clearly your body. We'd never have found it without your torch. It's your *twelfth*.'

I could see he was sorely tempted but though we boddicombing Boddicombers may not have a written code, we play things by the book.

'No,' he said, regretfully but firmly. 'You were first there, John. She's yours.'

That's what I call real moral fibre.

When I got back to the house, the Land Rover was parked outside. Lorna was sitting in the kitchen, drinking a glass of whisky.

On my way back I'd been working out how to play this. If she blurted everything out straight away, so be it. I'd do everything I could to cover things up. But in the long term, I doubted if this would do anything for our marriage. Shared guilt isn't a good basis for a relationship. What she needed was my unconditional love, not my complicity. And what I needed was hers, not a sense that she was in thrall to me.

So before she could speak I said, 'I'll have one of those. I've got some bad news, I'm afraid, dear.'

I told her about finding Maisie on the beach. When I told her about Maisie and Tony Simkin, I could tell from her reaction that she'd missed this too. Boddicombers might like their gossip, but they can be as discreet as doctors when it comes to keeping things from people they don't think should know them, like family.

'So poor Maisie must have just cracked under the strain. I thought she'd been acting a bit odd lately, even for her,' I concluded.

She sat in silence for a while. She looked pale and I guessed she was nerving herself to tell me the truth. Confession followed by expiation, that was the only route for a Boddicombe Baptist. Though if we could cut straight to the expiation, and it was painful enough, we might be able to put the confession on permanent hold . . .

But what form of expiation could I offer which would do the trick? How in the space of a few seconds could I weave a hair shirt fit for a guilt-ridden Baptist?

Then it came to me. Thank you, God, I thought. You've got yourself a convert.

I said, 'This has been a terrible shock for you, darling. You look whacked out. Have you had anything to eat yet? Why don't I rustle up something for both of us. And then we'll go round to Maisie's.'

She looked at me in fearful alarm.

'What for . . . ? I'm not sure . . . John, there's something . . .'

'To collect Samson, of course. You know how the poor beast doted on Maisie. He's going to be desolate. Someone's got to look after him, and if you don't, who will?'

'Samson? Look after Samson?'

I knew how she hated that dog, far worse than any dislike she'd ever felt for Maisie.

'Yes. Maisie would have wanted that, don't you think? Good job you're here to do it. Maisie will rest all the easier for knowing that dear old Samson's in good hands for the rest of his days. If you aren't around to do it, then who will? No, it would be the needle, I'm afraid . . .'

I was laying it on thick. No other way when someone's in search of a sacrifice.

She said again, 'Samson . . . look after Samson . . .'

For a moment I thought the prospect was going to be too daunting. But it was probably the very horror it roused that did the trick.

She nodded vigorously, even tried a smile.

'Yes, you're right, John. You're so right. That's exactly what Maisie would have wanted.'

As hair shirts went, Samson was going to be really scratchy for me as well as Lorna, I thought as I contemplated the single pork chop and recalled viewing the remnants of its one-time partner.

'Right,' I said. 'So let's have a bite to eat then I'll collect the dear little chap. Oh, there seems to be only one chop, dear.'

'Yes. It's yours. You have it. I'm not terribly hungry.'

She smiled at me as she spoke with more affection than I'd seen in her face for a long long time.

I smiled back at her. It was a long way back, but we were taking the first steps.

It suddenly occurred to me that while Lorna's will had been burned, Maisie's presumably hadn't, which meant her cottage and income would be coming to Lorna. Knowing my wife, she would do everything in her power to renounce the inheritance.

That was going to be my next test in diplomacy. Already I was seeing a way round it.

At the height of our anger, Lorna had sworn I would never get another penny of her money, and I had vowed that even if she begged me to take it, I would throw it back in her face.

Of course in our improved relations it would be easy to go back on both of those promises. But how much easier it would be simply to agree that whatever both of us had said in the past about her money, she need feel no compunction about giving nor I about taking what had once been Maisie's.

And with that little bit of help, I could soon be back on my feet again!

Foolish overconfidence? Why so?

I was a fully fledged Boddicomber boddicomber and my luck had changed.

I took a knife and sliced the chop in half.

'No problem,' I said. 'Let's share.'

Proxime Accessit

Proxime accessit.

'He nearly made it.'

The story of his life.

School saw the start of it. Collecting the tatty certificates while others strode off with the silver cups. Left in the shallows with a ripple of applause while others bore out to sea on a great surge of cheers.

University the same. Redbrick while his classmates were Oxbridge. A sound second while dimmer men got fortunate firsts. A teaching diploma while they did research degrees.

Once established, the pattern was unbreakable. Or so it seemed to Dennis Platt as his forties darkened to fifty. Here he was, still in his home town of Dunchester, deputy head of the same school he'd almost succeeded at as a boy, with seventy-five failed applications for headships behind him and a man ten years his junior over him.

Even his family seemed to fit the pattern. There was nothing wrong with them, and yet . . .

Pamela, his wife, had aged quite well, but somehow her dress sense hadn't matured with her figure. She was a good plain cook who had a habit of overreaching into disaster whenever they entertained. And she had more or less retired from sex after the birth of their third daughter. These were doubtless not uncommon flaws in Dunchester domestic life, hardly tragic in their scope. But Dennis knew, though he never shared the knowledge, that it was Lucy, her gorgeous younger sister, he had longed for, lusted after, and lost. Pamela was simply a consolation prize; the vellum certificate, not the silver cup.

He had hoped for a son and got three daughters. The youngest had just left home to join her sisters as a London secretary. Dennis had not been heartbroken to see any of them go. He was sure he would die in their defence, but he was less certain that he could argue for their survival in a balloon debate. Though not dull, they rarely sparkled; though not ugly, they erred on the Wimpey estate side of homely; and though not unmarriable, they remained steadfastly unmarried.

All this might have been endurable – indeed passed in a humdrum provincial Dunchester kind of way for enjoyable – if his bright young dreams had followed a natural course and faded completely, leaving his dusty middle-aged memory to the usual task of readjusting past targets so that present torpor might figure as some kind of success.

But how to adjust, how to forget, when day after tedious day, year after empty year, he saw his hoped-for life, his *true* life, the life in which all those bright young blossoms ripened into golden fruit, being lived before his eyes?

True tragedy lies not in missing your targets, but in having a best friend who hits them, every one.

It had been Tom Trotter who pipped Dennis for most of the school prizes; Tom Trotter who read Ancient History at Oxford while Dennis did modern history at Reading; Tom Trotter whose first play was instantly accepted by the same TV company who not only turned down Dennis's but lost the script. Soon Tom was appearing on chat shows, at media events, in colour supplements, and out of stretch limos at openings. He was prolific and energetic. He wrote plays, novels, short stories, travel books, and film scripts. He produced and directed. He won a Special Prize at Cannes and the lion's share in an Oscar. He bought a London penthouse, a California beach house, a Tuscan villa, and a Polynesian atoll.

Normally such success would have provided not only the reason for friendship to die, but the opportunity. The rising spiral moves ever more distant from the plane circle whose path it shared for a little while. But families are more cohesive than friends, and at the dark heart of Dennis's discontent lay the fact that Tom Trotter was his brother-in-law. He it was who inevitably had won the lovely Lucy, leaving his discomfited rival (whose awkward diffidence was such that no one actually noticed he was a rival) to salve his wounds by pretending that it was Pamela he'd been after all along.

Lucy Trotter was a nice girl whose niceness had survived the sudden inrush of wealth and fame. After a sojourn in California or Cannes, after shooting on location in Tijuana or Taiwan, her heart's desire was ever to return to Dunchester where her family and the friends of her youth still lived. Nor was Tom averse to modestly parading his success and honours down the thorough-fares of his childhood. Weddings, christenings, birthdays, funerals, none was forgotten and as many as possible were actually attended, while it was a sweetly proud boast of Lucy's that no matter what the distance or disarrangement involved, she had never missed a Dunchester family Christmas in her life.

Thus for Dennis there was no forgetting. He was a man who felt himself twice wronged. Not only had his 'true' life been stolen from him, but worse, instead of the peace of the grave which is the murder victim's usual consolation, he was condemned to watch the thief flaunting the usurped existence before his unavertable eyes. When the Trotters weren't actually in town, the local media provided an endless flow of news items about them, while a whole wall in the Platt kitchen was papered each year with Lucy's postcards from exotic places. And what visual detail her dense scrawl had perforce to miss out was mopped up by her video camera, to be laid before the family as a post-prandial Yuletide treat.

'Now this is a little party we had on the beach, that's Tom talking to Steve Spielberg, he wanted to help me edit these things properly but I said no, the folks back home prefer to see it just like it comes, warts and all, and there, if you look over Neil Simon's shoulder, there's Clint with the beer stein, he doesn't often show at these things, whoops! now we've jumped, this is Paris, no, it's London, of course, our apartment, a little dinner, I just couldn't resist taking a few shots through the door when I went to get the coffee, there's Margaret Drabble passing the After Eights to Harold Pinter, and that empty seat next to him, that's where Tony was sitting but he was in the loo being sick, and there's Vanessa and there to her left, with the big black beard, believe it or not, that's Salman!'

And Dennis would sit in the flickering shadows with a twilight song of hate keening in his heart, but when the show was over, he was always the first in his expression of admiration and interest, for he had long since realized that in this regard at least there must be no question of *proxime accessit*. Never by word or deed, by gesture or expression, by nod or by wink, had he given anyone the satisfaction of knowing the depth of his resentment. He was in all outward appearances Tom Trotter's greatest fan. He had first editions of all his books, videos of all his films, autographed first-night programmes of all his plays; and if anyone in Dunchester dared to hint criticism of the Trotter lifestyle or oeuvre, Dennis was down on them with a discipular fervour.

Nor were these attitudes altogether assumed. This, after all, was Dennis's 'true' life that Tom was living, and though a man may detest the thief who steals his jewels, the jewels themselves remain precious, whoever is wearing them. And Tom himself was not intrinsically dislikeable. A moment usually came on his visits when, unbuttoned and embeered, he would confide to Dennis that, in the wilderness of hype and hypocrisy he now inhabited, his old friend's words were the only totally honest and un-self-interested utterance he ever heard; and at such moments Dennis sometimes came close to forgiving the man his crime. Close, but no cigar, for there was always Lucy to remind him of the greatest theft of all, and yet it would have required a blindness darker than Cupid's not to see that her happiness was so inextricably bound up with Tom's that hatred of him must in some measure be hatred of her also.

So was struck a delicate balance of envy and admiration, of resentment and regard, of loathing and love, which looked to have a fair chance of bearing Dennis's painful double life undetected to the grave.

But it is strange what good a man may do in an existence he regards as wasted. Perhaps in an attempt to blot out the infinitely renewable pain of loss, Dennis Platt had resisted few calls on his time and energy in what he thought of as his shadow life. His work in the fields of youth clubs, young people's charities, and education in the widest sense, had won him golden opinions which he hardly noticed or, if he did, regarded as a kind of subtle mockery.

Until one day his headmaster said to him, 'Dennis, you realize that this year marks the twenty-fifth anniversary of your appointment to the staff here?'

'Good Lord. That long? If you add the seven years I was here as a kid . . .' Dennis shook his head, realizing he was drifting perilously near open bitterness, managed a laugh instead, and said, 'It doesn't bear thinking about.'

'On the contrary,' said the head. 'Lots of people have been thinking about it a great deal. Let me put you in the picture. Your colleagues had the bright idea of giving you a commemorative award at Speech Day. There was great enthusiasm in the school, and the governors and the old pupils' association got in on the act too. Things snowballed. It seems half of Dunchester are mad keen to contribute congratulations and cash! So get your thinking cap on, or come Speech Day, you could end up receiving the biggest clock you've ever seen!'

Dennis was genuinely dumbfounded. He felt moved, disturbed, even ashamed. Could it be that all this time he had possessed a pearl worth all his tribe without realizing its value? Was it possible that his shadow life had real substance? Here was a prize he had not striven for, and would not have felt cheated of if it had passed him by, and it was being offered, gratis and unsolicited, by his grateful fellow citizens.

For the first time ever he weighed solid civic virtues and values in the balance against the tinsel triumphs of Tom Trotter's world, and saw his 'true' life fly high, with no weight or substance whatsoever.

'I'm bowled over,' he said sincerely. 'I never thought . . . it's most kind . . .'

'No one deserves it more,' said the head heartily. 'It'll be a great occasion both for you and for the school. Oh, and just to put the gilt on the gingerbread, and I know how much this will please you, I've asked your old chum, Tom Trotter, to present the prizes and of course your award, and he has said he'll be delighted.'

A pearl dissolves in wine, they say, but it dissolves even more quickly in gall and wormwood, leaving only its seed of grit on the tongue.

Dennis smiled, and smiled, and bent all his resources of mind and will to make that smile genuine. It was *his* award, he told himself. It was to be given for *his* services to *his* school, *his* town. It was going to be *his* day.

But he knew in his heart that though the occasion might glitter, it would not be with his effulgence; though the cameras might click, it would not be to record his image; though paeans might be composed, they would not be in his praise.

Worst of all, Tom would do his best for him; and by his fulsome tributes win applause for his own generosity; and by his modest withdrawal take with him the best part of the media presence. So in the annals of great Dunchester occasions, it would go down as the day Tom Trotter presented the prizes, not the day Dennis Platt received one.

Tom rang from India to say how delighted he and Lucy were about the award and how thrilled he would be to present it. It was three o'clock in the morning, but Dennis dropped no hint of this as he expressed enthusiastic gratitude in a wide-awake middle-of-the-day voice, adding the hope that Tom wasn't going to disorder his far more important affairs for such a relatively trivial matter.

'Come off it!' said Tom. 'You don't think I'd miss something like this? In the world I live in, everyone's giving everyone else awards all the time. You've no idea what a pleasure it will be to present one that really matters to someone who really deserves it.'

Dennis recognized a rough-cut of the central theme of Tom's presentation speech. By a gentle rubbishing of his own success, he would attempt quite sincerely to emphasize the importance of Dennis's achievement. But it is not by conjuring up images of glittering Oscar ceremonies that you persuade people they are better off in a Dunchester school hall.

By the time he put the phone down he felt genuinely wide awake. He made himself a cup of coffee, sat at the kitchen table, and looked at his life. Or rather his lives.

It seemed to him that he was approaching a watershed. Some discontents may be divine, but at this moment he knew that his conviction that Tom Trotter had somehow stolen his 'true' life was merely destructive. He could not rid himself of what he recognized as a totally illogical sense of deprivation, but he could at least acknowledge that there was no way in fact or fantasy for him to regain what he felt he had lost.

That admitted, would he not do well to seek to be satisfied with what he had got? And was it so bad? He tried to reconstruct his feelings on first hearing about the special award, before his thoughts were muddied by news of Tom's involvement. He had felt good. He had felt complete. He had felt as a Dunchester deputy head with a faithful wife, three sturdy daughters, and the goodwill and high regard of his fellow citizens ought to feel.

In fact, he had felt like an achiever.

And it seemed to him, sitting in that cold kitchen at the dead hour of the night, that if only he could be allowed to enjoy that award, that ceremony, that day, unsullied by any reminder of that other lost life, he might be able to go forward as a whole man into a useful maturity and a serene old age.

He rose and rinsed his coffee cup. He felt strangely calm. God was showing him that happiness or at least contentment was still a possibility. All it needed was Tom's absence from Speech Day. And surely, when it came to ways of stopping a man in India from getting back to England, God was spoilt for choice. Airline strikes, mechanical breakdown, earthquakes, typhoons, civil unrest, contractual obligations, Delhi-belly – the list was endless. In fact, even without God's active opposition, the journey seemed almost impossible!

In the weeks that followed, he was a new man, or rather he was more genuinely than ever before the man he had always contrived to appear to be. When his wife said to him, 'This award really means a lot to you, doesn't it, dear?' he was able to reply with genuine affection and no hint of irony, 'Yes, it does. But only because of what it means to Dunchester.' And when the headmaster informed him that contributions to his award had topped the four-figure mark, his response was equally sincere and altruistic.

'I can't accept this,' he said. 'A token is all I require, a memento of people's kindness. But the bulk of the money I'd like to plough back into the community. That minibus we use for the disabled kids' trips – it's a disgrace. I've spent more time fiddling with that engine than the kids have spent at the seaside. It's time we had a new one. When people of Dunchester realize it's not just my beer money they're contributing to, we'll see how truly generous they can be!'

And they did. The money poured in. And even the news that Tom had rung the local press to say that he would personally double the total public donation cast only a temporary shadow over Dennis's newfound happiness. For he knew what no one else did: that he and God had made an arrangement whereby Tom Trotter was not going to make it to Speech Day.

His confidence held till eight o'clock the night before.

Tom had said they should arrive by six thirty, and with every minute that passed, Dennis offered silent thanks to God.

Then at eight the doorbell rang.

'That'll be them now,' said Pamela putting down her knitting.

'I'll go,' said Dennis with the serene certainty of one who knows it's the Jehovah's Witnesses or (just as unpalatable) some friend of his daughters, who had arrived earlier from London and gone out almost at once.

He opened the door.

'Evening, squire,' said Tom. 'Sorry we're late. Bloody brakes started playing up on the motorway.'

Years of role-play kept Dennis's face welcoming and his voice lightly concerned as he said, 'Good Lord. That could have been nasty. What was the trouble?'

'God knows. You know me, can't tell a plug from a piston. Can't have been much. The hire firm sent a grease monkey out, and he soon fixed it. Lucy, get a move on with those cases! I've done my back. Daren't risk the strain.'

'I'll help her,' said Dennis.

He joined his sister-in-law at the open boot. Tom didn't own a car, merely hired whatever was fast and comfortable wherever he went.

'Dennis, how are you? Big day tomorrow. I'm so glad they're appreciating you at last. You really deserve it.'

They kissed, a friendly family peck.

'It's great of you to make the effort to come,' said Dennis.

'We wouldn't have missed it for worlds. We know how much it must mean to you.'

For a mad moment Dennis toyed with the idea of telling Lucy the truth and inviting her cooperation in keeping Tom from the ceremony.

But how could he make her understand? And even if he succeeded, why should he imagine that her loyalty to Tom, not to mention her sister and her nieces, would allow her to join what must seem a pathetic, indeed paranoiac conspiracy?

He picked up the cases and carried them into the house.

After supper, Tom said, 'Now what's the game plan tomorrow?'

'It's quite straightforward,' said Dennis. 'The platform party assembles in the head's study at two o'clock, downs a quick glass of patriotic sherry, then processes to the hall where the drill will be much as it was in your time, Tom. Except that this time you're presenting prizes, not getting them.'

'They wanted to have a civic lunch beforehand,' said Pamela. 'But Dennis said no, he didn't want that.'

Dennis shrugged modestly. The truth was he'd seen his wife's proposed outfit and felt that the less public exposure it got, the better. He looked at Lucy, contrasting her elegant catsuit with the fussy cocktail dress Pamela had felt was a suitable garb for serving a disastrous boeuf en croute. And then, as evidence of the genuineness of his conversion, or reversion, to full-time Dunchester man, he felt a pang of guilt.

Lucy smiled back at him and said, 'Oh, you should have gone the whole hog and had the lunch, Dennis.'

'Just as well he didn't, as we couldn't have been there,' said Tom.

'Now, that would really have spoilt the mayor's day,' murmured Dennis.

Lucy gave him a slightly puzzled look and he realized he had come close to letting his number-one-fan mask slip. Injecting a dose of lively interest into his voice, he said, 'You've got something on in the morning, have you?'

'You know me. Always improving the shining hour,' said Tom. 'You remember those short stories I did way back? The ones set locally, about the two town lads who get caught scrumping apples by the old farmer, and then a relationship develops between them and the farmer's family?'

Dennis remembered them well, remembered especially that the initial story had been loosely based on an episode in their own young lives, except that his own fortitude and Tom's tearful terror had somehow got reversed in their fictional equivalents.

'I remember,' he said. 'They were really good. I always thought that they could have been developed into a great TV series.'

'I've always said you should have been my agent, Dennis,' exclaimed Tom. 'That's exactly what's going to happen. Now, the town sequences are easy. Good old Dunchester doesn't change. But we thought we needed a bit more of a contrast in the country scenes. I mean, it's really a bit scrubby round here and the local farmers look like supermarket managers. So I thought, let's widen the gap. Boys a bit scruffier, and the farmer an old-style landowner, perhaps with a title. And not a farmhouse they get taken to, but more of a country seat. And then I thought of Purbley Grange.'

He looked around triumphantly.

Pamela said, 'But that's fifty miles away, up on the moors.'

'My dear Pam, all we need is an electric point or two to plug our equipment into, and at a pinch we don't even need that,' mocked Tom. 'It's years since I've been there, but I can't imagine it's changed, except maybe to crumble a bit more. It's so dramatically situated. And that dried-up moat with the bridge and the arch! It's perfect, or at least so my memory tells me. But before I prise the money men out of their upholstery and ferry them up here, I thought I'd better take a look for myself and make sure memory wasn't deceiving me. It's empty at the moment and I've got the keys from the agent, so we'll be going to check the place out in the morning. And don't worry, Pam. I'll test the electricity supply!'

'I think,' said Lucy, 'that Pam was more concerned about tomorrow's timetable than your series, dear.'

She reached across the table and squeezed Dennis's hand.

'Don't worry,' she said reassuringly. 'I guarantee he'll get to the ceremony on time. I'll even take our togs along so we can change en route if we don't have time to get back here.'

Dennis smiled his gratitude, but behind the smile a wild sea of thoughts was surging.

Lucy's assurance itself was enough to have set a weaker man screaming. He already knew beyond all doubt that Tom's mere presence at the Speech Day would relegate his own leading role to a supporting part. But the presence of Tom preening himself at his own perspicacity after a successful visit to Purbley Grange, and bubbling over with the news that he was going to turn Dunchester into a prime-time telly town, would wipe Dennis off the cast list altogether.

But this was no longer the worst of his fears. Even if he got through Speech Day without running mad; even if he dug down deep and found strength enough to maintain his resolve to spend the years ahead giving substance to his shadow life, despite not having the longed-for launch pad; what hope was there of success if this proposed TV series took off? He had seen how these things could spawn an infinity of follow-ups. He knew areas which TV notoriety had turned into a tourist attraction. There could be coachloads of visitors, souvenir shops, postcards,

T-shirts. Dunchester – God help us! – could become the capital of Trotter Country. There could be magazine articles, TV documentaries. There could even – most terrible of thoughts – be a moment when he would be expected to emerge smiling from behind a screen to pour his pot of sentimental syrup into the glutinous gunge of *Tom Trotter – This Is Your Life!*

It must not be. It was no longer enough for Tom not to be present at the Speech Day. He must never be present anywhere again.

He looked at Lucy. For a second the old feelings of love and longing squeezed his gut. Then he saw her as what she would be without Tom – an even more potent threat to the new, worthwhile, honest relationship he was establishing with Pamela.

It no longer felt unfortunate that Lucy would have to go too; it felt necessary.

That night, as the Trotters slept the sleep of the jet-lagged and the Platt females slept the sleep of the just, Dennis slipped out of the house into the garage, where he picked up his bag of tools and inspection light. Do-it-yourself mechanics was a skill proper to a Dunchester man; only those who had made it into the 'real' world of executive jets and stretch limos could afford to boast their ignorance.

Tom's description of the trouble he'd had on the motorway had given him the hint. A car with a recent record of brake failure; a trip to Purbley Grange; the two things chimed perfectly. The road out to the Grange was a long uphill drag with not much reason for braking. But coming down . . . There were straights long enough for a man in a hurry to get up to eighty. And Tom would be in a hurry, wouldn't he? Lucy might nag him to give himself plenty of time, but Tom would leave it to the last possible minute, and then be determined to make the school with time to spare so he could proclaim, *Look, I was right, as usual!*

So, eighty down the straights, braking hard into sharp bends with steep fell on one side and a rocky slope into a deep gill on the other; accelerate, brake! accelerate, brake! accelerate . . .

It wasn't murder. God could choose to let the brakes fail as he backed out of the drive, or as he parked at Purbley Grange, or He could steer the car past the boulders and let it come to rest, no harm done, beside the chattering beck. God's choice, not Dennis Platt's.

He switched off the inspection light and slid out from under the car. Five minutes later he was slipping back into bed beside his gently snoring wife. He dug her in the ribs and she stopped. Then he closed his eyes and drifted smoothly off to sleep, knowing that he had done everything a man could be expected to do.

The following morning he woke, alert and refreshed, to the sound of a gusting wind blowing handfuls of rain against the window pane. There was a heart-stopping moment at breakfast when Lucy wondered whether it was wise to be driving to the Grange in such conditions, but Tom said, 'Nonsense. This is exactly the weather to see the place in. Don't forget your video camera. We'll have them drooling into their daiquiris in London.'

'Bye-bye, Dennis,' said Lucy as they left. 'See you at the school. And don't worry, I'll get him there if I have to carry him!'

By two o'clock, when the platform party began to assemble, there was no sign of the Trotters. At ten past two, the headmaster discreetly enquired if Dennis knew any reason why Tom should be delayed. Dennis explained that Tom had gone off to view Purbley Grange.

'Something to do with a TV film, I think,' he said vaguely. 'I'm sure he'll be here any minute now.'

He saw the head re-join the mayor and murmur reassurances. The sherry was recirculated. Another ten minutes passed. The head renewed his enquiries, this time less discreetly.

'Is there any way we can try to contact Trotter?' he asked across the room.

'I suppose you could ring Purbley Grange, though I'm not sure if there's anyone living there just now,' said Dennis dubiously.

'What's he want to go out to a godforsaken place like that for on a day like this?' asked the mayor, who worked at being a down-to-earth man of the people.

'Well, you know how it is in the media world,' said Dennis. 'Tom's awfully thorough when it comes to business. He likes to see everything for himself. And we shouldn't complain, not when it gets him into our neck of the woods for an occasion like this.'

It was a subtle reproof, defending Tom, but at the same time suggesting that the main reason he had come north was not the Speech Day but his own TV business.

The school secretary, dispatched by the head to try and contact the Grange, announced that the phone there had been disconnected. An envoy from the staff on supervisory duty in the hall looked in to say that a first attempt at a slow handclap by the impatient pupils had been quelled, but with even the parents and front-row guests beginning to shift impatiently, he feared a second insurrection could not be so easily put down. Dennis moved among the platform party, defending Tom vigorously and declaring that special allowances had to be made for the artistic temperament, and that of course it wasn't spoiling his own great day. Behind him he left a trail of admiration for his loyalty, sympathy for its betrayal, and indignation at the shabby treatment he was receiving from his so-called friend.

Finally the mayor approached him.

'Look here, Dennis,' he said. 'We can't hang about for ever. The headmaster's asked me to take over the prize-giving. I know it's a bit of a come-down, and that you in particular will be very disappointed not to . . .'

'No, no,' intervened Dennis. 'It'll be an honour and a privilege to receive my award from you, Mr Mayor. In some ways, to be honest, I'll prefer knowing I'm getting it from someone with a true appreciation of what civic service means to folks up here in Dunchester.'

'Well said, lad! It's big of you to take it like that. And you're dead right. At least I can guarantee that whatever I say will come from the heart, and I'll not be thinking about some half-baked television programme while I'm talking. Right, let's get to it.'

The applause which greeted the platform party was close to the threatened slow handclap, but disappointment at Tom Trotter's absence was clearly diluted by relief that at last the show was underway.

The school prize-giving was got through with such élan that when a fourth-year divinity prize-winner missed his name, his New Testament was given to the next on the list, a surprised-looking Muslim mathematician, and thereafter everyone got the wrong book. But that could be sorted out later, and now the mayor was launching into his encomium of Dennis. Curiously, it followed much the same lines as Dennis had anticipated from Tom, except that, couched in the mayor's honest earthy language, the argument that Dennis's station and achievement were much more admirable and praiseworthy than the passing triumphs of the media world rang out with real conviction and got the audience applauding Dennis for five minutes, then themselves for another five.

Dennis stood there, clutching the carriage clock he had accepted for himself and the large cheque he had accepted for the new minibus, and for the first time in decades felt totally himself, with no tinge of a Trotter presence. Below him even the cameramen, who had stayed in the hope that Tom would yet arrive, were carried away by the wave of local chauvinist feeling inspired by the mayor's speech, and clicked and whirred as if some great media celebrity were indeed standing before them.

Slowly, reluctantly, the applause faded and Dennis stepped forward to utter his thanks.

'Mr Mayor. Headmaster. Ladies and gentlemen,' he said brokenly. 'This is a moment I shall never forget . . . never . . .'

He was right. He never did forget it.

A door opened at the side of the stage and a buzz of interest arose in the hall which had nothing to do with Dennis. Out of the corner of his eye he glimpsed a uniformed figure intruding upon the platform. Even Marc Antony could not have competed with such an interruption, and, wisely, Dennis let his emotional pause stretch into infinity. The policeman was bending over the headmaster, whispering in his ear. The headmaster did not move after the policeman finished, and the officer held his stooped position as though in expectation of a whispered response. Together they formed a tableau which any Victorian narrative painter would have seized on with delight and entitled NEWS FROM THE FRONT. Then slowly the headmaster rose and with a stricken expression advanced towards Dennis.

'I'm sorry,' he said. 'It seems there's been an accident.'

The clock in Dennis's hand suddenly felt very heavy. He turned to place it on his chair, but it slipped from his fingers and crashed to the floor. The glass case shattered and the hands fell off. The audience exhaled a uniform gasp, but the head cut it off like a double-glazed window simply by raising his hand.

'Ladies and gentlemen,' he intoned. 'I regret to inform you I have just heard there has been a serious motor accident involving Mr Tom Trotter, who should have been our distinguished guest today, and his wife. In the circumstances I think we must consider these proceedings at an end, and I would ask you to leave the hall as quickly and quietly as you may.'

Suddenly a woman's voice rang out behind him.

'Dead? I don't believe you. Not dead!'

It was Pamela. At last her three daughters came in useful, and as she collapsed in hysterics, they led her away, leaving the other guests able to join the gentlemen of the press in demanding confirmatory detail from the messenger policeman.

'It was a farmer who got there first,' he said, relishing his role. 'He were up on the fellside with his sheep when he saw the car, going like a bat out of hell, he says, like the driver were in a desperate hurry to get somewhere. He could hear the brakes scream as he took the corners. Then suddenly the car were belting down to this sharpest bend of the lot and the brakes didn't scream. The driver, Mr Trotter that'd be, swung the wheel hard over, and he almost made it, the farmer says. But the car were sliding sideways on the bend, the road was narrow, and suddenly he was over the side. Not a big drop, but unfortunately there was a fire . . . If there hadn't been a fire, or if the road had been just a bit wider . . . he almost made it, the farmer says . . .'

His moving narrative was interrupted by the sound of high keening laughter.

It took Dennis a little while to realize the noise was coming from him.

'I'm sorry,' he gasped. 'It's just that . . . *he almost made it* . . .'
And then he was off again.

After the funeral, where the family mourners had to play a very subsidiary role to the few celebrity guests and the many celebrity wreaths, Dennis and Pamela re-entered their house in silence. Pamela went straight upstairs and Dennis went into the lounge and poured himself a whisky. So far he had refused to let himself know how he felt. Now for the first time he cautiously lifted the cover on his feelings and peered inside.

There was something down there, but he couldn't quite make out what. Cautiously he began to prod at it with the memory of these last days – the presentation, the news of the accident, the inquest, the funeral . . .

'Dennis? Are you all right?'

It was Pamela, with more of impatience than curiosity or concern in her voice.

'Yes, fine,' he said, slamming down the lid. She hadn't taken off her coat, he noticed.

He said, 'Are you cold? Shall I turn the heating on?'

'I'm leaving you,' she said.

His mind tried to pretend it hadn't registered the words but his eyes had already taken in the packed suitcase on the floor behind her.

'I'm sorry,' she went on. 'But after what's happened I can't stay.'

For a second he was certain she meant she knew what he had done to the brakes. The shock must have shown on his face for now she said with faint surprise, 'You look upset. Why? It can't be a total surprise, not after all this time. I've never been all that good at hiding my feelings.'

'What feelings?' he asked in growing bewilderment.

She considered, then said, 'Disappointment, I suppose. Dennis, this isn't a judgement session. It's not your fault. I opted for you in the first place. I thought, he'll be the one. Tom was flashy but flighty. You'd be the one with staying power, I thought. And so you were. But it was power for staying in Dunchester, I should have realized that. It's all you ever wanted, isn't it? To be someone here in Dunchester. I can't imagine you anywhere else, and I can't imagine how I ever could!'

'What the hell are you talking about?' he cried, baffled.

'I told you. Disappointment. And boredom,' she said. 'I know I've let it show. You must have noticed. I'm sorry. I just sometimes felt so stifled in this world of yours. But as long as Lucy and Tom were alive, it seemed bearable. They were news from another world, proof that there was life after Dunchester. But now they're gone. And the girls have voted with their feet, haven't they? Now it's my turn. Don't make a fuss. You'll be better off without me, Dennis. Just think, you won't have to be embarrassed by my clothes or my cooking any more.'

'Where are you going?' he asked desperately, trying to collect his thoughts.

'I'll stay with the girls till I get something sorted out,' she said. 'Lucy's left me a bit of money, so I won't need to trouble you much. I think that's my taxi now. Goodbye, Dennis. Take care. Dunchester needs men like you, and that's not a crack.'

She kissed him on the cheek, a friendly family peck, and then she was gone, before he could say anything, offer her any of the million revelations and explanations tumulting in his brain.

And yet, what was there to say which would not be too little too late, or too much too soon?

He poured himself another Scotch and sat in complete passivity for a while. No need now to lift the lid and poke at the thing in his mind any more. He knew why it wouldn't stir. It was dead. His life, his 'true' life, had died in that burning car on the high moors road.

And what of his shadow life? To live it out now without Pamela meant that it was going to be merely the shadow of a shadow.

Should he have told her what he really felt?

What he had really done?

He shuddered at the thought. There was a noise in the hall, and he rose almost in terror at the idea that she'd returned. But it was only the local paper.

They had an account of the funeral on the front page. There was a single reference to himself and they'd spelled his name wrong, as they'd done in the passing reference to his award presentation in the account of Tom's death. As for all those thousands of frames of film taken of him during the ceremony, not one had ever appeared.

Until now perhaps. When he opened the paper, he discovered an elegiac double-page photo-spread of scenes from Tom's triumphant career. And there, leading the rest, surely that was a shot from Speech Day?

The bottom left-hand corner of the picture was filled with a very out-of-focus human ear which Dennis was pretty sure he recognized as his own.

But what the photographer had been aiming at, and what he'd got with great clarity, and perhaps just a bit of touching up, was one of the Roll of Honour boards which lined the walls of the School Hall.

This one, in letters of gold on varnished mahogany, listed the prize-winners for the year 1959.

Highlighted was the school's premier award, *The Bishop Blaxton Cup for All-Round Merit*. Alongside it was the name *Thomas Trotter*.

Beneath this, not at all highlighted and in much smaller letters but still legible to the sensitive eye, was another name and inscription. *Dennis Platt. Proxime Accessit.*

Where the Snow Lay Dinted

Dalziel awoke. He knew nothing, remembered nothing, and felt neither the desire nor the will to activate cognition.

He lay unmoving and might have so continued for an indefinite period had not a physical sensation finally forced itself upon his embryonic consciousness.

His bollocks were cold.

Time to make contact with the waking world. Nothing rash, minimum risk. He opened his left eye just sufficiently to admit light in the smallest measure known to man, which is a single Scotch in an English pub.

Jesus wept!

Light poured in, white and blinding as if someone had indeed poured a glass of whisky on to his eyeball. He squeezed the eyelid shut and lay still until the dancing white patina had faded from his retina.

Sight no good, so try the other senses . . .

Touch . . . cold, he'd already established that . . .

Sound . . . voices, gently murmuring . . .

Smell . . . antiseptic . . .

Taste . . . BLOOD!

Oh God, I'm being operated on and the anaesthetic hasn't took!

'Nobody move!' he bellowed, sitting bolt upright and opening both eyes wide.

In a huge dressing-table mirror he saw a naked fat man with a split lip sitting up in a four-poster bed. On a bedside table stood a half-empty bottle of whisky and a half-full bottle of TCP. Through a tall open window drifted a chilling draught, a blinding white light, and a murmur of voices.

He rolled off the bed on to the floor, landing on a spoor of damp clothes which ran from the doorway to the bedside. After a while he pushed himself to his knees. When his head didn't fall off, he rose fully upright, took three uncertain steps towards the window and, catching hold of the pelmet to maintain verti-cality, he looked out. And knew at last where, and when, and why he was.

He was in the Hirtledale Arms Hotel on the Yorkshire Moors, it was Boxing Day morning, and it had snowed hard during the night.

It was a scene to touch even the done-over heart of a hung-over cop. The sky was delft blue and the still-low rays of the morning sun were gilding the horizoned hills, lending the curves and hollows the sensuous quality of female limbs in repose. Where the foothills gave way to pastureland, the varicosed lines formed by dry-stone walls were all that marked one field from another. Small trees and bushes sagged beneath the weight of their temporary blossom, while beech and oak and elm stood upright as judges in their wigs of white. About a mile away, the small village of Hirtledale had all but vanished under the sealing snow, but nearer still the fairy-tale turrets of Hirtledale Castle floated like something imagined by Walt Disney over the icing-sugared battlements.

Dalziel let his gaze drift down to the square of perfect lawn which was the pride and joy of Giles Hartley-Pulman, the hotel's owner. At its centre stood a bronze statue of little St Agnes clutching a lamb, saved from dereliction in Rome (according to the hotel brochure) by a nineteenth-century Lord Hirtledale, and planted here when the hotel building had still been the castle's dower house.

The perfect lawn was now of course a blanket of perfect white, and this seemed to be the focus of attention of the several guests standing on the terrace immediately below Dalziel's window, whose soft conversation he had mistaken for the blasé chit-chat of heartless surgeons.

So what was so interesting? wondered Dalziel.

He returned his attention to the lawn and as his eyes adjusted to the dazzling light, he saw that its surface was not perfect after all.

From the feet of the statue ran a set of small human footprints with alongside them another set of even smaller animal hoof-prints. The trail swung in a wide circle round the lawn, though always staying well clear of its edges, before returning to the base of the statue.

'Bugger me,' said Andy Dalziel.

His exclamation drew the attention of the watchers below to his presence. They looked up at him with expressions ranging from the amused to the amazed. Among them, he spotted Peter and Ellie Pascoe, who maintained the neutral faces of people who'd seen it all before. If so, they were seeing it all again, for it suddenly occurred to Dalziel that he was stark naked.

Time for retreat. Any road, miracles shouldn't be taken on an empty stomach.

He belched gently, gave a little wave, and called, 'See you at breakfast, I'm fair clemmed.'

As he showered and shaved, memory struggled back into his mind like the sea up a long shallow beach.

At low-tide level, things were pretty clear. This time last week, he'd had no plans for Christmas and didn't give a toss. Then Peter Pascoe had let slip that he was planning to spend the break at the Hirtledale Arms, and suddenly Dalziel realized how much he'd been relying on the usual Boxing Day invitation to lunch with the Pascoes.

He must have let it show. Or perhaps Pascoe just felt guilty, because he'd started explaining.

'Not my cup of tea, really, but Ellie's mum, well, you know she's not long widowed and she needs a change of scene, and it takes the pressure off Ellie . . .' Then, with the expansive generosity of one who knew the hotel had long been booked solid, he'd added, 'Look, why not join us? We'd all love to see you there.'

And God, who is a Yorkshireman, had grinned, nipped a guest in the appendix and made sure news of the cancellation reached the hotel five minutes before Dalziel rang.

When he heard the price quoted by Giles Hartley-Pulman (who immediately in Dalziel-speak became Giles Partly-Human), his Scottish/Yorkshire blood curdled. Then he'd asked himself, 'What are you saving for? a cashmere winding-sheet and a platinum coffin?' and booked. His reward had been the discovery that one of the things the inclusive price included was wine and liqueurs with Christmas Dinner. Somewhere between the turkey and the truffles he had a vague recollection of calculating that profligacy had turned into profit. And he thought he recalled starting on the liqueurs in alphabetical order, but now they sat like an oil slick on the tide of memory, turning it sluggish and opaque well short of high water. What he needed was some mental menstruum and he knew just the formula. First take a precise inch of the Macallan in a tooth glass and toss it straight down to avoid contact with your cut lip. Then add half a pound of streaky bacon, a black pudding, several eggs and a potato scone, and chew gently.

He descended to the dining room to complete the cure.

As he entered, a voice cried, 'Andy, good morning. Now the Great Detective is among us, the riddle of the perambulating statue will be solved in a trice. Or would you rather we all assembled in the library later?'

This was Freddie Gilmour, a young man who was something in the City and had been Christmassing at Hirtledale for many years with half a dozen like-minded friends. They had adopted Dalziel in a way which Peter Pascoe found offensively patronizing. But Dalziel's huge frame was lead-lined, and this imperviousness, plus his prodigious feats of consumerism, had brought these devout free marketeers to a wondering respect.

'Nay, Fred,' he said. 'I only solve real mysteries. Like if you put your hand in your pocket and found some of your own money there.'

Followed by a gust of laughter, he crossed the room and joined the Pascoes.

''Morning,' he said.

He couldn't have behaved too badly last night because both Ellie and her mother gave him a welcoming smile, though the former's began to fade as little Rosie Pascoe piped up eagerly, 'Uncle Andy, did you see? The statue went for a walk last night and took her little lamb with her.'

'I don't think so, dear,' said her mother, who, though having nothing against flights of imagination, was a natural enemy of anything smacking of superstitious credulity. 'I'm sure there's some other explanation.'

'No, they went for a walk, you can see the footprints in the snow. Isn't that right, Uncle Andy? Because anything can happen at Christmas.'

Dalziel looked from mother to daughter. The same dark, serious, unblinking gaze, the same expression of expectant certitude.

Pascoe was observing him with a faint grin which said, 'Get out of this one!'

'Aye, owt can. That doesn't say it will, but.'

Good try, but not good enough.

'But this *has* happened, hasn't it?' insisted the girl. 'You can see the prints.'

'That's right,' agreed the Fat Man. 'What I can't see is anyone to serve me breakfast.'

'I get the impression there's some sort of crisis in the kitchen,' said Pascoe.

'If there's not, there soon will be,' said Dalziel, glad of an excuse to escape Ellie's threatening glare.

He rose, went to the kitchen door, pushed it open and bellowed, 'SHOP!'

Giles Hartley-Pulman, deep in confabulation with his chef and three young waitresses, jumped six inches in the air. His lean ascetic face was creased with concern, but oddly when he identified the source of the sound, it relaxed ever so slightly.

There had been a moment last night when he would gladly have given half his kingdom for the privilege of never seeing Dalziel again. This had been when he bravely but foolishly attempted to slow if not stem the Fat Man's consumption of claret. To the applause of the other guests, Dalziel had flourished the menu, stabbing with a huge finger at the words *Wine and Liqueurs ad lib*, and saying, 'Here in Yorkshire we've got a word for a man who's not good as his word! We'll try another bottle of the '83.'

A good hotelier knows when to withdraw. He also knows how to get even if the chance offers, and now Hartley-Pulman advanced saying, 'Superintendent Dalziel, thank heaven. There's been a burglary. I was about to phone the police but of course with you on the spot, it seems a shame to drag someone out in these conditions . . . and I should hate for the press to get involved, asking impertinent questions about my guests . . .'

Meaning, I'd rather not have uniformed plods all over the place, but if I do, I'll make sure the world knows you were pissed the far side of oblivion last night!

Dalziel considered. Hirtledale was on the northernmost fringe of his Mid-Yorkshire patch so he certainly had jurisdiction, if he cared to assert it. On the other hand, he didn't care for Partly-Human imagining he could threaten him.

Postponing decision, he said, 'What's been stolen?'

'Well,' said Hartley-Pulman, savouring the moment. 'It's mainly . . . your breakfast.'

And in the dining room conversation ceased as a great cry of pain and loss exploded out of the kitchen.

Five minutes later, Peter Pascoe was summoned to join his boss. It didn't take long to put him in the picture.

'Partly-Human's making a list,' Dalziel concluded. 'You talk to the staff, lad. Use your boyish charm.'

'Yes, sir,' said Pascoe, looking unhappily at the chef who was breaking a bowlful of eggs into a pan. He didn't want to be involved in this, but if he was . . . 'Sir, shouldn't we seal the kitchen in case Forensic . . . ?'

'Stuff Forensic,' said Dalziel. 'There's nowt left but eggs and I need to keep me strength up.'

Sighing, Pascoe went in search of the waitresses.

Fifteen minutes later he returned to find Dalziel wiping the pattern off a plate with a slice of bread.

'You've got that aren't-I-clever look,' said the Fat Man.

'We've got a name,' said Pascoe. 'Remember little Billy Bream?'

'In the frame for the Millhouse break-in, but CPS got their knickers in a twist. Still, it gave him a scare and he dropped out of sight.'

'Hirtledale was where he dropped to. His old gran lives there. And Milly Staines, the waitress with the squint, she reckons she saw him hanging around here last night.'

'Grand. Owt else?'

'Maybe. Patty Strang, the pretty blonde, says she glanced out of her window just as the snow was starting and saw someone down the drive. No description except it was too big for little Billy and moving very slowly.'

'Even Billy 'ud move slow carrying this lot,' said Dalziel, producing a list.

Pascoe whistled. As well as twelve pounds of sausage, fifteen pounds of bacon, forty kidneys, thirty kippers, twenty-five black puddings and a kilo of salt, a dozen bottles of champagne had gone.

'One thing's certain, he must have left some tracks.'

'Let's take a look,' said Dalziel.

Close to the building the snow was already churned up, but a few yards down the drive they spotted two lines of footprints, one approaching, one moving away.

'How's your tracking, Pocahontas?' said Dalziel. 'Get your wellies and let's see where these lead us.'

Before they left Pascoe had a quick word with Ellie, who rolled her eyes in not-altogether-mock rage and said, 'Trouble follows the fat bastard, but I don't see that's any reason why you should.'

'We're just going to look at the tracks in the snow,' protested Pascoe.

'Yeah? With a bit of luck he might catch pneumonia. If he does, my sympathy's with the bacilli!'

Freddie and the Free Marketeers must have been earwigging on this exchange for, as Pascoe joined Dalziel outside the kitchen, they appeared in the doorway and struck up a rousing chorus of 'Good King Wenceslas'.

'Twits,' muttered Pascoe. 'Wouldn't surprise me if they had something to do with this.'

'Wouldn't displease you, you mean,' said Dalziel, acknowledging the carollers with a friendly two-fingered wave. 'Where's your festive spirit, lad?' And joining in their song at the line *Mark my footsteps good my page*, he strode off up the drive.

As Pascoe floundered behind already feeling the cold strike through his soles, the carol's words fell with heavy irony on his tingling ears. *Heat was in the very sod That the saint had printed.* No chance! You needed a saint for that and all he'd got was the very sod!

Where the drive joined the road, the prints turned towards the village and were joined by another outward set.

'Accomplice,' guessed Dalziel. 'Stayed here to watch.'

'Or someone who'd set out before the snow started laying,' Pascoe contradicted sourly.

But as they walked on and he began to warm up, the enchanted silence of the snow began to work its magic on his mood. This was what Christmas was all about, not the gluttonous consumerism of the telly ads but a brief interval in which all the filth and flaws of human existence were cloaked in a mantle of purest white.

As they were approaching the gothic archway marking the entrance to the castle estate, they heard the sound of a hunting horn and a merry chatter of distant voices.

'Must be the Boxing Day Meet,' said Dalziel. 'I could just sup a stirrup cup. Come on!'

He hurried forward, clearly with every intention of turning into the castle grounds and inserting himself among the huntsmen. But his haste was almost his undoing, for as he reached the gate there was a drumming of hooves mingled with shouts and laughter, and next moment a posse of red-coated riders erupted in front of them and galloped across the road into a wood. Pascoe, still in his master's steps, was protected from the worst of the spume of slush thrown up behind them, but Dalziel took the full brunt.

'Fuck me,' he said, coming to a halt. 'Rigid!'

He looked, thought Pascoe, like a snowman on a Christmas card, lacking only the carrot nose and old pipe to complete the picture. It was a thought he kept to himself.

Another horseman came through the archway, moving at a more decorous pace. This was a much older man, grey hair showing beneath his black cap. He came to a halt in front of Dalziel and examined him for a moment. What might have been a glint of amusement touched his bright blue eyes but didn't extend to his narrow patrician face as he said courteously, 'Sorry about that. Impetuous youth. I'll speak to them.'

'Aye, but will the buggers listen?' said Dalziel, brushing the snow away.

'Eventually, once they've ridden off all their festive excesses. No excuse, of course, but if we recall our own younger days and the tricks we got up to, perhaps we can forgive.'

This appeal seemed to strike a chord in Dalziel, who said, 'Aye, well, I'll not die of a bit of snow. Daresay some on 'em enjoyed themselves so much last night, they didn't even get to bed.'

'They were certainly still carousing when I went up,' said the horseman. 'I'd better get after them before they find a frozen pond to ride across. Again my apologies. And Merry Christmas to you both.'

He touched his riding crop to his cap and cantered on.

'Know who that was?' said Dalziel. 'Lord Hirtledale himself.'

'Well, roll on the revolution,' said Pascoe. 'Never thought you were a forelock-tugger, sir.'

'Long time since I had one of those,' said Dalziel equably. 'Thought you'd have been all for his lordship. Doesn't he chair that Bosnian relief gang your missus collects for? Cost me a fiver last time she rattled her can!'

'I don't see how that entitles him to prance around the countryside, slaughtering foxes.'

'Nay, lad, you'd best put that one to the Pope next time you write. Too deep for me. I just hunt villains. Tally-ho!'

They had no difficulty in refinding the trail beyond the hoof-prints, but when they reached the cobbles of the village High Street, it vanished completely.

'What now?' asked Pascoe.

Dalziel didn't answer straight away but thrust his great head forward and moved it slowly this way and that, like an old bear checking out the scents of the forest on waking from hibernation.

Then, showing his teeth in a hungry smile, he said, 'I reckon I'll follow my nose up here. You sniff around further along.'

He vanished down the side of a tiny grey cottage, leaving Pascoe to continue up the street, still scanning the trodden snow in search of the vanished spoor. But the combination of cobbled surface and the fact that people had clearly been out and about in the village made it an impossible task. Only on the doorsteps of some of the cottages fronting the street did the snow lay even enough to take a good print, and all you got here were the perfect circles left by milk bottles.

He turned to cross the street to see if he had any better luck on the other side. And halted abruptly as a puzzling thought came into his mind.

Surely even out here in the country where some trace of old-fashioned standards of service still remained, there was unlikely to be a milk delivery on Boxing Day?

Behind him a door opened. Something hard and cylindrical rammed into his spine, making him squeak with pain. And a harsh Yorkshire voice grated, 'Stand still, mister, and state thy business. Now!'

Dalziel meanwhile was pushing open a kitchen door, his nostrils flaring wide.

He found himself looking into the surprised eyes of a slightly built young man sitting at a scarred oak table, topping up a pint pot with Veuve Clicquot. In front of him was a huge plate piled high with the delicious freight of the full English breakfast.

''Morning, Billy,' said the Fat Man cheerfully. 'Cansta spare a sausage?'

Ten minutes later he emerged, chewing pensively. Looking down the street he spotted Peter Pascoe sitting on the low wall running round the churchyard, cradling a large plastic carrier bag.

'You look knackered,' said Dalziel as he approached. 'Should take more exercise.'

'Fails my heart I know not how,' said Pascoe. 'What are you eating?'

222

'Kidney. Billy Bream's back there stuffing his face and washing it all down with bubbly.'

'So why's he not here in handcuffs?' asked Pascoe without much passion.

'He says he found it all on his gran's doorstep this morning when he got back from the hotel.'

'And what had he been doing at the hotel that kept him all night?'

'You recall yon bonny waitress, Patty Strang? That's what he says he was doing at the hotel that kept him all night.'

'And you believe him?'

'Well, she looks a healthy young animal,' said Dalziel. 'Still, I admit that normally I'd have had him in for questioning so quick he'd have got indigestion. But when I opened my mouth to give him the caution, I found meself putting another sausage in. Peter, I think maybe I took a knock on the head last night and it's left me concussed. I've started imagining some very strange things. Tell me to get a grip on myself, then pop back in there and arrest Billy Bream, and I'll give you a big wet kiss.'

Pascoe smiled wanly and said, 'Sorry, sir, not even for such an inducement. You see, I've been having a strange encounter of my own too. With Miss Drusilla Earnshaw of this parish, age eighty-three, vegetarian and devout Methodist, who poked her walking-stick in my back and didn't take it away till she'd seen my warrant and my library card. Then she told me a very strange story indeed.'

'I don't think I want to hear it,' said Dalziel.

'I don't imagine you do,' said Pascoe. 'Seems she was woken by a noise outside her cottage not long after midnight. She got up, took hold of her stick and flung open her front door. A man was crouching on the step.'

'Description?' said Dalziel desperately.

'Her eyes are bad. Big, broad and brutish, is the best she can do. But her hearing's fine. To her question, "Who are you?" he

223

replied, "Never fret yourself, luv. It's only Good King Wenceslas."
Upon which, she hit him in the mouth with her stick and slammed
the door. When she opened it again this morning, she found
these on her step.'

He opened the carrier to reveal a bottle of Veuve Clicquot, five
sausages and a kipper. Dalziel looked at them, shivered, and touched
his wounded lip as the tide of memory finally broke clear of the
slick of liqueurs and ran clear and high and oh, so very cold.

He let his gaze rise to meet Pascoe's. And spoke.

'Well, here it is at last, lad. Your big moment. Ring the Chief
Constable, alert the Home Office, call out the SAS and get yourself put in charge of a nationwide hunt for a well-built man with
a cut lip and a bedroom floor covered with damp clothes who
might be staying at the Hirtledale Arms Hotel. Could be the
making of you.'

'No thanks,' said Pascoe, standing upright with sudden decision. 'I'm made already, I reckon. But here's what I do suggest.
You go back to the hotel, get in your car and head for town.
I'll say you've been called away on an urgent case. But first I'll
go round the village and collect as much of the stuff as I can
find. I'll tell Partly-Human that we lost the trail but are ninety
per cent sure it was some local lads, having a bit of a joke . . .'

Dalziel was shaking his head.

'Nay, lad. Good try but it won't work. Local lads means yobs
and poachers to the likes of Partly-Human. Vermin. He really
would want to call in the SAS to flush 'em out.'

'So what do you suggest?' demanded Pascoe, exasperated.

'Well, first off, I'm not going to take advantage of your loyalty
to get me off the hook. But I'm touched, lad. Deeply touched.'

His voice broke and he gave a choking cough.

'Please,' said Pascoe. 'No need . . .'

'Nay, I'm right. Bit of kidney got stuck, that's all. No, there
are times when a man's got to face up to consequences. What
is it I'm always telling you?'

Pascoe thought. None of the things that Dalziel was always telling him, such as he should eat more red meat, or that a university degree was what any convict could get between jerking off and sewing mailbags, seemed to apply.

'Can't think, sir,' he said. 'What is it you're always telling me?'

'Speak the truth and the truth will set you free!'

Pascoe couldn't believe his ears.

'You've never told me that in your life!' he cried. 'Besides, in this instance, it's rubbish. The truth will lock you up. You've got too many enemies, starting with Partly-Human . . .'

'Peter, you always think the worst of people,' remonstrated Dalziel. 'There's good in everyone, especially this time of year. Remember the carol.'

Seeking the tune, he began to intone, '*Wherefore Christian men be sure, Wealth or rank possessing . . .*'

'You won't have any rank,' insisted Pascoe. 'And precious little wealth. Andy, it's your career . . .'

But Dalziel was away down the street, the words now bursting out in a thunderous baritone.

'*Ye who now do bless the poor Shall yourselves find blessing!*'

Fifteen minutes after his return, he emerged from Hartley-Pulman's office looking solemn. Pascoe, waiting anxiously, cried, 'What did he say? What did you tell him?'

'I told him the truth,' said the Fat Man. 'And it's OK, lad. Like the decent chap he is, he listened, he understood, he forgave and now he's starting to forget. And I'm off down to the kitchen. All this confessing don't half make you hungry! And it's a shame to waste yon stuff you rescued from the old lady.'

He walked away smiling. He loved Pascoe dearly, but it did his heart good to see those intelligent sensitive features gobsmacked from time to time. Not that he hadn't been touched by the lad's willingness to cover up for him. But why tell lies when the truth was good enough? And in his dealing with Partly-Human he'd spoken nowt but gospel truth.

Of course what most folk forget is, there are four versions of the Gospel.

He'd said, man to man, 'I followed them tracks as far as the castle where I came across Lord Hirtledale and some of his young guests. High-spirited lads, but no harm in them. His lordship and I spoke briefly – man with a mind like that doesn't need things spelt out – and he apologized sincerely for any inconvenience his young friends may have caused. He said . . . but I reckon a chap like you doesn't need things spelt out either. Suffice to say, if you can see your way to keeping this business under your bonnet, you'd be highly obligating someone not a million miles away. No names, no pack drill. In fact the only name you need bother with is mine, 'cos that's the one that'll be on the cheque covering your losses. And I'll tell you, I'll be proud to sign it. What do you say? Draw a line under this lot? It won't be forgotten, I promise.'

Partly-Human was looking as if the Michelin guide had just awarded him three stars.

'Well, naturally, in those circumstances, I'm only too happy to oblige. And I must say I'm pleasurably surprised by your part in this, Superintendent.'

'Andy,' said Dalziel. 'Well, it 'ud be a sad world if them as are born to rule it couldn't sow a few wild oats. Tell you what, I bet his lordship 'ud be really chuffed if half the damages went to his Bosnian Relief Fund, eh, Giles?'

And Partly-Human to his credit hardly blanched as he said, 'I think that's a lovely idea, Andy.'

Driving home the next day, Dalziel grinned at the memory. All right, it had cost him, but he'd really enjoyed his break.

Best of all, though, had been the delight on Rosie's face, not to mention the dismay on her mother's, as they'd all stood on the terrace together before they left and examined the mysterious footprints still visible on the lawn.

'You see, the statue did walk, Mum,' insisted the little girl. 'Because it's Christmas. Isn't that right, Uncle Andy?'

'That's right,' said Dalziel, winking broadly at Ellie. 'Everyone gets what they want at Christmas, that's what it's all about.'

Everyone who had an Uncle Andy, anyway. It was funny, all these clever buggers like Pascoe, and not one of them had thought to speculate why the kitchen thief should have included a kilo of salt in his swag. But the salt had been the first and principal object of the raid. The Wenceslas idea had been an afterthought.

He'd trotted round the still snow-free lawn, marking out the trail of footsteps and hoofprints in salt. On the rest of the frost-hard surface the big flakes had soon started to settle, but for a while those that hit the salt melted away. And when the white coverlet was complete, the spoor of prints remained to baffle the adults and delight the little girl.

Andrew Dalziel threw back his head and laughed long and loud, and God, who is a Yorkshireman, looked fondly down on him and laughed too.

Rosie Pascoe, drowsy by her gran's side in the back of her dad's car, was also looking back on Christmas with much pleasure. Of course, any time spent in the close company of adults was bound to have its baffling elements. Like did her mum and dad *really* like Uncle Andy or not? *She* liked him, because he was funny, and kind, and never worried about being rude. Also, because he was a bit sad sometimes.

She recalled Christmas night when she couldn't get to sleep because of all the day's excitements. Finally she'd got up and looked out of the window. There on the lawn, she'd seen him, Uncle Andy, lumbering around like an old dancing bear with the snowflakes whirling like moths round his great grey head. He'd been pouring something on to the grass, she didn't know what.

But she didn't doubt next morning that it had something to do with the statue's supposed footprints.

Now, why Uncle Andy should want people to think the statue had walked, she didn't know. It was silly really. Statues couldn't walk, everyone knew that. But it was what he wanted, and that was enough for her to give him her total uncritical support.

Everyone gets what they want at Christmas . . . even Uncle Andy . . .

She fell asleep with her head on her grandmother's lap.

Bibliography

Reginald Hill's short stories often appeared first in newspapers, magazines or short story collections. This list attempts to catalogue the first publication of each story included in this collection.

'Dalziel and Pascoe Hunt the Christmas Killer', first published as 'A Gift for Christmas'. *Daily Express*. 24, 27 and 28 December 2004

'Market Forces'. *Northern Blood*. Didsbury Press, 1992

'The Perfect Murder Club'. *Perfectly Criminal*. Severn House, 1996

'The Thaw'. *Winter's Crimes 5*. Macmillan, 1973

'Brass Monkey'. *Ellery Queen's Mystery Magazine*. January 2003

'True Thomas'. *2nd Culprit*. Chatto & Windus, 1993

'Castles'. *Ellery Queen's Mystery Magazine*. July 2000

'Fool of Myself'. *The Detection Collection*. Orion, 2005

'John Brown's Body'. *Sightlines*. Vintage, 2001

'Proxime Accessit'. *New Crimes 2*. Robinson, 1990

'Where the Snow Lay Dinted'. *Northern Blood 2*. Flambard, 1995

Acknowledgements

HarperCollins would like to thank the Reginald Hill Estate for partnering with us to create this wonderful collection of short stories and Val McDermid for her typically insightful, thoughtful and generous foreword. We would also like to thank Tony Medawar for proposing the collection and assisting us by compiling the short stories from their original sources. Thank you, to Anne O'Brien for copyediting the collection, Janette Currie for proofreading it, and to Ellie Game for the cover design. More thanks go to Alexander Zapryagaev, Shunta Kakuyama and the staff of the Howard Gotlieb Archival Research Center of Boston University, as without their assistance this collection wouldn't have been possible. Finally, we would like to thank Becky Percival from United Agents for working closely with us on this collection.